1 MONTH OF
FREE
READING

at
www.ForgottenBooks.com

By purchasing this book you are eligible for one month membership to ForgottenBooks.com, giving you unlimited access to our entire collection of over 1,000,000 titles via our web site and mobile apps.

To claim your free month visit: www.forgottenbooks.com/free239740

ISBN 978-0-483-27527-0
PIBN 10239740

ESTBROOK PARSONAGE

BY

HARRIET B. M'KEEVER,

AUTHOR OF

"SIL· ·EN THREADS," "CHILDREN WITH ··· ··· ··· ··· WEDDI··," ···· ···

Third Edition.

NEW YORK:

HURST & COMPANY, Publishers,

122 NASSAU STREET.

WESTBROOK
PARSONAGE

WESTBROOK PARSONAGE.

BY

HARRIET B. M'KEEVER,

AUTHOR OF
"SILVER THREADS," "CHILDREN WITH THE POETS," "PIERCE'S
"WEDDING," ETC., ETC.

"Sir, we would see Jesus."

Third Edition.

NEW YORK:

HURST & COMPANY, Publishers,

122 Nassau Street.

PREFACE.

TO THE CRITICS.

THE writer of this volume is fully aware now severely these pages may be criticized in the heated state of feeling in our beloved Church on subjects of such momentous importance as those which now agitate her very depths. The advocates of Ritualism spare no pains in seeking to propagate their doctrines, and employ music, sensuous display, and the press, to spread the old superstitions. While there are many writers of tracts, stories, and hymns on one side of the controversy, the writer has met with nothing in the shape of a story, touching these subjects, on the other. It is not likely that young persons will read controversial articles; but it may be that a story embodying Protestant truth will interest many youthful readers, and lead them to read more deeply works that will enlighten the understanding and strengthen their faith, in the great religious issues of the day.

2047377

The writer has endeavored to deal with doctrines and not men, and trusts that no severe impugning of human motives can be found upon these pages. It is a cause of too much sorrow for bitterness ; but the time has come when we must answer the question, "Shall we, Christians of the nineteenth century, have *fossils* or a living Church?"

Aware that this volume must pass the ordeal of the Church press, one request alone is made, and that is: Spare the character of Dr. Hastings; for it is a picture of a holy man of God, who, thirty-five years ago, passed to his eternal rest, leaving behind memories fresh and green in the hearts of parishioners who yet survive. In these pages, an attempt has been made to show how that great and good man would have dealt with questions such as now agitate the Church that we love.

CONTENTS.

Westbrook Parsonage.

CHAPTER I.

A MILE-STONE IN LIFE'S PILGRIMAGE.

"And this stone, which I have set for a pillar, shall be God's house."

IT is an early morning hour: a carriage is standing before the door of one of the merchant-palaces of the great metropolis: several handsome trunks strapped behind indicate a journey; and in a few minutes, a young lady in travelling costume appears at the door, accompanied by a gentleman in clerical garb.

There is a serious expression on the sweet, young face, and large tears are in the dark gray eyes, for Emily Warren has bidden adieu to home, parents, brothers, and sisters, and is about to enter upon a new life, as the wife of a minister in a rural district, about a half-day's journey from her home.

The mother and sisters are standing behind the curtains of the drawing-room windows, looking out for the last time at the young bride. Servants are in the hall,

and Mr. Warren is handing his daughter into the carriage.

"God bless you, my child," said the father, as he
stood a moment on the pavement. "Be tender, Edward; she is a good daughter, and has never known any
hardship."

"With God's help, I trust that I may," was the reply.

"We must be quick, sir," said the driver, "or we
shall miss the train."

Closing the door hastily, the carriage drove off, conveying the young couple to the cars which would lead
them to Westbrook Parsonage.

"That is a sacrifice, mamma," said Gertrude Warren,
as she seated herself upon the sofa. "I cannot understand Emily. Think what she has rejected for that
country parson — a house in the Fifth Avenue, a carriage
and pair, a country-seat, and every luxury that heart
can wish!"

"I agree with you, my daughter," was the reply;
"but ever since Emily has been attending at Dr. Woodville's church, she has been a complete enthusiast, and
here she has thrown away her youth, beauty, and talents
upon an obscure minister, a mere nobody."

How little could these worldly spirits understand the
purity and holiness of the tie which united the young
pair, nor the simple-hearted piety which led Emily
Warren to choose what seemed to them a lot so humble
— to her, so high and holy.

The Warrens were members of a fashionable church, where sacramentarian theology was proclaimed from the pulpit, and mingled as much with its services as the Prayer Book seemed to allow; for in those days reverence for its hallowed forms exceeded what was accorded to the Word of God; and there were many who, following the teachings of Newman and Pusey, were ready to build the structure of mere formalism on the one word so unfortunately retained in some of our offices by the early Reformers; for that word *priest* seems to have been the fruitful seed out of which has sprung all that has followed since those early days.

Let once the idea of a sacrificing priest prevail, then must follow the altar, the sacrifice, the adoration, absolution, and salvation through a human priesthood.

And this was all taught at the Church of St. Agapius, where there was much to attract the worldly : fine music, and a showy church, but none of that holy unction of the Spirit which renders the gospel precious and powerful; for it was not in the ministry at St. Agapius; and to such the Spirit bore no witness.

Christmas came, with its bright evergreens and inspiring music—Lent, with its sackcloth and ashes, when there was a great hurrying up of parties and balls before the season; then came the fasting and daily service, to be followed by greater worldliness when what had been observed as a penance had been rigidly performed. Easter, too, came with all its high and holy hopes, but where the glory of the Master was hidden behind a veil of mystic theology : there was no real Christ-life, no vital union effected by *faith only* in the crucified Lord.

Such teachings had satisfied all of this household but Emily Warren, who had often felt a longing for a deeper and a holier life; but there was nothing here to guide the young inquirer.

The annual Confirmation was approaching: Emily heard the notice — she was then sixteen, and felt that the call was to her.   Carefully she read the service, and saw that there must be something more than a mere form in the vow which promised to renounce " all the vain pomp and glory of the world, with all covetous desires of the same, and the sinful desires of the flesh, and to lead a sober, righteous, and godly life."

With trembling steps, she sought her pastor's study, expecting to be questioned thoroughly as to her experience of the great moral change.

But all that Dr. Thurlow asked was literally her knowledge of the Creed, the Lord's Prayer, the Ten Commandments, and the Church Catechism — nothing that answered to the cravings of an awakened spirit, no pointing to the blessed Saviour, no words of earnest pastoral prayer.

Her name was registered among the candidates, and Emily returned to her home still more deeply convinced than ever that the Christ-life meant something more than that.

For she was an earnest student of the Holy Scriptures, and there she read of the new birth of "Christ within, the hope of glory," of the "new creature in Christ Jesus," of a "life hidden with Christ in God."

She felt that she had committed herself to a very solemn step; and, as the day approached, the fear of taking a false vow increased, until the agitation of her mind preyed upon her frame, and on the morning of the confirmation, in attempting to dress for church, several times she was compelled to lie down from weakness, until utter inability obliged her to give up the idea of presenting herself among the candidates on that occasion.

About this time, a young friend, formerly a member of the same school with herself, called to renew a previous acquaintance. Emily soon found that she had met with a congenial spirit; for Mary Cruthers, like herself, was a seeker after truth, and attended upon the ministry of Dr. Woodville.

To one of his evening lectures Emily accompanied her friend. No priestly arrogance marked the deportment of that good pastor; for he did not imagine that he bore about with him the power of forgiving sins, or the still more solemn power of dispensing the real body and blood of Christ. A shepherd to lead to the still waters, a guide to point the way to heaven, a father to sympathize with the trials of his people, an ambassador for Christ — this was Dr. Woodville.

2

Emily Warren felt especially drawn toward the serene and holy countenance, the sweet, persuasive tones of Christian love, and when the whole congregation joined in singing

"O! happy is the man who hears
Religion's warning voice,"

she felt, "This is my Christian home, here are the pastures where I must feed."

Great opposition was made at home; but, after a year's patient waiting, consent was given that she should join the flock that worshipped at St. Matthias'; and when the next confirmation season arrived, it was with very different feelings that she bowed beside Mary Cruthers, to take upon her young and ardent soul real Christian vows, with an intelligent understanding of what she was about to do. It was a solemn Sunday morning, and the occasion was one not soon forgotten.

About fifty candidates presented themselves for that holy ordinance. Seated in the front pews, the aged and the young, in simple garb, with reverential aspect, they assumed these deeply solemn vows; and from that holy day, Emily's course was onward and upward in her Christian life.

In this church connection, she formed the acquaintance of the Rev. Edward Hastings; and, after a season of determined and protracted opposition, the father was the first to yield, until, at length, she was permitted to follow the bent of her own inclinations in the choice of a partner for life.

Back again to this mile-stone in her young pilgrimage, we will return to the travellers on their way to Westbrook. Their road lay through a tame and uninteresting country, until toward the close of their journey, when hill and dale appeared before them, and touches of beauty peeped out now and then upon the landscape.

Leaving small towns behind, clumps of forest-trees dressed in their early spring robes appeared—bright carpets of the same fresh color covered the fields, where the young lambs sported in their innocent joy — the clouds, through the early part of the day chased over the heavens in sweeps of long, feathery forms, toward evening piling themselves up in banks of snowy cumuli, the summits of which reflected the rays of the declining sun, looking like glistening mountains of snow.

Suddenly above the trees appeared a church-spire, glittering in the sunlight. "There is Westbrook, Emily," said the husband, "and that is the spire of St. Barnabas'."

"I am so glad that the church-spire is the first object that I see, Edward ; it looks so like a haven of rest, always pointing upward to our real home."

"May that thought ever be present, Emily. That church-spire is a very dear object to me, for I am so completely wedded to the people of St. Barnabas', that I feel as if my earthly ministry should begin and end here.   Let this sacred object mark the first mile-stone in our union."

The young bride was looking at everything now through Claude-Lorraine glasses, for the prospect of a Christian home, with a congenial spirit, where there would be freedom to serve her Master, flooded her young heart with happiness, and, viewed through such a rosy medium, everything wore a look of beauty.

"What pretty rural lanes, Edward! and what neat little cottages!   I suppose that piety flourishes here."

The husband smiled as he replied, "Unfortunately, the same carnal enmity is found here as in the city, and I fear that many of your pretty pictures will dissolve when you draw nearer.   But there are, nevertheless, many lovely examples of piety among the people."

Just then the cars stopped at the dépôt, where Dr. Lacey's carriage was in waiting, and soon they were rolling on through rural streets, where beautiful modern houses, surrounded by tasteful pleasure-grounds, greeted the travellers.   Turning somewhat out of the more pub-lic streets, they came in sight of the loveliest part of Westbrook.

"There, Edward! that is the house that I admire," said Emily, as she directed his attention toward an old graystone house, with five gables, windows with small panes, and a long piazza stretching across the front of the house.   On one side smiled a flower-garden; on the other a fruit orchard, separating the house from a graystone church, embowered in a grove of grand, old trees. In front lay a fine lawn, with well-kept shrubbery; and back, the vegetable garden, joining a field which sloped down to a creek winding its way between green, shady banks, bordered with bushes and trees dipping their bending branches into the transparent waters of the stream.   Trees that looked a century old shaded the back of the house, and two of the noblest towered up in front.

The minister enjoyed the pleasure that beamed in his young wife's countenance, and remarked, with a smile, "That is Westbrook parsonage, Emily, and there is St. Barnabas'."

"That is indeed delightful: it looks exactly as if it were an old country-house, and those modern dwellings had all crept gradually around."

"That is just so, Emily; but we shall always have these pleasant grounds, and that will be a little taste of the country still."

The carriage is at the gate now, and a respectable middle-aged woman, with her clean, white apron and thin muslin cap, is standing on the piazza, waiting for the party.   It is Debby, a faithful family-servant, who has lived with Mrs. Warren all her married life, and who has now come to take charge of Miss Emily's kitchen.

"You are welcome home, Miss Emily," said the woman; and then, correcting herself, added, "It will be a

2 *   B

long time, I am afraid, before I can call you any
thing else, ma'am; for it seems only yesterday that I
used to rock you to sleep, and now you are a married
lady."

"We are a little tired, Debby. I hope that supper is
ready," said the husband.

"It has been waiting for half an hour, sir; but shall
I show you to your room, Mrs. Hastings?" and leading
them up the stairway that led directly from the hall,
the young lady soon found herself in her own room,
which, with the parlor, had been newly furnished by her
parents in a neat and comfortable manner.

"I will show you through the house on Monday,
ma'am," said Debby. "I have tried to arrange everything as well as I could. There is a good lot of old
furniture, but I have cleaned it all up, and it looks quite
decent, though a little different from the Fifth Avenue."

"Everything is delightful to me, Debby. It is such
a nice old country-house, and such fine trees and pretty
grounds — and then so near the church, that I am quite
happy."

After tea, the pastor led his wife into a small room
on one side of the hall, where a low porch led out into
the apple-orchard.

"This is your own apartment, Emily. I believe every
thing is here that you valued, even to the carpet in your
own room at home."

It was filled with birthday and holiday gifts from

dear friends ; and Emily looked around with a grateful heart and swimming eyes.

There were her rosewood work-table, her pretty secretary, her Chinese cabinet that contained so many articles of taste, her own lounge, her rocking and her sewing chair, all the pictures that she valued, and many little statuettes and rich vases that adorned her own room at home, and, added to all, a larger chair for another occupant.

"That is yours, Edward; pray be seated," said the happy bride. "Now, this is really home. I hope that I shall often see you in that chair."

"Another glimpse through a Claude-Lorraine. There is not much lounging time in a minister's life, Emily. This bower of ease is very inviting, but one who has the care of souls has not much rest upon earth. This pleasant bower looks very much like the one where Bunyan's Christian lost his roll."

"I will never interfere with your duties, Edward. You are the Lord's servant, and, by the grace of God, I will help, not hinder."

"This evening, however, I am at your disposal for an hour or two. Suppose that we walk out into the orchard."

It is Easter-eve, and the bright paschal moon is shimmering through the leafy branches, shedding a flood of silvery light upon the church windows and along the soft grass of the fragrant orchard.

Seating themselves in the summer-house at the other
end, through the openings of the branches, they watched
the pale moon sailing on so quietly through the cloudless
sky.

"I wonder if it shone upon the new tomb in the
garden of Joseph of Arimathea, eighteen hundred years
ago," said Emily. "It seems so associated with our
most sacred hopes that it always leads me back to that
first resurrection, and forward, Edward, to our own."

"Just so it affects my mind, Emily. This is indeed a
mile-stone in our pilgrimage, and I think Easter-eve
will ever be remembered with reference to this one in
our mortal life."

Crossing the stile leading into the field adjoining,
they made their way down to the creek bordering that
side of Westbrook, so secluded among such thick and
heavy shade that one could scarcely realize that a short
walk could lead to a place inhabited by so large a
population.

Seated on its grassy bank, they communed together of
the things of a better world, and of that blessed time
when sin should be banished forever, and the reign of
holiness be perpetual on the ransomed earth.

Happy, blessed union thus commenced below, to be
made perfect forever in heaven!

Their household consisted of four: a young girl,
named Jane, to assist Debby, with husband and wife.
On their return, at the sound of the bell, this little group

assembled in the parlor, and there Edward Hastings dedicated his family to God.

Emily had fine musical talents, and, seated at the parlor organ, she led the music of the household, singing the good old hymn which has formed the evening worship of so many saints now in glory:

"Glory to thee, my God, this night,
For all the blessings of the light;
Keep me, oh! keep me, King of kings,
Under thine own almighty wings."

Doubtless some of the winged messengers of the heavenly host descended that night to watch over the inhabitants of Westbrook Parsonage, for are they not all ministering spirits, sent to minister for them who shall be heirs of salvation?

"I must leave you awhile, Emily," said the young minister, "to make some preparation for to-morrow, for the people will look for the Easter sermon."

CHAPTER II.

ST. BARNABAS'.

"And daily in the temple, and in every house, they ceased not to teach and preach Jesus Christ."

EASTER morning, the queen of days — for thus it appeared to Emily Hastings, as she stood at her chamber window, inhaling the delightful fragrance stealing in from the delicate apple-blossoms, and listening to the carolling of the sweet spring birds! The atmosphere was full of the resurrection melody; it seemed as though the kiss of peace rested upon cloud and tree and flower — it certainly had left its impress upon the calm and holy countenance that turned to speak to her husband.

"'Brother, Christ has risen;' that was a beautiful custom of the early Christians, Edward, on Easter morning: it seems as if every human creature should echo the sentiment."

"Yes, Emily, the bursting buds, the sweet, fresh green, the smiling sky, all are eloquent in their declaration of this holy truth; for not long since, dreariness and cold and death seemed to reign, but now all is typical of the coming glory."

22

It was with full hearts that the little family sang their Easter hymn on that hallowed morning.

All was new to Debby, for the religion of the Warren household seemed to have very little to do with the family, and there was no domestic altar there; but here, everything appeared linked with another world, and none could quite forget beneath this roof that they were immortals.

The young wife made her first appearance at church on that holy day, and as she moved so reverentially up the aisle upon her husband's arm, dressed in the simple costume of a Christian lady, feelings of involuntary respect followed the stranger, whose whole deportment seemed to say, "The Lord is in his holy temple."

The church was an old building, with none of the modern decorations; but there was an air of solemnity around the capacious chancel, where the *communion table*, and not the *altar*, occupied the chief place. The reading-desk and pulpit were both draped with crimson velvet, and the chancel and aisles carpeted with the same warm color. The music was everything that a devotional spirit could desire, and such as enabled the worshippers to join in this delightful part of the church service.

The Easter sentences were sung with touching effect, and the time-honored service of the old Prayer Book was *prayed* — neither read in a drawling, lifeless manner, nor intoned in mumbling accents that none could un

derstand; but earnestly, devoutly prayed. Edward
Hastings loved the Master that its sacred services revealed, and the heart meant and felt the power of spiritual worship. The deep devotion of his own spirit
raised the tone of the worshippers, and Emily felt that
her lot had indeed been cast in one of the "heavenly
places in Christ Jesus."

Then the sermon was so impressive — full of Christ
and his resurrection, replete with practical teachings;
for his whole ministry was such as exalted Christ, the
Great Head of the Church. Around Jesus only, re-
volved all the hopes and joys and labors of the people
of St. Barnabas'.

There were several notices read, which declared the
activity of this busy hive of earnest workers — an evening lecture, a mothers' meeting, and cottage services;
so that Emily felt that "daily in the temple and in every
house" her husband "ceased not to teach and to preach
Jesus Christ."

Then the communion was so sweet, so solemn; the
singing of the Trisagion so elevating — for was she not
really singing "with angels and archangels"? — was
she not truly worshipping "with all the company of
heaven"? A very thin veil separated the church militant from the church triumphant. Who knows how
near the heavenly worshippers may be on these communion days?

The tone of her spirit inclined her to avoid introduction after service, but many a pleasant smile of welcome passed over the faces of numbers who recognized the young rector's wife now as one of the flock of St. Barnabas'. But there were censorious tongues here as elsewhere; and we will follow two, who, even from the feast of love, indulged in this miserable practice.

"Did you take notice of the lace shawl and the handsome silk dress that Mrs. Hastings wore, Hetty?" said Miss Prudence White.

"Yes, indeed; and the tasty little bonnet, too," was the reply. "I am afraid that our minister's wife is decidedly worldly. There is no one at Westbrook who has such a rich shawl as that. She will need some one to tell her what is expected of the pastor's wife."

"I have heard that her father is one of the wealthy merchants of New York, and that she has been brought up in great extravagance."

"That will not do for Westbrook," replied Miss Hetty. "The minister's salary will never support such articles of taste."

"I wonder that Mr. Hastings did not make a choice from among the young people of his own flock. I had often hinted to him about Mary Lacey or Sarah Hartwell, but he only smiled."

We will take leave of the ladies, and return to the unconscious subject of these remarks. She has folded up her handsome lace shawl, the wedding-gift of her

8

mother, without one thought of its offensive character changed her silk dress for a muslin wrapper; and, with a heart filled with love for her husband's flock, has joined him in the parlor.

"How is it that you have such delightful music, Edward?" inquired the lady.

"I am very fond of sacred music, Emily, and especially watchful of my choir, every member of which is a communicant. I meet with them weekly, and some of my most happy hours are spent on those evenings."

"It is a pleasant thought, Edward, that this most delightful part of our worship is not performed by irreverent and worldly spirits; for I have often witnessed sad desecrations in city choirs, when seated with Sunday-school children in the gallery. I have frequently seen its members eating in the intervals of the service, talking to each other, and, during the sermon, seating themselves in groups, whispering and laughing, or leaving the choir for the Sunday-school room, evidently no more interested in the preaching of the Gospel than the outsiders who desecrate the Sabbath openly."

"You will never see such a state of things at St. Barnabas', Emily, for I regard the music as a most important part of Divine worship."

In the afternoon, the young stranger was introduced to the Sunday-school, where the marks of a master mind were manifest in the cheerful alacrity with which everything was conducted — the teachers in their places punctually, the children following their example, a bright, earnest superintendent, and deeply interested classes. There were the infant department, the Sunday-school, the Bible-classes, and all the machinery belonging to an efficient school in active operation.

"Shall we hope for your co-operation, Mrs. Hastings?" said Mr. Hartwell.

Emily glanced toward her husband, as she replied, "I must consult my husband as to my post of Christian duty, ere I make any hasty promises: it has always been one of my chief pleasures to labor among the lambs of the flock."

Everywhere marks were seen of an efficient, earnest ministry.

When Edward Hastings first took charge of St. Barnabas', it was in a cold and lifeless state, for his predecessor had been a dull, formal preacher, and the congregation was then comparatively small.

Dr. Lisle's rigid adherence to what he deemed the rubrics of the Prayer Book had repelled newcomers, and kept back the spirit of progress.

The present minister had been there three years, and great changes had followed in his footsteps. He had made a deliberate and intelligent choice of the Episcopal Church as his own, where he delighted to preach the Gospel, as taught in her precious articles of faith. Its chaste and reverent decorum appeared to be

most m accordance with the simplicity and spirituality
which should distinguish public worship; but he saw
nothing in its rubrics, or its laws, to stifle the free,
familiar breathings which should prevail in more social
gatherings. The beauty of its public offices became as
it were a part and parcel of the current of his devotional
spirit, and made up the golden tissue that tinctured
all his approaches to the Triune God.

He was not ashamed of the name Protestant Episcopal, for there was no hankering after any of the popish
practices that marred the Church before the days of
reformation. He did not consider those doctrines and
practices non-essentials for which the martyrs died, and
loving his Church with a pure and holy love, he longed
to see her purgèd entirely of even the appearance of
sympathy with Rome; and therefore the word priest
always jarred upon his feelings, lest it should convey
false ideas of the Christian ministry. He knew that
purification must come, for was she not a branch of the
true Vine? and the Saviour has declared of the Church
collectively, as well as of individual Christians, that He
"purgeth every branch, that it may bring forth more
fruit."

Not in vain had he used the name of Jesus — appearing in every prayer, permeating every office, conspicuous in all the Articles and Homilies of the Church he
loved: baptized by the Holy Spirit into a deep experience of real, manly faith, he preached with power and

unction Jesus all in all, Jesus only as the sinner's hope; and the Spirit bore a constant witness to the power of such a truly apostolic ministry.

When he baptized, it was to bring not simply to an ordinance, but to Jesus; when presenting his spiritual children for confirmation, it was to draw still nearer to the Master; when he administered the consecrated bread and wine, it was to lead his people as near to Jesus as mortals could be on this side of heaven; and this was the apostles' doctrine and fellowship taught at St. Barnabas'.

Thus Edward Hastings lived the Christ-life among his people, and thus he drew increasing numbers, by lifting up, *not the Church, but the Cross* as the refuge of the soul. His Prayer Book had taught him to value above all things the revealed word of God: that was first and foremost, as it was God's — the Prayer Book second, as it was the work of man.

It was his constant practice to bid his people prove all things by the word of God, and then to hold fast to that which was truly good and spiritual.

These were the steps by which he led immortal souls — first, to self-abhorrence at the foot of Sinai, then to Jesus at the foot of Calvary; thence to the Church, that spiritual home left upon earth by the Saviour, to nurture his own children, and not the children of the flesh. Thus he gathered around him a company of laborers

3 *

truly consecrated to the service of God, because sealed
by the Holy Spirit of God.

To the poor and afflicted he was especially a minister
of consolation, and to the community at large a beloved
and respected minister ; for he had large and catholic
views toward all who loved his Master.

Every Sunday he repeated that article of his faith,
"I believe in the holy Catholic Church, the communion
of saints ;" and his comprehensive charity stretched out
its arms to all who reflected the image of Jesus in their
daily lives.

To his spiritual mind, this invisible army, throughout
the whole world, marching on to glory, composed the
band of Christian brotherhood, and as such his warm
heart loved them, and his benevolence co-operated in all
works of good for man which did not compromise his
fidelity as an Episcopal minister. His evening lectures
were numerously attended, not only by his own flock,
but by many otl.ers, who were glad to enjoy his more
social meetings for worship.

Railroads had of late years brought Westbrook so
near the great metropolis, that many families made it
the place of their summer residence, and at that seasรn
the church was crowded to its utmost capacity. Here,
in this blessed home, Providence had cast the lot of Emily
Hastings.

It is now Monday morning, and the young wife is
walking after breakfast in the garden among her flow

ers, stooping now and then to pluck a lovely blossom to add to her bouquet for the parlor. Suddenly, a pleasant voice accosts the young lady:

"This is Mrs. Hastings, is it not?" said the visitor, standing by her side in the garden path.

"It is, madam. And my visitor?"

"Mrs. Lacey, the doctor's wife, your nearest neighbor. You see that there is a gate between our gardens, intimating that we are open to calls at any time. Your good husband has frequently made use of it, for I have tried to be a mother in his bachelor estate."

It was an agreeable countenance that smiled upon the young lady. A short figure, somewhat inclined to stoutness, and a general appearance of health and cheerfulness, prepossessed Emily at once in her favor.

Mrs. Lacey held a bouquet of choice flowers in her hand.

"I presume that we are alike in our love of flowers," continued the lady, as she offered them to Mrs. Hastings.

"Thank you," replied the listener. "They are really lovely! I shall often come for hints how to nurse my own garden."

"Please remember the open gate, my dear. You are a new housekeeper, and you will always find me ready with motherly hints, never intruding my advice."

"You are very good, Mrs. Lacey; and I dare say that I shall often avail myself of your kindness."

"We are glad that our young pastor has taken to himself a wife, for I know that he has been very lonely in the parsonage. He is so good and useful that we think he deserves every earthly blessing."

"I am glad to hear you speak so, Mrs. Lacey, for that is just what I think," said the young wife, with a modest smile upon her face.

"You have no idea what changes have been wrought under his ministry. St. Barnabas' was high and dry enough before he came. Now we are all alive, and a blessing follows Mr. Hastings everywhere. But I must not detain you, for I dare say that you have household duties to attend to. We are neighbors now, and I hope often to see your hand upon the latch of our gate. Good morning, my dear." Then, turning hastily back, she added: "Be ready at four o'clock, to-morrow. I want you to ride with me, for I have some pleasant spots around Westbrook to show you."

"It will give me great pleasure, madam. I shall be ready."

And the two parted — Emily to look through the parsonage, and Mrs. Lacey to report at home the interview — mutually pleased with each other.

Debby was quite chagrined at what she deemed the plainness of Emily's establishment, for, compared with home, it seemed rustic indeed.

"I don't know how you are going to put up with so

many privations," said the woman; "it is all so different."

The young wife smiled as she replied, "You can have
no idea, Debby, how little those things that you value
so much, have to do with my happiness. I am sure that
my parlor and chamber are just as neat as I could wish;
all the furniture is new, and my own sitting-room is
charming, Debby."

"How in the world are you going to do without a
carriage? you can't walk about much, the roads are so
dusty, and the distances so long."

"We can do very well, Debby. The good people will
sometimes call for me to ride with them, and I can very
well dispense with that luxury."

They are now among the bed and table linen, of
which there was an excellent supply, furnished by
Emily's parents.

"I took good care of all this, Miss Emily," said
Debby, as she turned these articles out of the chests,
with a proud look upon her honest face.

Suddenly the door opened, and Mr. Hastings made
his appearance.

"You had better be ready for visitors, to-day, Emily;
I am pretty certain that you will have some calls. I
have many visits to make, for several of my people are
sick."

Accordingly, the young wife prepared for visitors, and
had not been long seated in her sitting-room ere she

heard the latch of her front gate, and looking up perceived a small lady, under a large, green umbrella, coming up the garden walk.   It was a neat, dapper little figure, with precise step, and quick, bustling motions.

A profusion of crisp, gray curls, piercing black eyes, a nose not remarkable, but the pleasant smile around the mouth almost redeemed the other unpleasant features.   Emily saw all this as the lady stepped up on the front piazza.

Received in the pretty sitting-room, Emily saw that she looked around uneasily, as she introduced herself by the name of Miss Prudence White, one of the oldest members of St. Barnabas'.

"You have undertaken a very weighty charge, my dear," said the lady.

Emily smiled as she replied, "Not so very weighty, I should think, for we have only four in our family."

"I did not allude to your private duties, my dear; I referred to your position in the church."

"I have no very imperative duties there, for I believe the vestry called my husband to the charge, and not his wife."

"You certainly mean to take some part in the benevolent operations of the parish?"

"My husband will advise me, Miss Prudence; I am a novice in my new position, and he is my best counsellor."

"You have a great many fine things around you

here," continued the lady; "quite showy for a minister's house. I hope that they will not make you worldly."

"They are chiefly gifts, and valued on that account. I have been used to such things all my life, and do not find that they engross either my time or thoughts, Miss Prudence."

"You will find a great variety of people here, Mrs. Hastings; and I will give you a few hints about some of them, to put you on your guard. There is Miss Jane Proctor, the greatest talker in Westbrook; and there are the Westons, as proud as Lucifer — they will want to patronize the minister's wife; and there are the Browns, stiff high-church people."

"They are all members of my husband's flock, Miss Prudence, and as such entitled to kindness and courtesy. I dare say that I shall find many amiable qualities in all of them."

"I hope that you will not be disappointed, my dear: you had better not be too unsuspicious."

"I had better think too well of them, Miss Prudence, for we all need forbearance from our fellow-creatures."

"You talk just like all young people, but you will learn better, some day."

After making many rude inquiries about the cost of many pretty things in the room, Miss Prudence took her departure, leaving behind some troubled ripples upon the atmosphere of the parsonage, and the lady inspector quite defeated. Mortified by her discomfiture, Miss

Prudence stopped on her way home to see her friend, Miss Hetty Van Zandt. "I don't know what to think of the young thing," was her report to inspector number two. "I could make no impression there; she was very polite, but I felt somehow as if her manner said that she had an excellent counsellor at home. I wonder if she is not a little proud."

On Mr. Hastings' return, he laughed at Emily's account of the visit, saying:

"There are many phases of human character in a parish like ours, but we must learn to 'be wise as serpents, and harmless as doves;' but I must not forget to say that with all Miss Prudy's unpleasant peculiarities, there are many valuable traits of character, for she is always ready to give time, money, and sympathy, wherever there are misery and want."

"I'll remember that, Edward, and try to forget the oddities."

"Dear, precious wife! May this sweet spirit guide and bless you always," replied the husband, as, pressing a fond kiss upon the fair forehead, he left the sitting-room to prepare for dinner; and the young wife sat a moment where he had left her, with hands folded and a soft smile of perfect content resting upon the lovely face.

The next day brought a different experience, for the ride with Mrs. Lacey was so very delightful. Emily found her to be sensible, refined, pious, and was charmed with the kind and charitable accounts that she gave of many of the people of St. Barnabas'.

"We have a mothers' meeting that meets on every Wednesday evening at the Bible-class room. Would you not be willing to take charge of it, my dear?"

"Who directs it now, Mrs. Lacey?"

"That has been my pleasure until a better is found."

"Then it must just continue under the same direction. I should be happy to attend the meetings, and aid in your benevolent work, but your experience must not be lost to the people by my blunders."

The ride was through a delightful country of hill and dale, where beautiful country residences greeted the eye on every side; and Emily could easily see why so many citizens had chosen their summer residence among these green hills.

"Do many of these families attend at St. Barnabas'?' inquired Emily.

"Quite a large number," was the reply; "and it helps the parish very much. There is one place where we must waive ceremony and make a call," continued Mrs. Lacey. "Stop at the next place, John; we will get out for a few minutes."

The carriage drew up to the gate of a neat cottage; and, on the ringing of the bell, an old servant presented herself at the door.

"How is your mistress, Susan?" inquired the lady. "Can she see company to-day?"

4

" Walk in, ladies; I will see."

Leaving the visitors in the parlor, Susan left the room, and in a short time a venerable lady of at least seventy entered.

"Mrs. Raymond, this is our minister's wife. We thought that we must not wait for your visit."

"That is right, my dear. I pay very few now, and am really obliged to you for coming." Turning to Emily, she took her hand, and said:

"May the Good Shepherd guide and bless you in your new calling!"

Emily was struck with the aspect of the venerable lady. Clad in a black silk dress, with her silver hair parted on her smooth forehead under a fine lace cap, she thought that she had seldom seen an aged face where so much of peace and resignation shed their holy calm.

"You are just entering upon life, my dear; I am going out. You are looking forward probably to a life of usefulness and happiness. I have outlived all my children; but I have the hope of meeting them in heaven, for they were all Christians. Come into the next room, and I will show you their portraits."

Four lovely children, two daughters in young woman-hood, and two others in the very bloom of manly youth, one in military garb.

"They were lovely in their lives and happy in death. I shall go to them, but they will not return to me "

Emily looked at the saintly face of the old lady, and thought how precious is the faith which can sustain the soul under trials like these.

"I have not one word to say, because my Master did it. Time is very short, and eternity is long. I shall have them all that long, long, happy life. Meanwhile, I wait patiently till my time comes."

They returned to the parlor, and Susan soon entered with some sponge-cake and cool beverage.

"This is excellent, Mrs. Raymond," said the doctor's wife.

"Susan made them both," was the reply. "I don't know what I should do without her."

"That will never be, Mrs. Lacey, so long as I live," said the faithful woman. "Mrs. Raymond has been good and kind to me ever since I was a young thing, and I shall never forsake her."

"You will come often, my dear," said the old lady, addressing the pastor's wife.

"It will give me the greatest pleasure, madam," was the reply. "I shall not soon forget this afternoon's visit."

"Remember me most kindly to your good husband," continued the old lady, "his visits are very precious to me, and he never forgets the afflicted."

"I call that little cottage 'The Chamber of Peace,'" said Mrs. Lacey, when seated in the carriage, "for it

always takes me back to that resting-place in the Pilgrim's Progress."

" Well named," was Emily's reply ; " for I think that
I never saw more of the peace that passeth all understanding than rests upon the face of that dear old
saint."

The week was occupied chiefly with receiving visits
from her husband's parishioners. Miss Hetty Van Zandt
was among the callers, patronizing and scrutinizing, for
she was rather near-sighted.

Emily was quite amused at the manner with which
she examined the bijouterie of her sitting-room, (using
her nose almost as much as her eyes,) and more so with
her remarks, for she soon perceived that Miss Hetty had
come on a tour of discovery.

When Mrs. Hastings gave the lady her first donation
to the Missionary Society, her visitor's prejudices were
quite disarmed, for Emily remarked, smiling, " You
have my first donation, Miss Hetty."

" Miss White will not like that much, for Prudy
always must be foremost." And off started inspector
number two to show inspector number one how she had
been preferred.

How much of wood and hay and stubble are to be
burned in the great day of purification ! But how blessed
to feel that Jesus sees even the *small grains* of real faith,
which through the abounding riches of divine grace will
be owned in that sifting day.

Many tokens of good-will reached the parsonage, sometimes in the shape of a basket of fresh vegetables, sometimes a pair of spring chickens, or, at others, a dozen of new-laid eggs; and the young wife's first week was, upon the whole, one of general satisfaction. In the afternoons, she generally accompanied her husband on his visits to distant parishioners. Not having a carriage of his own, he was obliged on these occasions to accept the loan of his neighbors' vehicles.

"How different this is from home, Edward!" said the young wife, as she took her seat by her husband's side on one of these pleasant afternoons.

"Better, happier, Emily?"

"Infinitely; for here, in this peaceful home, there seems nothing to separate us from our Lord."

"There may be, Emily, for bosom foes follow us everywhere in our earthly pilgrimage."

"Yes, but Jesus is nearer here than in the Fifth Avenue, where all was so worldly: it seems just like Bethany here, Edward."

"Why, Emily?"

"If Mary and Martha and Lazarus are not here, there are those whom Jesus loves, and that makes Bethany."

"But we shall find the little foxes that spoil the tender grapes everywhere, Emily, but especially in the little world of a minister's parish."

4 *

"We won't let them worry us, Edward, when we have so many blessings; for I think that we can both say, thus far, that we have met with many more of the Saviour's lambs than Satan's foxes."

"Dear, hopeful wife, live in the sunshine, for the candle of the Lord is shining brightly around your young footsteps."

CHAPTER III.

FATHER MORGAN.

For he was a good man, and full of the Holy Ghost.

IS the little chamber in order, Emily?" inquired her husband; "I mean the one facing the orchard, that we call the prophet's chamber, and is frequently occupied by a dear old friend, who is a kind father to me. I am expecting Father Morgan every day now."

"Why do you call him by that title, Edward?"

"He is the oldest member of our Convocation, and all the brethren call him by that name, for he is a man of ripe experience, and we all look up to him as to a father. That is his likeness over the sideboard in the dining-room."

"He has been a handsome man, Edward, in his youth I shall be glad to see him, for your sake."

"My parents died when I was young, Emily, and left me penniless: you do not know what Father Morgan has done for me; at once he adopted me as his own son, bore all the expenses of my education, and is always the same devoted friend. I know no other father."

"I will see that all is comfortable, Edward."

"There are a wrapper and a pair of slippers in the

closet, kept expressly for him; be sure to lay them out, and have some warm water in his room every night, to bathe his feet."

"There is a carriage at the gate now — Edward, a low vehicle, odd and old-fashioned enough."

"It is our friend, sure enough."

Hastening down the path, the young minister wel comed the old gentleman, but was surprised to see a ragged boy of ten sitting in the carriage.

"Well, Edward, you have another bird in the nest, I hear. How do you think that you are going to support a family on your salary? And then I hear that you have brought home a dainty lark, not used to the privations of a country parsonage."

"You must judge for yourself, father. I know that in a few months you will think Emily Hastings a choice blessing in a minister's lot. But let me take care of the horse: you must be tired after your long ride."

"Not I — no one waits on Pete but myself, Edward; I know just what he likes; he's a pretty saucy chap; I have to take his own bucket along, for he will not feed from any other. Run into the house: I'll be there as soon as Pete is comfortable."

Knowing the old minister's peculiarities, he was not interfered with.

Putting his head in the kitchen door, Father Morgan took Debby by surprise by his abrupt address.

"Here, Biddy, help me out with these things: I want

them put away in an eye-wink, without the knowledge of the mistress."

Debby wondered who this could be, who with such an air of authority gave his orders.

"I am not certain that I ought to, sir, for I don't know where they came from."

"You needn't ask any questions, just do as I bid you. And give this boy something to eat: he's hungry, I know, by this time."

Without farther dispute, the stores were safely deposited in their proper place. and the boy fed, as directed.

In about half an hour, Father Morgan made his appearance in the parlor, where the mistress of the parsonage was ready to receive him.

Mrs. Hastings was struck by the aspect of her visitor —rather tall, with a fine, open countenance, a benevolent, winning smile, and broad, expansive forehead. crowned with silver hair.

The modest deportment, and bright welcome on the sweet, young face, at once interested the old clergyman's warmest feelings.

"I suppose that you know this is my son, young lady," said her guest; "and as a matter of course, you must be my daughter: as such I give you my blessing, child."

"I know what you have been to Edward, Father Morgan, and are entitled to our warmest love."

"I bid you take care of these husbands, daughter: it all seems very sweet during the honeymoon, but by-

and-by you'll see the staff of authority; then take care!"
and a humorous smile passed over the old gentleman's
face.

"I shall never be afraid of my husband's staff, father,
for it is my pleasure to follow its leadings."

"Where in the world did you pick up that ragged
boy, Father Morgan?" inquired Mr. Hastings.

"Sitting by the road-side, as I came along, crying bitterly, just to worry me, I suppose; and on making inquiries, he told me that he had lost both parents: you
know, Edward, that I could not leave an orphan by the
road-side; Hannah conceives that we want a boy to help
in the kitchen, and so I brought him along."

"And what has become of Jacob?"

"Oh, he's about yet, but I have a place in my head
for him at neighbor Jones'. I have had him now for
two years, and he is quite a good gardener now."

"When did you leave New York, Father Morgan?"

"Last Friday, Edward; and a miserable visit it was,
to be sure. I am concerned for our beloved Church, for
she has enemies among her pretended friends. There is
decidedly a strong disposition to favor the sacramentarian theology in more quarters than one; there is, moreover, a weekly journal advocating the new doctrines, or,
rather, the old fossils dug up; and it is all so agreeable
to unrenewed human nature, that I fear many will be
led into the snare."

"These are days of trial, father, and it behooves us all to be on the watch-tower."

"This corporate idea of the Church, Edward, reminds me of what I have heard of the practices of the Romanists in South America, where, in crowded churches, with consecrated mops, the priests sprinkle the masses with holy water."

"We are not in danger of such gross ideas as these, but of something more refined; for there is much in the Newman tracts to interest the intellectual, and draw them after the teachings of that school, especially when promulgated by men of high character, such as Drs. Pusey and Newman; but most of all, I fear the future: some of our brethren say, let them alone — that opposition creates friends; but I cannot agree with them: this is the seed of deadly error; if we allow it to germinate, bitter will be the fruit. It has commenced with the intellect, that affects the few who wield the power; by-and-by it will pander to the sensuous and imaginative, that will sweep the masses, especially in America. Choke the thistle-seeds, Edward, and there will be no harvest of weeds."

"Did you ever hear any positive teaching, father?"

"I did hear the doctrine of priestly intervention between the soul and God openly taught; and, moreover, I saw the raising of the patten after consecration, and the bowing of heads among the people, that indicated serious, vital departure from Protestant truth."

"Did you visit St. Matthias' during your stay?" inquired Emily.

"I did, my daughter; and it was truly refreshing to the spirit to hear the clear, decided teaching of that pulpit; but Dr. Woodville is sorely traduced by many of his brethren as a Methodist, a Presbyterian, anything but a churchman. There is one comfort, however; God will take care of His own Church, and bring her in safety through all the days of tribulation."

"Are n't you tired, father?" inquired Emily. "We should have thought of that before."

"I am somewhat, and should like to go to my little room."

Emily led the way, and the old man looked around with a pleasant smile as he surveyed the marks of attention to his comfort.

"Edward has told you about my notions, I see. Now you 'll please not to disturb me until dinner-time, for I should like to be alone."

Passing the door about an hour afterward, Emily heard the voice of supplication in deep, earnest tones, and felt how blessed it was to be the subject of such faithful prayers. Next morning, the good man walked around the place in company with the pastor, surveying everything with fatherly interest.

"This is a fine fruit orchard, and quite a good vegetable garden; but they must have some one to take care of them, or they will be useless to you."

" Yes, I know that," was the reply; "but I cannot afford to keep a man."

" And then how are you to go about with your wife without a carriage? She can't take long walks in the country; and besides, it is absolutely necessary."

" It is quite out of the question, father. The cost of a horse and carriage would be a great addition to our expenses."

The old gentleman was seated in the summer-house with the pastor, leaning thoughtfully upon his cane, and talking in low tones to himself.

" She seems such a good little thing. It's such a pity that she has n't these few comforts."

" Who are you talking about?" inquired Mr. Hastings.

" About Emily, to be sure — my daughter. She must be made comfortable."

The old gentleman was much amused by the look of surprise with which Debby surveyed him seated at the dinner-table.

" I guess she wonders who I am," said the visitor; "but she'll get used to me after a while. Where did you meet with her, Emily?"

" She has lived with my mother all her married life," was the reply, "and is very much like a housekeeper here."

" I suppose that she wondered who the old man was that ordered her about yesterday in the kitchen."

"She is a faithful woman," was the reply, "and will respect every one that we value, I am sure."

After dinner, Emily led the way to the parlor, and opening the organ, asked her old friend if she should entertain him with some music.

"That is my chief recreation, daughter. Can you give me some of the old chants?"

Both had fine voices, and Father Morgan sang a good bass yet. The music brought Debby and Jane to the parlor-door; for it was something more than common melody that filled the room. Grand old hymns and some sweet modern airs followed. The old man was in his element.

"I pity the Quakers, Emily, don't you? They lose so much of holy joy in this part of public worship; but I think that they'll be among the loudest singers in heaven, to make up for the silence here."

"The young people of that sect are just as fond of music as we are; for I have had visits from several such, and they are never tired of the organ."

"What must be the worship of heaven, children, when the whole church triumphant joins the angelic choir? That idea is a fine one when comparing it to the voice of many waters."

"I must be going to-morrow, Edward," said the visitor; "for I have preparation for Sunday to make; and Hannah will be troubled if I do not come on the day appointed."

The morning came, and Father Morgan led the family prayers. The holy, heavenly fervor of that sweet service seemed to rest upon the family for days, and Emily said to her husband, as the carriage drove out of sight:

"It seems as if a benediction were left behind, Edward, by that good old man: how is it that he is so much attached to you?"

"In his youth, he loved my mother — they were separated by money-loving parents. My mother married, and died young, leaving but one child, and that one he loves for my mother's sake; for he has never married. A rich uncle left him all his property, and he uses his wealth for the glory of God and the good of man."

On the Monday morning of the following week, Jacob drove up to the gate in a neat country carriage with seats for four. Fastening the horse to the gate, he asked for the minister, and handing him a letter, stood waiting with hat in hand. The young pastor's lips quivered as he handed the letter to his wife, who read:

"My dear children will accept this horse and carriage from their friend, with the services of Jacob Grant, who I know will prove a faithful servant. Regard this as a gift from the Lord. Jacob's wages will be paid monthly, and all other expenses attendant upon the keeping of the carriage. It is a great pleasure to do this for a servant of our dear Lord and Master."

"Take the carriage to the stable, Jacob," said the

pastor, and then turning to his wife, he said, "'Goodness and mercy have followed me all the days of my
life.' Let us thank Him, Emily."

Shutting themselves up in their own room, their full
hearts poured out their gratitude in words of earnest
praise and consecration.

Jacob was older than they had supposed, and was
well qualified to take care of the garden, as well as the
horse and carriage.

"Who would have thought that Mr. Morgan was such
a rich man?" said Debby, when informed of the gift. "I
thought he was some old driver, belonging to a grocery
store, when he first came here, for he brought such a
load of stores. I could not make out how it was, when
he told me not to tell until he had gone; but now I
must show you, ma'am," and leading the way to the
store-room, there were fifty pounds of coffee, the same
of white sugar, a box of tea, and a small kit of superior butter."

"This is just like Father Morgan," said her husband;
"always going about with his open hand of munificence."

The good clergyman lived about twenty miles from
Westbrook, where he supplied two country churches.

He had a very comfortable house, kept by Hannah, a
faithful housekeeper, who knew exactly how to make
the master happy. One might suppose that she had but
little to do, in so small a family; but Father Morgan
was "given to hospitality," and was never without some

one to enjoy his bountiful board. Always one or two orphan children were permanently lodged, often temporary pensioners, and not unfrequently a minister's family when without a charge, were members of his household. His was a warm and generous heart, filled with the love of Christ, and loving the whole household of faith for his Master's sake. Perhaps some, dwelling in smaller Christian circles, might have been scandalized when hearing that the whole family of the Presbyterian minister were received into his house when the father was suddenly removed. The parish was poor, the minister had been a valued friend, and when the successor was about to enter upon his duties, Father Morgan opened his house to receive the widow and orphans, until something was permanently arranged for their support. So large and unusual were his charities, that Father Morgan was esteemed as the friend of the whole community, for he was truly "a good man, and full of the Holy Ghost."

5 *

CHAPTER IV.

LITTLE FOXES.

"The little foxes that spoil the vines: for our vines have tender grapes."

THE stream of life was so different now to Emily Hastings! In the dawn of her voyage to the New Jerusalem, her course lay through troubled waters, where rocks and shoals met her little bark constantly as it struggled on through numerous impediments.

Now the atmosphere within the parsonage was peaceful as was the face of nature without. She was daily making new acquaintances among the people of St. Barnabas', the ministrations of the sanctuary were refreshing, and it might well be said of her present experience that "I *sit* down under his shadow with great delight, and his banner over me *is* love."

There were some families, however, where it was an especial privilege to visit, and old Mrs. Raymond's was such.

Once a fortnight, it was the good pastor's habit to visit the invalid; for there were many marks of decline daily visible.

"Always welcome," said the old lady, as she met the

two on one of these occasions. "I don't know what I should do if I lived among some of the lofty ministers in the city. A friend was here last week, who was giving some account of the doings of the Tractarians, and I could not help thinking how different it must be from the Master, who encouraged sinners of all classes and grades to come directly to Him."

"That is the blessed privilege of the true Gospel, Mrs. Raymond; and when I hear of priestly intervention, I think of the precious words of the apostle when he says, 'Let us come boldly to a throne of grace, that we may obtain mercy, and find grace to help in time of need;' for 'there is one mediator between God and man, the man Christ Jesus.'"

"Blessed words, Mr. Hastings. What should a poor, trembling sinner such as I do now without this assurance? I believe the precious message, and so I dwell in an atmosphere of peace."

"Thanks be to God for His 'unspeakable gift,' Mrs. Raymond."

"Here is my monthly payment to the church fund, Mr. Hastings. The objects are all marked; and I only wish that I had more to give to Him who gave Himself for me." Then, turning to the young lady, she continued, "Do you feel at home among us, my dear, by this time?"

"I should be very ungrateful, if I did not," was the

prompt reply; "for I have received nothing but kindness ever since I came to Westbrook."

"I have something for you, my dear;" and going to a closet, she brought out three bottles marked "Raspberry Vinegar." "We had a fine crop of fruit this year, and Susan made a good quantity of it. It is a delicious summer-drink, mixed with ice-water; and many a sick and feverish patient enjoys this beverage."

The old lady had heard of Father Morgan's gift, and looking out of the window, remarked, "What a comfort your little equipage must be, Mr. Hastings! I was so happy when I heard of the good man's kindness."

"It has been a great blessing; for Emily and I can now visit freely among our people, which we could not do without it. He is one of the good stewards of the Master's bounty, and considers his wealth not his own. But we must go now: shall we have a farewell word of prayer before we part?"

Susan was called in, and the four enjoyed a short space of sweet communion with God, leaving with the dear old lady a holy benediction.

"Ripening for the kingdom, Emily," said her husband, as they drove home. "I can see the dear old saint drooping and fading at every visit, and it will not be long ere she joins her departed children."

On returning home. Emily perceived several trunks in the hall, and entering the parlor, was surprised to see her mother and sister Gertrude.

"This is an unexpected pleasure, mamma," said the young lady.

"It is beginning to grow warm, Emily; and Gertrude and I thought that perhaps you could accommodate us for a few weeks. We have brought Maria with us, so that we shall not make much more work in the family."

"You must be tired, mamma: shall I show you to your room?"

"Debby showed what she called the spare room, Emily; but I really don't know how two of us can occupy that small room."

"We will make some other arrangements, then. Our room is much larger; you can take that, and we will go into the spare room."

"I have always been used to a dressing-room, Emily, can't we have the two together?"

"Yes, mamma, if you say so; and we will take the prophet's chamber."

"What shall we do if Father Morgan comes, Emily?" said the husband, when alone.

"I should be very sorry not to accommodate him," was the reply. "I should not know what to do, unless Mrs. Lacey will give him a room. I should not be afraid to ask her; she is so truly benevolent and obliging."

It was a real inconvenience to be shut up for several weeks in so small a room; but there was no appearance of annoyance.

On retiring for the night, Emily remarked, "We have prayers before breakfast, mamma; the first bell rings for rising, the second for worship, the third for breakfast."

"You need not expect me at the second, Emily; it is a Puritanical practice, at any rate. We find the daily service at church to meet our views on that subject."

"It is so sweet, mamma, to surround a family altar together. Won't you sometimes come?"

"I may in the evening, perhaps; but your ideas and mine will never correspond, Emily."

Next day, the young wife led her mother and sister through the parsonage.

"And this is your home, Emily," said Mrs. Warren. "Plain enough — half of the furniture is worn out. There is nothing in the house worth looking at, except the rooms that your father furnished. What a fool you have been to reject George Le Roy for Edward Hastings!"

"I am very happy, mamma. We have every com fort, church privileges which are invaluable, and a husband kind and good as man can be. My employ- ments are all congenial, and I consider my lot much to be envied."

Emily soon found that the peace of her happy home had been sorely invaded by the newcomers. Not only did they refuse to attend upon morning prayers, but fre- quently the breakfast-table was kept waiting until nine o'clock, an hour and a half after the usual family meal, and all the household rules disturbed. Then the meal was uncomfortable; for it was impossible that it should be otherwise when standing so long. The ladies frequently ordered away the meal, making Emily most unhappy by their conduct. When such was the case, the two were ill-natured all day. Then especial pains and expense were bestowed upon the dinner, which was criticized likewise by Mrs. Warren. Here were the little foxes spoiling the tender grapes of domestic peace and comfort.

"I am going to lecture to-night, mamma," said Emily, when the evening arrived. "Won't you accompany us?"

"Perhaps I may," was the ungracious reply.

Dressed in high fashion, the mother and sister of the pastor's wife excited much remark as they sailed into the humble lecture-room of St. Barnabas'. Forgetting that they were in God's house, they took no pains to conceal their disgust at the service, scarcely joining at all in the responses, making themselves conspicuous by their low bows, not only in the Creed, but the Gloria, wherever it occurred. Such things were uncommon at St. Barnabas', and Miss White accosted her friend after church in high indignation.

"Did you ever see such airs, Hetty?" said the lady. "What did they mean by all that bowing?"

"That's the new fashion, I suppose," was the reply. "I have been told that in New York there are churches where this is done wherever the Gloria occurs in the service."

"Is it in the Prayer Book? I never saw it, I am sure."

Miss Hetty smiled.

"There is much done by these new-fangled church people that is not found in our good old book, and I am afraid that much will follow."

"Don't ask me to go to that lecture-room again, Emily," said her mother. "Why on earth don't your husband have public worship in the church? I felt as if I were in a Presbyterian meeting-house."

"Edward thinks that for our more social services the lecture-room is better — where the people are brought more closely together, and the elements of sympathy more cultivated."

"The people are brought too close to the minister for me, Emily. Reverence for the sacred ministry suggests the idea of distance between the two. Let the priest and the people be separated; so say I."

"And yet, dear mamma, we are invited to draw very near to the Great High-Priest of our profession, assured that the sacrifice, once offered, is forever perfect, and we forever sure of acceptance. If we may draw near to the Holy One, certainly we need not fear to approach His ambassadors; for we have no other priest than our anointed Saviour."

"We can never agree, Emily; I see that."

In a day or two after this conversation, Father Morgan made his appearance at the parsonage, and was much disappointed on finding that he was obliged to lodge at Dr. Lacey's instead of in the prophet's chamber. Mrs. Warren was greatly amused by the old minister's peculiarities, and sometimes not a little afraid of his sarcasm. Staying over Sunday, he assisted the young pastor in the public services, and saw much in the deportment of the two ladies in church to excite his displeasure. Meeting at the dinner-table, Father Morgan turned abruptly to Mrs. Warren, and said:

"Can you inform me, madam, by what authority the new interpreters of our beautiful service bow at the Gloria?"

"It is an expression of reverence for the name of God; so I use it."

"Is the mode authorized by our Book of Common Prayer? If so, I have never been able to discover the rubric."

"It is not forbidden, I believe."

"Miserable sophistry, madam! That reasoning would bring in a host of practices among sober-minded Episcopalians, each worshipper being his own interpreter. We should have but little of common prayer left if that principle were tolerated."

"You will not deny that it is an expression of reverence, Father Morgan?"

"I am certain that it is not in all cases, madam; for,

6

last winter, I was at church in New York, sitting near
a lady who was very particular in all these observances,
when my attention was drawn to something of a bright
pink color lying close by her side, which she raised frequently to her lips.   Very soon, to my disgust at her
mummery, I saw that she was eating; and as it was
Christmas morning, I discovered that it was a bonbon
that she had brought to church, and, in the intervals
between the bowings, regaled herself with this confec-
tionery.   You do not pretend to say that these were acts
of reverence."

Mrs. Warren looked confused as she replied, "I certainly do not justify such proceedings, but I never saw
anything like that."

"I have sat near young ladies, too, madam, who were
among the best dippers in church, who, even in the act
of such performances, were occupied in whispering behind their prayer-books, in a manner most scandalous to
devout worshippers around.   You do not call that reverence?"

"By no means; but you are prejudiced."

"Very much, madam, against all such innovations of
our Book of Common Prayer.   When I go to the house
of God, I desire all its services to raise my thoughts to
heaven, and must own that these exhibitions drag them
down to earth, and sometimes excite a class of emotions
incompatible with spiritual worship."

Arguing from different stand-points, it was impossible

that two should agree where one advocated the sacramental, the other, spiritual religion: the gulf is impassable, *never* to be bridged over — *never*.

During the following week, Miss Hetty Van Zandt was announced as a visitor at the parsonage. Father Morgan had seen her tall, thin figure coming up the gravel path, and turning to Emily, said, smiling,

"Inspector number two, my dear: get your defences ready for an attack."

Miss Hetty was peculiarly erect, her lips peculiarly rigid, her eyes peculiarly bent on that occasion, as she took the proffered seat.

"All well, Mrs. Hastings?" inquired the lady.

"Quite well, thank you," was the reply.

A silence of a minute, a clearing of the throat, then an opening of the battery:

"Your visitors must be quite a trial, I should think, Mrs. Hastings."

"They are my mother and sister," replied the lady, with quiet dignity.

"Yes, I know. Tractarians, are they not?"

"They attend upon such a ministry, Miss Hetty."

Another silence, then another discharge:

"If I were you, I would advise them to refrain from their singular bowings, at St. Barnabas'; it is very offensive to the people, especially in the pastor's pew."

"It would not become me, I think, to interfere with their ideas of public worship."

"It gives great offence, Mrs. Hastings, and excites not a little ridicule: then they are such a very dashing pair, that their conduct is peculiarly disagreeable."

"I am sorry that you feel so, Miss Hetty; but, really, it is not in my power to interfere."

"While I am speaking, I might as well be a little plain, my dear. Do you know that there is a great deal of talk in some quarters, about the dress of our minister's wife? Old Mrs. Lisle was a very plain lady, and the contrast is quite striking."

"I was not aware that I was stepping out of the bounds of moderation becoming my station as a Chris tian lady, Miss Hetty."

"You wear articles of jewelry, and other tasty decorations. Let me repeat a few passages of Scripture, which you may have overlooked: 'Whose adorning, let it not be that outward adorning of plaiting the hair, and of wearing of gold, or of putting on of apparel.'"

"I have often read the passage, Miss Hetty, and a kindred one, also, which enjoins the 'women to adorn themselves in modest apparel, with shamefacedness and sobriety; not with broidered hair, or gold, or pearls, or costly array.' Mr. Hastings and I have often discussed them, and I have concluded that they are intended to check the tendency of that age and people; and while we must pay some attention to the customs of the world in which we live, whatever is contrary to the rule of

Christian shamefacedness or sobriety, must be avoided, as becometh saints."

"And so you justify the wearing of rings and breast-pins, Mrs. Hastings?"

Emily smiled at the look of surprise on the face of inspector number two.

"I have a few, the gifts of dear friends, which, in wearing, I do not feel that I offend against the law of Christian simplicity: at all events, Miss Hetty, I think my husband is the best interpreter of Scripture at St. Barnabas' — he is to me, at least."

Miss Hetty drew up her neck to a still greater degree of erectness, as she replied, "I am sorry that my advice is thrown away."

"By no means, Miss Hetty: your motives may be all right, and a little free discussion is good for Christians, at all times."

"You would have much more influence if you would only pay a little attention to my hints, my dear. But I must be going: I have many calls to make to-day. Good morning, Mrs. Hastings. No offence, I hope, my dear?"

"None whatever, Miss Hetty; I am getting accustomed to free remarks."

Father Morgan had overheard all the conversation, and entering the room with a smile, he said, imitating Miss Hetty's manner to perfection:

"No offence, I hope, my dear," as, with an erect head

6 *   E

and precise, measured step, he crossed the room, and then
returning, continued:

"Pretty well done, my dear. I don't think Miss Hetty
will come again with her budget of advice."

Mrs. Hastings was laughing heartily at the exact
imitation of her late visitor, head erect, eyes bent, and
hands folded.

"I don't mind them as much as I did Father Morgan;
but I own that they do disturb my temper, sometimes,
and I feel very much like excusing myself to some of
these meddlers."

These were the little foxes that spoiled the tender
grapes of Emily's peace, not her piety.

There were many trials connected with Mrs. Warren's
sojourn at the parsonage, and when the visit was at an
end, it was with a quiet sense of relief that Emily
returned to the sweet and holy calm of her daily life.

It is the evening for the meeting of the choir, and
very soothing was the heavenly music to the rector and
his wife. There were several fine voices belonging to
the choir, and united as the group was in Christian faith
and hope, none of the church gatherings were more
elevating than this, for were they not celebrating praises
that they hoped to sing forever in the better land? The
echoes of the melody reached Mrs. Lacey's parlor, and
stealing softly across the garden, she stood outside of the
window, enjoying the harmony. Mrs. Hastings thought

that she heard footsteps by the window, and opening the shutters, she recognized the doctor's wife.

" Come in, Mrs. Lacey," said the lady; "you are always welcome at these meetings."

The evening was closed with fervent prayer, and each member felt it a privilege to join this weekly gathering at the parsonage.

" There is a message from Mrs. Raymond," said Emily to her husband; "she is very ill, and wants to see you at once."

The good pastor hastened to the bedside of the dying saint, where, sustained by faith in Jesus, not in sacraments, he found her gently passing to her everlasting rest.

" God bless you, my dear pastor, for all your kindness and fidelity to me," said the faint, weak voice. "I am going to my Saviour and my God, where I shall meet the dear ones that have gone before: prepare to follow me to that better land. I have remembered dear St. Barnabas', for it has been a sweet haven of rest to me, in my pilgrimage."

Mr. Hastings told Susan to get a room ready for him, for he should not leave the house until all was over.

A night of wrestling with the death-angel brought a morning of release to the sufferer; and as her pastor closed the eyes of the departed, he said, " Blessed are the dead who die in the Lord."

A solemn funeral at St. Barnabas', a quiet resting

place beneath the shadow of its sacred walls, and the last will and testament of the departed was read — bequeathing five thousand dollars to St. Barnabas', a settlement upon her faithful servant, Susan Roberts, the principal, at her death, to go to the poor of the church that she loved.

Thus life flowed on at St. Barnabas' — the pastor and his young wife identified with all the joys and sorrows of its people; their own Christ-life deepening and widening amid the numerous cares and duties which met them in their daily walks. The bond between pastor and people was daily strengthened, and it was difficult to imagine what could break the tie which bound Edward Hastings to St. Barnabas'.

The sacramental host of God's elect were marching on to glory, under the guidance of a holy pastor — the trials of daily life, mellowing and softening human asperities, and bringing the real children of God nearer and nearer to the Master; wheat and chaff growing together until the reaping day, the chaff then to be consumed, and the wheat to be gathered into the heavenly garner.

Blessed are they who are ready for the sifting!

Wheat and chaff! solemn words! Which am I! Reader, which art thou?

CHAPTER V.

FRAGRANCE.

"Behold, how good and how pleasant it is for brethren to dwell together in unity."

EIGHTEEN mile-stones have been passed by the dwellers at the parsonage since last we met them. The rector of St. Barnabas' has received many calls since then to leave his parish — some from city churches, to more extensive fields of labor, holding out large inducements to tempt him from the church of his early love; but to all he had the one answer:

"How can I leave the children that I have baptized, the flock that I have seen confirmed? How can I part from those with whom I have held such sweet and heavenly communion at the table of our Lord? I love my people. Many I have joined in the holy bonds of matrimony: I have travelled with them through their first trembling steps to the Cross; have watched their succeeding march along the heavenly way; have rejoiced over my spiritual children when they walked in the truth, or mourned over them when they have taken backward steps in their Christian course. I have prayed with them by the death-bed of their loved ones, and have committed their precious dust to the silent grave, in the hope of a glorious resurrection.

"I cannot leave them! Let me labor for the dear people of St. Barnabas' so long as I have health and strength. They are a kind and faithful people. As my family has increased, so has their bounty. No, no! I cannot leave St. Barnabas'. I am theirs for life, or as long as they can use me. I looked out of my study window this morning, and watched the pigeons flying around the steeple, flitting in and out of the loop-holes that afforded the pretty creatures a shelter. I love the innocent birds that make their home in my Father's house, and tears filled my eyes at the thought of hearing their cooing no more."

Mr. Hastings writes thus to Father Morgan on the subject:

"I took the call to St. John's, and read it in the summer-house. I looked up at the dear church-spire pointing ever to the way that leads to heaven, and then round upon the grand old trees; and great, large tears filled my eyes at the thought of the time when I might look upon these dear objects no more.

"I went into the church, for it was time for evening service. I walked up the aisle, and felt the clasp of childish hands, and saw the loving beams of sweet, familiar eyes. Seated in the chancel, I looked at the dear old pulpit and the reading-desk. I glanced along the aisles at every pew, and thought of the occupants that had sat there during all my ministry ; and, with a heart bursting with emotion, I said, No! Dear St. Barnabas'! I must not — cannot leave you. Just then the organist entered, and, unconscious of my presence. played the hymn I love so much, and which for so many years we have sung at our Friday-night lecture :

"Far from my thoughts, vain world, begone;
Let my religious hours alone;
From flesh and sense I would be free,
And hold communion, Lord, with thee."

I covered my face with my hands, and yielded to the emotions of the solemn hour. No, no ; I cannot leave St. Barnabas'. I passed into the vestry-room, and prepared for evening service, relieved at the thought that I was not to leave the people that I loved."

And thus the pastor was wedded anew to his devoted flock.

Great changes have passed upon the parsonage, two wings having been added to the building, one opening on the orchard, the other on the garden. There is quite a family there now, and we will take a peep at the group out in the fruit orchard on a pleasant afternoon in spring.

Apple-blossoms are covering with their delicate bloom the low, green trees, and filling the air with their sweet fragrance, while the rays of the late afternoon sun are streaming in through the opening branches from the western sky, lighting up the fresh greensward and the group of happy children scattered over the pretty orchard. Not more fragrant, however, is the sweet perfume of the lovely blossoms than the odor of sanctity filling the atmosphere of Westbrook Parsonage ; and it is more than probable that, in the dim future, the same delicate perfume will always bring back to that household the memory of that holy, blessed home. Let us make the acquaintance of the youthful inmates.

Warren, a boy of fifteen, is stretched upon the grass, face downward, poring over a book. He is tall and slender, with an intellectual face, dark-brown hair and eyes, wearing a look of deep, earnest thought. Allan, the second boy, is drawing his brother Edward round in a carriage. Alice, a girl of eleven, is amusing her sister Lucy with a book of bright pictures. It is a lovely group scattered over the soft, mossy carpet of living green So thinks the mother, who is looking at them from the window of the sitting-room in the new wing.

Suddenly Alice raises her eyes, and crying out, "Papa! papa!" drops her book, Allan the carriage, and they all scamper off, save Warren, who is intent upon his book, and follows slowly. A gentleman is coming up the path, carpet-bag in hand. Lucy seizes one hand, Alice the other; Allan and Edward dance on before to announce the arrival. But Margaret, a girl of seventeen, is before them, and, seizing the carpet-bag, hastens

in to call mamma; but she is coming, with a frail, delicate infant in her arms.

The joy of reunion expresses itself in tender caresses and words of sweet affection. Eighteen years of labor have left their marks upon the pastor's holy countenance: the face is pale and worn, the light brown hair is thin and scattered; there is a look of spirituality over the whole countenance, and a want of elasticity in the slow and measured footsteps very different from the buoyant tread of the first years of his ministry at St. Barnabas' — all marks of ripening for the heavenly inheritance.

The pastor's wife is changed also. Sweet young womanhood has given place to the more sober aspect of the Christian matron; there is a sweet smile of perfect peace upon the still lovely countenance — that look which we see upon the face of the Madonna.

They have shared life's joys and sorrows, and together they have trod those blessed paths which lead home to heaven. They have learned much of the preciousness of Jesus under the teachings of that blessed Spirit whose office it is to reveal the Saviour to the thirsty soul; and Emily Hastings is learning each day to know and love her Lord still more and more.

The Master hath wisely set Christians in families as beacon-lights to the world around; and such is the household at Westbrook Parsonage.

Composed of human beings, not angels, sharing the

7

common taint which has passed upon all the race, they
know the value of the fountain of a Saviour's blood,
and daily do they lead the dear ones committed to their
care, at least within reach of its drops of sprinkling.

The children are like others — neither worse, as is so
often uncharitably asserted, nor better naturally than
others. Seated on a pinnacle, it is true that they are
more observed than the children of private families;
hence the criticisms which follow them. These, at least,
are in better circumstances than many others; for they
are daily viewing the Christ-life of their parents, daily
the subjects of earnest, believing prayer.

We are in their midst now; and, seated on a lounge
between his wife and daughter Margaret, the good pastor is telling about his visit:

"We have had a precious season, Emily. The brethren of our convocation are so united, and had much to
tell of the work of the Spirit among their flocks; and
we are always happy when the work of the Lord is
prospering."

Margaret watched the wearied look on her father's
face, and said, "You are tired, papa; if you will go up
to your room, I will run out and hurry up an early
supper."

"Papa has come, Debby," said the young girl.
"Make a good cup of chocolate; you know he is fond
of that when he is tired."

The good woman was always glad to wait upon the

nead of the family, and replied, "I'll have a nice one in a very short time, Miss Margaret; you may be sure of that."

Seated around the table, all had something to tell of what had passed in papa's absence. Warren was somewhat of a quiz, and sometimes, like other elder brothers, took pleasure in teasing the younger ones.

"Do you know, papa," said the youth, "that Sir Charles and Lady Anne have had a falling out? I neard a great noise in the attic on the last rainy day, and listening at the keyhole, I found Miss Lucy delivering a long lecture to the two on the wickedness of their conduct. I opened the door, and behold the two were placed back to back, having had a dreadful quarrel."

"It was only play, papa; and I don't think that it is kind in brother Warren to make fun of our sports."

These worthies spoken of were two pictures left by the former residents, dressed in the costume of the last century, and which afforded much amusement to the children on rainy days, personating all sorts of characters.

"What book is that which you were reading so intently in the orchard, Warren?" said the father.

"Volney's Ruins, papa," was the reply.

"Where did you get it, my son?"

"From Dr. Arnold's library. He has given me the free use of all his books, papa."

"I would rather that you should not read books of that class, Warren, until you are older."

"It 's just the kind of book that I like : it sets me to contradicting, and asking questions, papa."

"Contradicting what, my son ? "

"Everything, papa.   I always like the opposite side."

The father looked troubled, for this cast of mind had developed itself in the days of earliest childhood, when Warren, in lisping tones, asked "Who made God ? " and "Who made Satan ? " and " Why did God let sin come into the world. Is n't God stronger than the Evil One ? '" and " Why did He let him into the garden ? "

Just such knotty questions had the boy asked all the days of his life, and the father feared that the soil of Warren's heart was only too well prepared for the seeds of unbelief.

Warren sat playing with his knife and fork, his eyes bent thoughtfully upon his plate.

"Ought n't we to read both sides of a question, papa ? "

" Whom do you mean by we, Warren ? " and the father smiled at the consequential pronoun.

"Every one that has the power of thinking, papa."

" When the mind is well stored with Scripture truths, the judgment formed, and the imagination under proper control, then, perhaps, it may be safe to read on both sides of difficult questions ; but not in the crude days of hot boyhood, Warren."

Turning to his second son, he asked, " And what have you been about, Allan ? "

"Margaret and I have learned two new pieces, papa: we will play them for you, after tea; and I have commenced a new piece of drawing, too."

"And Alice?"

"I have hemmed two pocket-handkerchiefs and two bands for you, papa, beside all my lessons at school, and helped mamma, by playing with baby when she was busy."

"And Master Edward?"

"I—I—" and the boy looked up to the ceiling, with a puzzled expression. "Well, papa," counting his labors on his fingers, "I've fed old Boss every day, and learned my lessons for mamma, and I tried to put things to rights in your study, papa; but—but—I broke the large inkstand, and stained the carpet."

"There, there, that will do, Edward."

"Now for Sunbeam," and the father turned to Lucy, with a loving look.

"I made some iron-holders for Debby, to keep her poor old hands from getting burned, learned lessons for mamma, stringed the beans—and I didn't forget my prayers, papa."

"Now, children, what are the texts for the week? for you know that I have been away for five days."

"The subject was the character of God," replied Margaret.

"Well, what have you to say, my daughter?"

7*

"'God is a Spirit, and they that worship him must worship him in spirit and in truth.'"

"And yours, Warren?"

"'God is from everlasting to everlasting,' and 'I am that I am.' That is a deep thought, papa. How is it? —without beginning, and without end —how can that be?"

"That is a description of the unfathomable God, Warren: it is not for man to answer how such a Being can exist."

Then, turning to Allan, the father asked, " Now, my son, what have you to say?"

"He is the Rock, his work is perfect; for all his ways are judgment: a God of truth, and without iniquity, just and right is he."

"And Alice, my love?"

"'The eyes of the Lord are in every place, beholding the evil and the good.'"

"I am ready for yours, Edward."

"'God is love; and he that dwelleth in love dwelleth in God and God in him.'"

"And Sunbeam's?"

"'But ye have received the spirit of adoption, whereby we cry Abba, Father.' 'The Spirit itself beareth witness with our spirit, that we are the children of God.'"

"Very good texts, my dear children; yet this is only a glimpse of his infinite perfections; but you have learned something. Now these are solemn Scripture truths, for from all these passages we learn some duty: if, therefore, God is a Spirit, Margaret, what duty does it require?"

"That we must worship him in spirit and in truth; is it not so, papa?"

"That is correct, my dear. Can you tell me who only worship him thus?"

"The true children of God, papa — those taught by the Spirit."

"Now, Warren, what do you learn from the passages on the eternity of God?"

"I learn to stand in awe of such a mysterious Being, papa."

"What from his justice, and truth, and holiness?"

"To trust him with everything, and know that all his doings are perfectly right. I learn also to fear sin, since God hates it," replied Allan.

"What from his omniscience, Alice?"

"That we must fear to offend in deed and thought, because he is always present to read our hearts."

"Can Edward tell what his beautiful passage teaches him?"

"That we ought to love such a kind and gracious God with all our hearts, papa."

"Sunbeam's is the best of all," said the father, "for she has learned that we may call this great and good and holy God our Father. Which of you can tell me how that can be done? for by nature, we are the children of wrath, and at war with him."

"By adoption, papa," said Margaret; "for we learn that by a true and living faith in Jesus, we are adopted into the family of God, so that we can call him 'Abba, Father.'"

"Blessed and holy privilege!" said the pastor, as he looked around upon those he loved. "May you all be His, my dear children."

Then came the sweet service of family prayer, the father presiding at the organ, while with full hearts they sang the precious hymn:

> "Lord, with glowing heart I'd praise Thee
> For the bliss Thy love bestows;
> For the pardoning grace that saves me,
> And the peace that from it flows."

Happy household! brought so close unto the Father in these impressible days. How many of our most eminent men date the dawn of their spiritual life from such family altars as this! Here are the seeds of imperishable truth sown. Here are wafted down the gales of the Holy Spirit. Here descend angelic spirits to ward off harm from the dwellings of the just; and here is inhaled that sweet fragrance of piety, never to be forgotten in the days to come, when the perfume of sweet apple-blossoms will always return laden with the memories of these blessed orisons at Westbrook Parsonage.

CHAPTER VI.

SOWING BESIDE ALL WATERS.

"Blessed are ye that sow beside all waters."

I HAVE just had a visit from Miss White," said the wife, in meeting her husband at the dinner-table. "She came to ask me to take charge of the Bible class, which now is without a teacher. But I do not see how I can leave home so early in the morning, and do my duty by the children."

"Our first duties are to the church that is in our house, Emily, and to this we must be faithful."

"There are six to prepare for Sunday school. Margaret aids me, it is true ; but I never allow Edward and Lucy to go without reciting their lessons, and then it is time to prepare for church. I have taken Mrs. Lacey's place in the mothers' meeting, for those I can meet at home."

"It is a blessed field, Emily, for there you can give the benefit of your experience."

"It is very interesting, husband, and I trust that there I may do good among an humble class of society — the women are so grateful. Then little Emily is so delicate, that she requires my constant care; but she is better now, and I think that we might venture to take her to church next Sunday : she is five months old, and ought to be baptized."

"If the day is fine, let it be so, Emily."

Accordingly, on the following Sunday, the little lamb was received into the congregation of Christ's flock, and signed with the sign of the cross, "in token that here-after she should not be ashamed to confess the faith of Christ crucified."

"What does the service mean, papa?" said Margaret. "When it says, 'Seeing now that this child is regenerate, does it mean that the child is spiritually renewed?

"That is not my interpretation. I think the following clause does much in the way of explaining, when it con-tinues 'and grafted into the body of Christ's church. Spiritual renewal may sometimes accompany the ordi-nance; but not invariably, as experience proves abun-dantly; for how many baptized children grow up wholly destitute of spiritual piety!"

"That is true, papa; but as there are two Christian sacraments, there must be some benefit derived from what the Saviour instituted himself."

"True, my daughter: by this sacrament. children are received into the outward fold of Christ's church on earth, are the subjects of the prayers of Christians, and, if the parents keep the vows made at that time, are trained in the paths of piety, to which God has promised his blessing. If such an important doctrine as spiritual regeneration were connected with this sacrament, would not the Saviour have made it very clear at its institution ?"

"When was the idea first connected with the sacrament, papa?"

"Not in the days of the apostles, Margaret, for in all the records of the New Testament it is like all the institutions of our Lord, impressive and simple. All the mysteries which have since been crowded upon it have been added by man. What more simple than the language, 'baptizing them in the name of the Father, and of the Son, and of the Holy Ghost.'"

"It seems a pity, papa, that the word should be kept in our Prayer Book, if no such thing is in the New Testament."

"It was retained at the time of the compilation of the English Prayer Book, and may bear several interpretations. We would explain it by the *Bible;* others explain the Bible by the Prayer Book. It is a great privilege and a sacred duty, Margaret, to be allowed to bring our children to Jesus, certain that a blessing will attend upon the service, if we only come in faith, believing."

"Now our little Emily is a Christian child, papa."

"In one sense she is, my dear, a member of the household of Christ."

"When was the Prayer Book arranged, papa?" inquired Allan.

"In the days of Edward VI. many important alterations were made, but in the days of Queen Elizabeth, still more. In her reign, the word table was substituted for that of altar, for the idea of a sacrifice was entirely repudiated by the Reformers of those early days. It is a pity that the word priest has been retained in some of the offices; for we love our Book of Common Prayer, and desire to see it just as perfect as a human composition can be made."

"I wonder that the Reformers did not see what these words must lead to," said the wife; "for they had clear views upon vital points, and regarded them worth dying for."

Touching the book that lay upon the table, the pastor replied:

"Let us love the book, my children, that came to us from men like these—only, love it intelligently and scripturally, not superstitiously: the Bible, first and best, always; the Prayer Book, as it reveals the truths of Scripture, and guides our devotions."

"I have been to other churches, papa," answered Margaret, "but always came back to my own, thankful that we have forms so beautiful in which to worship our God."

"It is a privilege, my daughter; but never allow yourself to doubt the piety or wisdom of those who differ from us; for some of my most valued friends are in other earthly folds than ours, but there are the same heart-throbs of love to a common Master, and it is quite impossible for a true Christian not to love that image, wherever it is found."

Thus did this faithful servant of the Lord sow the seeds of truth and love beside all waters, the Spirit sealing the words as they sank into the hearts of the children of the parsonage.

Watchful to embrace all occasions, the mother withheld not her hand in scattering the same precious seed.

We find her, one morning, entering the church, while the sexton was busy in cleaning it, to get the box of bands from the vestry-room. Passing along the aisle, she perceived Edward running about from pew to pew, evidently annoying the sexton by tossing the books and cushions out of their places as fast as they were arranged.

"Don't do so, Edward," said the sexton; "it gives me a great deal of trouble to put them all back again, and I know that your papa would not allow it."

Straightening himself up, proudly, the boy replied, "Do you know who I am Mr. Robb? I am Edward Hastings, the minister's son."

"Yes, and the more is the shame that you behave so badly."

By this time, Mrs. Hastings had reached the boy; directly taking him by the arm, she led him out of the church, saying, "Come with me, my son, I have much to say to you."

Edward hung his head, for he knew that he had behaved badly to the sexton.

"What did you mean, Edward, by your speech to Mr. Robb?"

"I meant, mamma, that he had no right to reprove me; for am I not the minister's son?"

"Suppose that you are, Edward, does that make it proper that you should speak so rudely to a respectable man, attending quietly to his business?"

"I guess I must be a little better than a common boy, mamma, for Miss White always makes a fuss over me and Lucy, and brings us loads of candy, and says that we are pretty and smart."

"And so, Edward, this foolish idea of yours has led you to be impertinent to the good sexton. Now you must go directly into the church, and make your apology."

Edward hung his head. "He's a working-man, mamma, and it seems hard to ask his pardon."

"You have brought it upon yourself, Edward: it must be done."

Taking him quietly back to the church, she led him to the sexton's side. "Edward has something to say to you, Mr. Robb," said the lady, with a grave look on her face.

"Mamma says that I have been a bad boy, Mr. Robb. I hope that you will excuse me this once."

"That 'll do, my little man: children are very apt to

got foolish notions in their young heads; but you've got a dear mamma, to teach you what is right. May God bless you, and make you like your father, my son!"

Edward looked up into his mother's face, pressing her hand more fondly, for the boy knew that this was true.

" We must lay an interdict upon the children's seeing general visitors, Edward," said the wife, when relating the incident. "I have often thought that the foolish flattery of some of our good people might be injurious: now I am convinced that it is so, and we must do as we think for the good of our dear children."

"Miss Prudence may be offended, for she has been very kind to us, Emily."

" I will be candid, husband, and tell the truth: she may not like it at first, but that will wear off."

And thus the interdict was wisely laid upon general intercourse with the parishioners.

The four elder children of the family were in attendance upon Dr. Arnold's school, a select establishment, where a few boarders were received, in addition to about twenty-five day scholars; the domestic department being under the care of his two sisters. Dr. Arnold was a prince among teachers, well qualified to conduct the education of youth, and one whom Mr. Hastings could trust entirely. Much attached to the children of the parsonage, he was most careful to make no distinction in the government of his pupils, and it is certain that his just, impartial course secured the universal respect of all his scholars. His school was daily on the increase, for many were anxious to secure a place for their children in this favored establishment.

"I wish that you could have seen Bob Winter, when he came into school, to-day," said Warren; "he looked like a great, awkward booby, with his long legs and arms sticking out of his old clothes; we could n't help laughing at him, but the doctor gave us a lecture for it afterward."

"Not more than you deserved, Warren," said the father, "if you let the boy see that you were ridiculing him. Remember that he is the only son of a poor widow, but a good and faithful boy, and ought to be respected."

"Did you see that mean fellow, Richard West," said Allan, "how he followed Jenny Chase about at inter- mission-time? He knew that she had some good sponge-cake, and he never stopped until he coaxed away more than half of it."

Then Alice joined the critics: "Did you ever see any one like Mary Hope? She never knows her lessons, and there she sat shaking and stuttering, while the rest were looking on."

"Perhaps it was just because they were looking at her that prevented her from reciting well," said Mrs. Hast- ings.

"This is very unkind talk, children," said papa. "Suppose that we change the subject."

Next day, the good pastor was walking around the back of the house, in company with the family group.

"Did you ever observe how that gable is covered with moss, Warren?" said the father, pointing to that part of the roof.

"Yes, papa: how beautifully green it is!"

"Do you know what is underneath, my son?"

"A mouldering roof, is it not, papa?"

"Yes, beautiful to the eye, it still conceals much that is offensive and decaying: it reminds me, children, of a verse in the Bible, which says: 'for charity shall cover the multitude of sins.' I thought of it yesterday, when you were talking so freely about your school-mates: doubtless there are many human frailties visible in that little world; but think how many you have yourselves. Why can't you be like that soft green moss, covering so beautifully the decaying roof?"

"I wish I were, papa," said Allan.

Warren was silent, but only because he felt deeply the power of this gentle reproof. Walking quietly away, he took his seat in the summer-house, evidently thinking over his father's words.

We will step in at Dr. Arnold's next day. Bob Winter was the same bashful boy as on the day of his first entrance. Seated by himself at recess, he was puzzling over a difficult example, and, large boy that he was, Warren saw that every now and then he would steal his hand up quietly to wipe the moisture that would come.

"Shall I help you, Bob?" said Warren, taking a seat by his side.

"I am a little puzzled," was the answer, "and would be very thankful for just a few words of explanation; I must do the work myself, though."

Warren was a bright mathematician, and, by a few clear words, set the boy upon the right track. Raising his large, dark eyes, Bob Winter spoke his gratitude. Warren walked away happy, and thought of the soft green moss.

Poor little Mary Hope was in trouble too: she had failed again in her lessons, and was seated at her desk, her face bent down upon her small fair hands.

"What is the matter, Mary?" said Alice. "Can I help you? Do you study your lessons, Mary?"

"I am not idle, Alice: I learn my lessons, and say them perfectly to my mother before I leave home; but I get frightened, and then I can't say one word, and the girls all laugh at me, and think me stupid."

"Forgive me, Mary; I was one," said Alice; "I thought you were lazy; but I won't do so any more, Mary. I'll ask Miss Darling to let us sit together, and I'll put my arm around you when your turn comes, and try to be your friend. Don't cry so, Mary."

Then the gentle girl pressed a kiss on the little trembler's cheek, and thought of the soft green moss, as she led her out into the play-ground. Allan too remembered the lesson, as he heard Lewis Barr recounting the wrong-doings of Harry Seymour.

"Would n't it be better to say nothing about them, Lewis?" said the boy, as he stopped a moment at the desk — and all the way down stairs repeating the sweet words which his father had quoted the day before: " for charity shall cover the multitude of sins."

"What is the subject for to-day, children?" said papa at morning prayer.

"The immortality of the soul, and our accountability," replied Margaret.

"What have you, my daughter?"

" 'And the Lord God formed man of the dust of the ground, and breathed into his nostrils the breath of life, and man became a living soul.' "

"What do you gather from the word 'living,' in that passage?"

"I suppose, papa, that God breathed into Adam a part of His own nature, and thus man became immortal."

"That is correct, my child. Now it is your turn Warreu."

" 'But now is made manifest by the appearing of our Saviour Jesus Christ, who hath abolished death, and hath brought life and immortality to light by the gospel.' "

"What have you found upon the subject, Allan?"

" 'And fear not them which kill the body, but are not able to kill the soul.' "

" What has Alice on the subject of accountability ? "

" ' For we must all appear before the judgment-seat of Christ.' "

" I am ready for Edward's now."

" ' For God shall bring every work into judgment with every secret thought, whether it be good, or whether it be evil.' "

" Now my little Lucy's."

" ' So then every one of us shall give account of himself to God.' "

" These are solemn truths, my children; let us remember them every day and hour of our mortal lives."

" If we are to give account of our most secret thoughts," said Margaret, " who can stand in the last awful day, papa ? "

" Not one, in his own righteousness, my child ; but clothed in the perfect righteousness of the Lord Jesus Christ, we need not shrink from one who is not only our Judge, but our Advocate with the Father; so that when accused by our conscience, or by our fierce adversary, we may say, ' Who is he that condemneth? it is Christ that died.' "

Very earnest and believing was the precious prayer poured out on that hour of morning devotion by the father of the household, and very sweet and tender the deep emotions of more than one young spirit seeking to clasp its tendrils around the loving Saviour.

Living epistles of Christ, the children read in the lives

of their parents the blessedness of serving the Master — attracted by the picture, and not repelled by the caricature of his matchless holiness and love.

"As the small rain upon the tender herb, and as the showers upon the grass," so gently did the dews of the Holy Spirit fall upon these tender lambs of the flock. Well may it be said of the future for these dwellers at Westbrook Parsonage, that "they that sow in tears shall reap in joy;" for "He that goeth forth and weepeth, bearing precious seed, shall doubtless come again with rejoicing, bringing his sheaves with him."

CHAPTER VII.

BETHANY.

"Now Jesus loved Martha, and her sister and Lazarus."

LITTLE RUGBY stands amid the shade of forest trees, for Dr. Arnold has been careful to select a spot of beauty, where there is at least a miniature academic grove. He has named it Little Rugby, not from any vain comparison between himself and the celebrated master of the English Rugby, but from a real love for that model teacher whom the world honors. The house is a stone building, with several porches, each shaded by clustering vines of fragrant roses, honeysuckle, and clematis; the most beautiful flowers covering the large bay window of the parlor, opening on the side of the garden.

Father Morgan admires and loves the accomplished head of this institution, and seldom visits the parsonage without dropping in at Little Rugby. He has just returned from such a visit, and, according to his custom, he has found his own name for the pleasant home.

"I have just come from Little Rugby, Edward," said the good man, "but I have a better name than that; I call it Bethany, for here dwell Lazarus, and the sisters Mary and Martha; and I am sure that it is a household that Jesus loves."

"It does seem appropriate," was the reply, "for I always feel the sentiment when sitting in the pleasant parlor."

Richard Arnold was a man of thirty, of high culture, deep piety, and remarkable wisdom in the profession which he had chosen. He had taken orders in the Episcopal Church, but finding that his voice was not equal to the demands made upon it in the ministry, and being an enthusiast in his love for the young, he has wisely devoted himself to the business of education, for there is no more useful man connected with St. Barnabas' than this faithful teacher of the Youths' Bible Class. He is a deep student of the Scriptures, and eminently a man of prayer. We will step in a moment into his class-room, on Sunday morning, where he has just gathered as many as the room will hold. He has singular power in fastening the attention of this wayward, excitable company; for there is that in the full, dark eye, in the sweet, loving smile around the firm mouth, and in the penetrating tones of a voice mellowed with earnest feeling, which fascinates and controls the whole.

Then the rich treasures of learning and piety ever at his command, the convincing power of the words that come from a heart that has experienced their preciousness, and the constant presence of the Holy Spirit so earnestly invoked, make this little room often a holy Bethel to the members privileged to meet there.

Not only does this spiritual unction rest upon the hearts of Christians here, but even the most worldly acknowledge that there is no hour of instruction through-out the week so full of interest as this.

From this band — generally ranging at fifty, some-times more — have come out several youthful soldiers of the cross; and the most useful among the Sunday-school teachers are always drawn from this training-class.

Richard Arnold is the friend of each; for many of them are members also of Little Rugby; and to its master, with all their perplexities and mental struggles, they eagerly come. He is among the most trusted and valued of the pastor's friends, is one of the leaders in the meetings for social prayer, an influential manager of the Missionary Society, a member of the vestry, and in all things a warm supporter of the pastor of St. Barnabas'.

Martha and Mary are younger sisters; and, singular enough, their names correspond to the Scriptural de-scription of the sisters of Lazarus. Early made orphans, their affections have clung around their brother, and it is to their efficient supervision that Little Rugby has attained its popularity in its domestic department; for there are twelve boys beneath its roof, and members of the family. Martha is the active, energetic housekeeper, and Mary, living so near the Master, delights to gather the boys around his dear feet by her gentle, holy influence. They are very fond of the Hastings children, who are on terms of private intimacy at the academy. Margaret is an especial favorite, and it is understood that she is to graduate at Little Rugby. Richard Arnold is peculiarly qualified to guide the young girl in her search after truth upon all subjects.

She is now seventeen, and has grown up to be a fine, interesting girl, thoughtful beyond her years, and, moreover, lovely in her appearance, wearing in her face that look of purity which so distinguished her mother in her early days. Dr. Arnold is often found fastening upon the young girl a look almost of mournful interest; and, one evening, addressing his sister, he said:

"Martha, is there any one that Margaret Hastings reminds you of especially?"

"Daily, more and more of our sainted Laura. Even the tones of her voice thrill me sometimes."

"I am glad that you see the likeness. It is remarkable!"

"There are the same lovely traits, too, Richard; the same conscientiousness and gentleness and truth. No wonder that we all love her."

Warren, too, is a great favorite. Dr. Arnold understands the boy's character, and sympathizes with his mental questions; for he remembers having passed through just such a season in his early youth. He is not met with harsh rebuffs, even when he comes with

9   G

the carping conceits of young boyhood, but with the
patience of Christian rebuke.

We often find Warren and the professor, on summer
evenings, with arms encircling each other's waist, walking up and down under the green trees, the youth pouring out his crude, undigested thoughts, and the preceptor
instructing, guiding — often removing doubts and perplexities from the young and ardent mind.   Warren
regards Dr. Arnold with perfect confidence, concealing
nothing of his mental struggles, not afraid of uplifted
eyes of holy horror, nor of the word "infidel" from his
preceptor's lips; for Richard Arnold loves the youth,
seeing, amid all that is almost chaos now, as regards his
religious faith, light struggling with the darkness of the
natural man, his doubts not so much in the head as in
the heart, the real seat of carnal enmity.   He remembers
that, from earliest infancy, he has been under the teaching of most spiritual and holy guides, and living in an
atmosphere of prayer.

"Do you know, Dr. Arnold, that I sometimes get
really disgusted with long faces and cant phrases of
people that live horrid lives?   There is old John
Naseby.   You would suppose that there never was such
a saint born, if you would trust his sanctimonious ways;
when I know that he is such an old miser that he hardly
gives his children enough to eat.   I often share my
lunch in school with the boys."

" Unfortunately, there are such specimens, Warren;

but the very fact that it awakens your indignation shows that you have stored away somewhere in your cranium a picture of something better — a reality. Where did you get it, Warren, if not from the Bible?"

The boy did not reply; for this silenced the doubt that was almost on his lips as to the power of Christianity.

"One word let me add, my boy. Give up the study of poor frail humanity, and turn your thoughts to the bright example left by our Master. Study that, Warren, until you feel your soul abased by its conscious sinfulness and weakness, stretching up its wings to reach after that matchless holiness. You will then have neither time nor inclination to come down from such a study to scrutinize the caricatures that are seen around us." And then, as though soliloquizing, he continued, "When will Christians learn to say, 'I have a great work to do, therefore I cannot come down from the holy mount to quarrel with fellow-pilgrims'?"

There were three boys connected with the family at Rugby, whom we must notice in the progress of our story. Archie Murray, a boy of fifteen, the son of a departed sister of Dr. Arnold, somewhat lame from a hip disease — an interesting, a promising boy, whose great desire seemed to be to fit himself as soon as possible to support his darling sister Annie, two years younger than himself, now living with an aunt, not very happily, however. Harry and George Seymour, two of the chiliren of wealth, whose parents passed the summer at Westbrook, their winters in New York, devoted wholly to the world, and having placed all their children away at school, had abundant money and leisure, which were engrossed by the world and its empty vanities.

It is drawing very near a summer vacation now, and Dr. Arnold is meditating a pedestrian tour in company with several of his pupils, having selected the Hastings boys first.

It is the favored hour of morning prayer at the parsonage. The precious Bible is on the stand, and the father's eye glances around for the daily texts.

"Who is ready?" asked the kind voice.

"I, papa," was Margaret's reply. "The subject is the law of God — and mine is, 'The law was given by Moses, but grace and truth came by Jesus Christ.'"

"There was law before that, Margaret: can you tell me when?"

"The law in Eden, papa, was it not so?"

"That is correct; there was the first expression of the law of God. Is there any one who can tell me anything about its nature?"

"I, papa," replied Allan: "'The law is holy, and just, and good;' and 'By the law is the knowledge of sin.'"

"Very good, my son. Now something of its use."

"I have a strange text," replied Warren: "'Therefore by the deeds of the law there shall no flesh be justified in his sight.' If that is true, of what use then is the law?'"

"I can tell," replied Alice: "'The law is a school-master to bring us to Christ.'"

"That is an excellent choice, my daughter. What has Edward to say?"

"Margaret selected mine, papa: 'Cursed is every one that continueth not in all things written in the book of the law to do them.' That seems a very hard text."

"And Sunbeam's?"

"Allan searched for mine. He said that was the way Paul felt after he became a Christian: 'For I delight in the law of God after the inward man.'"

"Very good, my children. Thus you see that the law of God is a picture of his holiness, for 'it is holy, just, and good'—but since the fall, not one has, or ever can keep the law in its strictness."

"If so, papa, how can we be justified?" asked Margaret.

"By a new and living way, my dear: as there can be no perfect human obedience now, our God has mercifully made another way to heaven, whereby we can be justified freely by His grace, bestowed upon all who exercise a true and living faith in Jesus as our substitute. Now we will sing our morning hymn"—and the sweet voices sang intelligently—

"Ah, how shall fallen man
Be just before his God!
If he contend in righteousness
We sink beneath his rod.

9*

"Ah, how shall guilty man
    Contend with such a God?
None, none can meet Him, and escape,
    But through the Saviour's blood."

Then, bowed in prayer, the father brought his beloved ones to the feet of Jesus, and prayed that, "justified freely by his grace," they all might have peace with God on earth, and blessedness in heaven.

Allan and Alice were walking out on the piazza in the pleasant hour after evening worship, when they heard the front gate open, and saw the face of a welcome friend.

"Here is Dr. Arnold, papa," said Alice, running out to meet the preceptor, and taking his hand, led him into the parlor.

Always welcome at the parsonage, the family gathered around him, all having some pleasant words to say.

"Vacation is drawing nigh, Mr. Hastings," said the visitor, "and I have come with a novel request, which I hope that you will grant. It has been a year of intense mental application, and I feel the need of an unbent bow. I propose a pedestrian tour to the Adirondacks, and if it meets your approbation, would like to have Warren and Allan for companions. Archie Murray is going, and Mr. Seymour has requested me to take the boys, for they are off on a pleasure tour, and desire entire freedom from care."

Mr. Hastings looked at the boys. Warren's dark eyes

and Allan's blue were dancing with delight; and the impatient tapping of young feet upon the carpet betrayed the eagerness with which they listened for an answer.

"Dear papa," said Allan, leaning upon the back of his father's chair, "please say, Yes."

"I see no objection, boy, with Dr. Arnold for a guide; but what says mamma?"

"Yes, by all means. I think it would be a great benefit to the boys in every way."

Father Morgan was on a visit to the parsonage, and gave his voice for the projected trip.

"I wish I were a boy again, Dr. Arnold, or even a little younger. Nothing could afford me more pleasure."

"Can't you go, Father Morgan?" said Warren. "We should be so very glad!"

"To walk among the Adirondacks, boy! Too old for that, my son; but I shall be glad to see you start on such a tour. But what can be done with Archie?"

"We must take a mule for our tents and baggage; and Archie can ride Dick over the rough places."

Nothing else was talked of now but the summer tour; and mamma was busily employed in brushing up some of the old winter suits for the cold nights in the mountains. Ere Dr. Arnold took leave of the party, Father Morgan sought an opportunity to place a pocket-book in his hand, with the whispered words:

"You may want something additional for contingencies. Use it freely; for these are my boys."

CHAPTER VIII.

THE ADIRONDACKS.

"O Lord, how manifold are thy works! in wisdom hast thou made them all: the earth is full of thy riches."

IT is a warm summer day, early in July, the day for starting on the projected tour. The boys are full of their journey, and the subject of the daily text seems to make but little impression on the giddy young travellers. They are assembled, as usual, at morning prayer, and Margaret mentions the subject of original sin.

"I have several, papa," said the young lady. "'They go astray as soon as they are born, speaking lies;' and 'There is none that doeth good; no, not one.'"

"Have you a passage, Allan?" inquired the father.

The boy blushed, and hung his head; for it was the first time that he had been negligent.

"I forgot all about it, papa. Pray, excuse me."

"I am sorry, my son. And Warren, too?"

"I suppose that we must all be pretty bad; for thus saith the Apostle Paul, 'We are a set of good-for-nothing fellows, and there is no health in us.'"

The father looked grieved and very sternly upon Warren, as he said:

"Jokes are unbecoming here, my son. If you **too** have forgotten the subject, at least be silent."

Then Alice repeated, reverently: "'All we, like sheep, have gone astray: we have turned every one to his own way.'"

"This is a most important and solemn subject, my children; for upon right teaching here depends all our views of the great salvation. When we are conscious that we are sin-sick, we shall welcome the Great Physician, and not before; but my words to-day must be few, for I fear that preoccupied hearts leave but little room for serious thoughts."

The morning hymn was sweet and solemn, and the prayer full of a father's longings for the spiritual good of his offspring, closing with a blessing on the dear boys about to leave the parental roof for a few weeks. On rising from their knees, Warren instantly advanced to his father, with an ingenuous blush upon his bright, young face:

"Excuse me, dear papa. I did not mean one word of disrespect; but I am intoxicated with delight to-day. My feet are full of dancing steps, and my head brimful of nonsense."

"Try to put some restraint upon yourself, my son; for reverence should always mark our approaches to Deity."

But Dr. Arnold, with the three boys, are at the parsonage gate now, accompanied by Hector, a favorite dog, and Dickey, the mule—both panniers heavily laden. The boys were all in high glee; but the oldest and most merry was Dr. Arnold himself.

"How long will you be absent?" inquired the father.

"Not less than a month; perhaps more," was the reply.

"Can we hear from you?"

"Yes; there is a post near the Adirondack Iron Works, and here is the address."

Attired in loose blouses, with broad-brimmed straw hats, and carpet-bags on each of the traveller's arms, they took leave of the party at the parsonage.

"Be careful of them, Dr. Arnold," said the mother; "they have never been away before."

They had all exchanged the parting kiss, when Warren ran back to fold Alice, his darling pet, once more in his arms.

"Write, dear little sis!" said the boy. "I don't know how I am to do without you so long."

At the same time, Dr. Arnold was taking a more tender leave than usual of Margaret Hastings, whispering a word that left a blush on her sweet face. In another minute, they were speeding along the street, with flying steps, to the cars.

So wholly preoccupied were the boys with their anticipated pleasure that, if it had not been for Dr. Arnold's watchfulness, they might even have forgotten the laws of courtesy which their preceptor was so careful to inculcate.

"Don't you see the woman with her baby, Warren? I think that you had better give up your seat to her, and come join Archie."

"Certainly, dear sir; I did not see her;" and rising immediately, he placed her comfortably, where she could be near a window, and took a seat himself inside, by Archie Murray.

"You are very good," said the woman, "for my little boy has been sick, and I am anxious to give him all the fresh air that I can."

"You are quite welcome," was the quick reply, for in Warren's sunny frame of mind, it really gave him pleasure to confer a favor.

Staying but a short time in New York, the party were soon sailing up the North River, never tired of admiring the charming scenery as they passed along, for this was their first peep at the lovely river. At a place appointed, they took passage in a rough wagon across the country leading to the mountains, hitching Dickey on behind, and taking Hector in when he seemed tired.

"We shall soon meet our guide," said Dr. Arnold, for the peaks of the Adirondacks were now in sight.

"Who is your guide?" inquired the driver.

"His name is Nichol Lescure, a Canadian hunter."

"I know him," was the reply, "and a clever fellow h

is — one of the best guides found in this neighborhood. Where are you to meet him?"

"At a little hut, near the first glimpse of Mount Marcy."

"We are there," was the reply, as, suddenly turning a corner, the rude dwelling was in sight, and, standing at the door, was a man clad in skins, leaning upon a gun.

"Is this Dr. Arnold?" inquired the guide.

"It is — and this is Nichol Leseure?"

"That is my name. You have chosen a fine season for your journey, sir; but these young chaps will find it hard work to scramble up these mountain heights, where one can sometimes wash his hands in the clouds."

Nichol was accompanied by a large dog, who did not appear to be very friendly toward the newcomer.

"What is your dog's name, sir?" inquired the hunter.

"Hector — and a fine, intelligent fellow he is. How shall we make them friends?"

"You'll see. Come here, Leo."

The large animal came bounding to his master's side.

"Do you see that dog, sir?" — and taking him by the ear, not roughly, he led him close to the stranger, both growling and showing their glittering white teeth. "Come closer, sir — this is a stranger, Hector, and you must treat him well — mind what I say."

But Leo still continued growling, although lying down close to the ground.

Taking a piece of meat out of his hunting-bag, Nichol

threw it to Leo. "Hand that to Hector — don't eat it, sir."

The dog crouched closer and closer to the ground, and then commenced crawling toward the stranger, holding the meat in his mouth. When close to Hector, he pushed it toward him, and Nichol threw another piece, which Leo began to eat, and Hector did the same.

"Let the dumb beasts only eat together, peaceably, and they'll be friends: I always find that out."

To Dr. Arnold's surprise, after Leo had finished his meal, he walked quietly around Hector: they then examined each other for a minute or two, took another piece of meat in company, and the quarrel seemed at an end.

Taking leave of their driver, they made preparations for their long walk. Mounting Archie on the mule, with carpet-bag and long pole in each hand, they commenced their toilsome march. Soon they were ascending heights which to their inexperience seemed almost insurmountable. Nichol smiled at their exclamations. "This is nothing, boys; wait until you try Mount Towanus: you'll have something to say then." Very soon they were in the deep, solemn woods, far, far away from human habitations. Even their young spirits were subdued by the perfect solitude of this mountain forest. The mournful music of the woods gradually silenced the youthful party. The rustling of the leaves, the soft sighing of the summer winds among the trees, now and

10

then the whistle of a wild bird among the high branches, or the swift passage of a deer in the distance, all lent new charms to this forest tramp. Nichol was highly amused at the silent rapture of the boys, as step by step they advanced into the deep shadows, to them so full of unuttered mysteries. All day they travelled thus, stopping at noon to regale themselves from the contents of the panniers. Cold chicken, ham and biscuit, fruit and domestic summer beverage, proved a delicious meal, up in these mountain solitudes. Nichol looked on surprised, as Dr. Arnold reverently asked a blessing before partaking of their lunch. After resting about an hour, they again took up their line of march, and late in the afternoon came to an opening, where the curling of smoke into the clouds indicated a human habitation.

"This is our stopping-place," said Nichol, "and that is my cabin." Just then they came in sight of the low dwelling, and in the next minute, a girl of fourteen came running out of the hut.

"I am glad to see you, father; for I was very lonesome last night. I heard the wolves howling not far off; and all night I had to keep the fires burning."

"This is my daughter Nan," said the hunter. "Hurry up, my girl, and get us a good supper, for we are all hungry."

Away she ran, and the sound of the axe called the boys to her help.

"Here, Nan, let me have that axe," said Warren. 'It's a shame that a girl should do such work as that."

She smiled as she replied: "It's nothing; I'm used to it, and I guess I can hit a better stroke than you any day."

Nan smiled at Warren's efforts, who belabored the log without producing any impression.

"Here! see what I can do," said the girl; and seizing the axe, she raised it far above her head, planted her foot firmly on the log, fixed her eye intently for one moment, and at one sharp stroke clove the log.

Warren seized the axe again, and now that there was a cleft in the wood, made some headway; Nan sitting by on another log, laughing at his efforts. All the boys went to work with a good will in carrying in a heavy load of fire-wood, and Nan thanked them in her rough way, adding, "You shall have a good supper in the twinkling of an eye for that, boys."

Pretty thoroughly tired, and lounging upon the greensward around the cabin, with carpet-bags for pillows, they awaited the summons to supper. The sound of the grinding of a coffee-mill was comforting music to the travellers; and the savory smell of cooking meat the sweetest of all perfumes just now to the sharpened appetite.

Leo and Hector were good friends now, for a march through the woods together had entirely banished th' last vestige of canine cumity.

"Supper is ready, boys, come in," said the hunter, leading the way into the cabin.

It was a one-story building, with three large rooms; the floors laid with rough planks, and the walls composed of rougher logs. A large fireplace stood in the family room, the smoke finding its way out through a chimney made of stones and mortar. In the centre stood a wooden table, on which was spread a most inviting meal. Around the room were rude benches; one arm-chair alone gave any promise of comfort for a weary back. The entrance was crossed by two sets of fine antlers, and around the room hung the skins of animals, powder-flasks, hunting-bags, guns, spears, and every variety of hunting implements. From the rafters were suspended venison, hams, and dried meats, in great abundance.

The boys were all surprised to see what an excellent meal had been prepared by Nan Leseure in these mountain solitudes. There were rich coffee and cream, broiled venison steak, mashed potatoes, a dish of birds, and the very nicest bread and butter.

Nichol made good provision for his family, for twice a year he went down to the nearest town and laid in his stores, leaving Nan at Farmer Hughes's, on the lake. Added to this, he kept a cow, and Nan had learned to make good bread and butter.

Dr. Arnold reverently asked a blessing on the meal ere they partook of it, and Nichol remarked, "We have nothing of that up here in these mountain parts, sir."

"God is here, Nichol, in all the majesty of his works: one would think that the full heart ought to worship Him in such a grand chapel as these wooded cloisters."

"Somehow we forget Him, sir."

The listener thought how much of just such forgetfulness prevailed among humanity, surrounded by Christian churches, amid the blaze of the Gospel. Truly, the soul unrenewed is everywhere alike — dead to God — dead as regards spiritual life.

"You had better not camp out to-night," said the hunter. "With your blankets and our skins we can spread up sleeping room for all the party: it's too cold on the mountain at night. I suppose that you must be very tired, and would like to go to rest early."

"First, with your permission, we will have evening prayer. Our boys have fine voices: I think that you would like their music."

"Do just as you please, sir; my little cabin is yours while you are with us."

Nichol and Nan sat on a bench near the door, listening to the delightful music as it filled the cabin on this summer evening, the first time that the worship of Almighty God had ever been observed beneath that roof. Dr. Arnold selected a portion of the Sermon on the Mount, read it in an impressive manner, and then engaged in solemn, fervent prayer — remembering the dwellers at

10 *   H

the cabin, the two sitting reverently with their faces bowed upon their hands, while the rest knelt around the mercy-seat. Had an angel stopped at Nichol Lescure's humble cabin on that summer night? for so wondered the rude hunter as he silently wiped the moisture from his eyes.

"That was a grand sermon that you read, sir," said the man; "who preached such good words as that?"

"The Lord Jesus Christ, Nichol, when he was on earth, more than eighteen hundred years ago."

"I remember, when I was a little chap, my mother used to take me to a church in Canada, and there I used to say my prayers before a crucifix, and heard now and then about Jesus, but more about the Virgin; but it has been so long, and I have lived such a wandering life here in the wilderness, that I have forgotten both."

"He will not forget you, Nichol, for He is coming again to judge the world, and if you have not made Him your Saviour here, He cannot be your friend then."

The hunter listened attentively, and then replied: "I have been very careful to lead a pure and honest life in all my dealings, sir; and would n't do what some of the Christians down below are not ashamed to do."

"That will not do for a plea there, Nichol; for, 'Except a man be born again, he cannot see the kingdom of God.'"

Stretched out upon the cabin-floor, the weary travel-lers slept more delightfully than they could have conceived of, apart from the comforts of civilized life, and by the peep of day were up again; and, after a hearty breakfast, following their guide, were off on their march, singing, at the top of their young voices, " A life in the woods for me!"

A half-day's journey through the woods brought them to the clearing of the Newcombe Farm, commanding a magnificent view of the chief mountain summits of the Adirondacks, looming up to heaven in all their melancholy grandeur.

Travelling on still, they reached the shores of Lake Henderson ; and the boys were greatly excited by the appearance of a young fawn, startled by the appearance of human beings. True to a hunter's instinct, Nichol took aim at the innocent creature before one word could be said, and, wounding the leg, disabled the poor thing from walking. The party were hungry, and therefore the advent of the fawn was welcome as Friday to Robinson Crusoe. When poor Fan crept to Nichol, lying down at his feet, and looking up timidly into his face with her full dark eyes, the hunter patted the pretty creature's head ; Dr. Arnold turned an inquiring look at each of the boys, who shook their heads at an unspoken thought.

" Not to-night, nor to-morrow, nor next day, poor Fan : we would rather all be hungry," said Dr. Arnold.

" There are fine trout in the lake," said Nichol ; " let us try our luck. I couldn't see that poor thing killed."

It was a successful effort, and a good supper of trout

rewarded the humanity of the travellers, which Nichol speedily prepared.

Taking a boat after supper, they had a charming view of the Indian Pass, an opening between two of the loftiest mountains of the group, Echo Mountain and Mount Towanus, both in full view. Just before them, on the shore of the glassy lake, stood three splendid deer; their branching antlers, towering above their graceful heads, elevated as though listening for enemies: one sight of the travellers was enough; for dashing into the lake, they were speedily out of sight.

"I wish that we could see a hunt," said Warren.

"It is n't unlikely," said Nichol, "for a party of hunters is out now."

Suddenly, the cries of the hounds came across the lake.

"There they are," said the guide.

Soon after, a gallant buck, with antlered head erect, was seen standing upon the cliff opposite, and in the next minute, the panting creature was battling with the waters, the hunters all in hot pursuit.

Nichol is watching too, with lifted rifle—fires—wounds, but does not kill his game at the first fire: another shot is more successful. Bringing the boat near, the poor thing was taken on board, and carried to a thicket near. It was time to think of arrangements for the night. With the help of the boys, the stakes were driven into the ground, the canvas tightened as a covering, the gum-elastic spread upon the ground, and pillows of the same material for the head; and then the boys thought that it would be grand to sleep thus in the wild solitudes of the Adirondacks.

It was a moonlight night, and the party stood in solemn silence viewing the grandeur of the scenery — the moon sailing in her majesty over the transparent lake, whose clear waters reflected its silver rays upon its quiet bosom.

Dr. Arnold uncovered his head as he repeated:

" The heavens declare the glory of God; and the firmament showeth His handy-work.

" He telleth the number of the stars: He calleth them all by their names.

"Praise ye Him sun and moon: praise Him all ye stars of light:

"Mountains and all hills, fruitful trees and all cedars,

" Praise ye the Lord."

The first night's rest beneath the glittering firmament was a new feature in the pilgrimage. Comfortably disposed of, they slept soundly, and by early dawn were astir again, for they actually contemplated the ascent of Mount Towanus, the Indian name meaning "the sky-piercing."

Nichol gave dismal accounts of the undertaking, but young spirits were not to be deterred. While they were discussing the propriety of the movement, several hunters joined their party; each having some terrible account to give of dangers to those attempting the ascent. One told of a fearful snow-storm that had overtaken him at this very spot and season. Another had been overtaken, the year before, by a mountain flood, which so filled the brooks with rushing waters, that he found it impossible to descend; and seeking another route, was lost in the wilderness so long that even the dogs did not know him when found. A third, on waking from sleep, had found himself surrounded by rattlesnakes; and another had made a narrow escape from a bloody panther.

The boys heard it all; but, listening to the songs of birds in the tree-tops, looking down upon the gentle moss and tangled flowers, out upon the vistas of valley and hill, and upward to the soft sunny skies above them, they laughed with provoking incredulity, and waving their banners, said, "Let us try: others have succeeded; why not we?"

The trouble was about poor Fan, for, unable to walk yet, they were obliged to carry her wherever they went.

"We cannot leave her: she is a light little thing," said Warren; "I guess we can manage among us."

Full of spirits, they started, expecting to be gone two days, with one night in the woods, on the way. It was an interesting study to Dr. Arnold, to watch the different characters of the boys in their efforts to overcome obstacles. Warren, with his strong, indomitable will; Allan, with his quiet, determined perseverance; Archie had but little effort to make, for Dickey did the work for him, Harry Seymour, with his weak, irresolute, fitful efforts; and George, with his constant calls upon his companions for help.

Over many immeasurable miles, over rude rocks and treacherous bridges of the mountain torrents, up and down, around and among the chasms of the pathless forest, onward the party tramped.

At the close of the first day, Harry and George begged to be left behind.

"What would become of you, boys, all alone in these dark forests?" said Dr. Arnold. "That can never be: you must exert yourselves a little more. What say you to going back, Warren?"

"Going back, Dr. Arnold, after having reached such a height! My motto is, Excelsior!"

"And mine, too," said Allan, "though I am very tired."

"We must kindle fires to-night," said Nichol, "for these mountains are infested by wolves and panthers at all times."

"Suppose the fires go out, Nichol," said Warren.

"That must not be: I will keep watch."

They had not been long in their tent ere a singular noise, like the crying of an infant, was distinctly heard.

"What is that, Nichol?" said Warren, putting his head out of the tent.

"That's one of the varmints, boy, a genuine panther; but I'll keep him off: he'll not come anear a fire, not he."

"Are you sure, Nichol?" said Harry Seymour, his teeth chattering with terror.

"Purty sartin of that, boy; they don't like fire. Go to sleep, boys: I'll take kere of the tent."

Early in the morning, off again, the difficulties increasing as the top was nearing. Many a time in the course of the day did the boys have to stop, panting and breathless, to wipe the sweat from their brows.

"It will take another day, sir," said Nichol: "the boys can't stand it — and must stop two hours in the middle of the day."

His prophecy was correct, for it was not until the middle of the third day that the guide pointed out the height.

Seizing his banner, Warren planted himself firmly by the side of his guide, and was the first to reach the summit; where, with glowing countenance and exulting voice, he placed his flag upon the top of Mount Towanus, calling out, "Hurrah! hurrah! we're here at last!"

And there, from that mountain height, they surveyed the glorious landscape. After resting several hours, they commenced the descent; and after a day's repose, visited the Indian Pass — a wild gorge precipitously walled in at one point by the colossal cliffs which impart such features of grandeur to the landscape. And now they were ready for a return to the hunter's cabin.

Strange what effects contrasts have upon passing

objects! When first our travellers came in sight of Nichol's cabin, it had seemed to them like a wild wilder-ness, indeed: now they hailed its curling smoke as an indication of returning civilization, compared with the wild and awful solitudes which they had left. They were glad to rest once more upon the grassy sward before the hunter's cabin, reading letters from home, which had been brought to Nan in their absence.

Dr. Arnold and Warren are in deep conversation, the latter stretched out upon the grass, looking upward to the grand scenery around him.

"Look at those magnificent trees, Dr. Arnold: how much more impressive than any church that I have ever visited! Here is stupendous height, and that leads the mind upward; here is breadth immeasurable, and that, too, aids our attempts at worship; and look through those arching branches, forming such mysterious cloisters: the woods are full of thoughts of God."

"That is all true, Warren; but this worship of nature that you speak of, does not reach the wants of man: it might have done in Eden; but not now, upon this polluted earth."

"You remember Horace Smith's Ode to the Flowers, Dr. Arnold?"

"I do, Warren, and own that it is exquisite poetry; but we need more than that. Our Father knew what was in man, and therefore he planted a church upon earth, organized it, and called upon the children of men

11

to enter its fold, and feed upon the food which it offers to weary pilgrims: beside, Warren, there is a social bond connecting us all, and by the closeness of the church relation we are bound together as one family, having common joys and sorrows, common wants, common hopes, and a common home: hence our Book of Common Prayer. How long do you think that Christianity could exist upon earth, if man everywhere worshipped only nature?"

Warren lay silent for a while.

"I wish I did not think so much, Dr. Arnold — so many doubts and difficulties chase each other in my head."

"They can all be settled by the word of God, Warren, but by nothing else — remember that. Come, boys, let us sing our evening hymn.'

And, seated around upon the grass, they joined in singing:

> "Softly now the light of day
> Fades upon my sight away;
> Free from care, from labor free,
> Lord, I would commune with Thee."

They are spending several days now at the cabin, only going off far enough to return every evening; and many interesting conversations do the boys have with Nichol and Nan about their wild, adventurous life.

"How do you get along in winter, Nan?" inquired Allan.

" Dreary enough, until I learned how to read."

" How did you learn ? " inquired the boy.

" When father goes away to sell his game and buy stores, he leaves me twice a year at Newcombe Farm, on the lake ; and there I met with a kind lady, who taught me how to read, and gave me a heap of good books."

" How do you get your clothes made, Nan ? "

" Mrs. Hughes gets them made for me when I go down. I have nice times there, for she has a girl, named Susan, about my age ; and we are so sorry when I have to go back to the mountain."

" Shall you always live here on the mountains, Nan ? " inquired Warren.

" I don't know : father wanted to send me to school last year, but I could n't leave him all alone here in this lonely place, and so I don't know what is to become of me : maybe father 'll go back to Canada some day ; he says I have an aunt there."

Dr. Arnold lost no opportunity to speak to Nichol upon this subject, and obtained from him a promise that he would not keep Nan here always, for he saw that it was " a hard lot for such a young thing, with none of her own kind to speak to."

It is now the last night before their return. They are all stretched out upon the green grass, with Fan among the group. She has recovered the use of her limb now, can skip about as merry as any of them, and there is not one who would be willing to leave the fawn behind.

"It seems as if we had been away six months, instead of a few weeks," said Warren.

"We shall all feel the benefit of our journey after our return," said the preceptor, "when we recover from our fatigue."

Warren wore a peculiarly thoughtful look, and Dr. Arnold continued: "What are you thinking of, Warren?"

"Of the future: I wonder where we shall all be ten years hence? I shall be twenty-five then."

"Have you ever thought of a profession yet?"

"Not exactly, Doctor: but there is a future of fame and honor, where I hope to make my mark. No yard-sticks nor clerk's desk for me."

"And you, Allan, what do you desire?"

"A life just like my father's — to be just as good and useful."

"And Archie Murray?"

"A quiet Christian home in the country, where, with dear sister Annie for my housekeeper, we can serve God together."

Harry Seymour was lounging upon the stump of a tree, toying with the trinkets of a gold watch-chain, a slight sneer upon his handsome face.

"And you, Harry? Let me know your thoughts."

"All I want is plenty of money, that I may enjoy myself — buy fine horses, beautiful pictures, live in style, travel, dash, with nothing to do."

' And then ?'" said the preceptor solemnly.

" What do you mean, Dr. Arnold ?"

" All this must end, Harry; and then, when this short lrfe is over, do you ever think what follows ?"

" I don't trouble myself about such things, now ; time enough for that."

" Has George any aspirations ?" asked the gentleman, with a serious look.

" I want to make money, to be busy among the bulls and bears of Wall Street, to heap up piles of gold, and to be called one of the millionaires of New York."

" And these are the aspirations of immortals — of beings destined for eternity! Allan and Archie alone have objects worthy of their nature. Warren may reach the pinnacle of fame; but that will not make him happy. Harry may revel in self-indulgence, but the satiated senses will be his tormentors; and George will spend sleepless nights fearing to lose his gold; while Allan and Archie will enjoy the blessedness of a life spent for the glory of God and the good of man here, and the unspeakable bliss of endless happiness hereafter."

" I should like to know what we are all to be," said Warren. "Suppose we agree to meet at Little Rugby ten years hence, and truly relate our experience ?"

" Agreed," said all the boys.

" That is, if we are all spared," interposed Dr Arnold.

" That of course,' replied Warren.

11 *

Each one then noted on his tablets the date of this engagement. The remainder of the evening was spent in settling accounts with Nichol, distributing books and tracts, and reminding the father of his duty concerning Nan, obtaining his promise to write to Westbrook, if any trouble should come upon the poor girl. Early in the morning, they bade farewell to the Adirondacks, and returning as they came, the boys soon recovered their merry spirits, which had been somewhat subdued among the grand and sombre objects of nature by which they had been encompassed. They found it rather diffi- cult to take home with them three animals instead of two — for Warren said that Alice must have the fawn ; and it cost Dr. Arnold some trouble to find a freight- car, where animals were conveyed comfortably.

At the end of four weeks, we find them all at home once more ; Alice charmed with her pet, and the family group highly entertained by accounts of their summer travel in the Adirondacks.

CHAPTER IX.

THE PASTOR'S AID.

"He that hath pity upon the poor, lendeth unto the Lord; and look, what he layeth out, it shall be paid him again."

THE summer tour has been both profitable and delightful; but the children eagerly return once more to their pleasant household ways. The memory of the grand mountain scenery, with its wild, romantic features, will remain powerfully impressed upon the hearts of the young travellers; but the music of the birds in the low trees of the orchard, and the perfume of the sweet flowers around the parsonage were never so precious as on this morning, when they met again around the family altar.

"What is our subject to-day, Margaret?"

"The duty of benevolence, papa."

"A most delightful theme: and what have you gathered from the Holy Book?"

"'Whatsoever ye would that men should do to you, do ye even so to them: for this is the law and the prophets.'"

"And yours, Warren?"

"'He that soweth little, shall reap little; and he that soweth plentifully, shall reap plentifully. Let every man do according as he is disposed in his heart, not grudgingly, or of necessity; for God loveth a cheerful giver.'"

"Let me hear yours, Allan."

"'God is not unrighteous, that he will forget your works, and labor that proceedeth from love; which love ye have showed for his Name's sake, who have ministered to the saints, and yet do minister.'"

"This is mine, papa," said Alice. "'Whoso hath this world's goods, and seeth his brother have need, and shutteth up his compassion from him, how dwelleth the love of God in him?'"

"I am ready now for Edward's."

"'To do good, and to distribute, forget not, for with such sacrifices God is well pleased.'"

"Now Sunbeam's?"

"'Blessed be the man that provideth for the sick and needy; the Lord shall deliver him in the time of trouble.'"

"A blessed and pleasant duty, dear children, we have been considering, and one that seems especially pleasing to our common Father. By-and-by, when we have more time, I want to talk over this matter."

After family prayers, the good pastor is passing down the lane, bent on an early errand of mercy to a suffering member of his flock.

"Can't you spare a minute, papa?" said Alice. "Just go with me to the summer-house: my head is brimful of thoughts, and I want you to help me get them in some order."

Mr. Hastings took out his watch : then, with a smile, said, "I can spare a half-hour, daughter."

Taking his hand, she tripped lightly over the green orchard, and seating himself, said pleasantly : "Now for the labyrinth, Alice."

"Well, you see, papa, we each have a little bank of our own : Father Morgan always leaves us something; Aunt Gertrude and Aunt Helen send us frequent presents; and I have been thinking how much good we might do, if we only knew how. We always give something to the missionary fund at Sunday school ; but then I want something here at the parsonage, just for our own family."

"What would you like to do, Alice?"

"I have three questions to ask, papa—When? How? What?"

"Now, Alice, I shall not at present answer your questions; but I'll just leave you to think how objects of nature work, and then come again and tell me your thoughts. But good morning now, my love," and the father stooped to imprint a kiss upon the sweet young face, that looked so lovingly in his. She ran on before him, opening the garden-gate for him to pass out, and

I

then, slowly turning back, whispered to herself: "I am to look around on what God has done."

"What are you about, Alice?" said sister Margaret. "You appear to be dreaming all day, and mamma wants us, I know."

"Does she, Mary? then I am ready;" and away tripped the child, having found something to do.

"I have all these aprons to make for Lucy; can't you help me?" said the lady.

"Gladly, mamma; just show me how;" and soon the child was seated by her mother's side, busily plying her needle, while her sweet voice sang:

> "The mite my willing hands can give,
>   At Jesus' feet I lay;
>   Grace shall the humble gift receive,
>   Abounding grace repay."

When the task was done, Alice was out in the summer-house again.

"I wonder what papa means? There is the sun, how does he work? All day long, and what for? just for the good of man. There are the moon and stars, they shine at night, and what for? for the good of man and glory of God." Many other thoughts came crowding into the young brain, as she mused all day about the puzzling questions of doing good: repeating again and again, "When? How? What?"

At worship, the father detained the family group

awhile, and smiling, said, "Alice has been puzzled to-day: now we must all help her; she wants to be doing good, here at the parsonage, in a little band, I suppose?"

"Yes, that's it, papa; but now I want my first question answered: When?"

"Can any one help Alice to an answer?" said the father.

"Whenever we have opportunity: is not that so, papa?" said Margaret.

"That is an excellent answer."

"Now, daughter, let me ask a question — have you been looking around to-day?"

"Yes, papa, and thinking so very nard: I watched the sun, papa."

"And what did you find out, Alice?"

"That he shines all day for the good of man."

"What of the flowers; can you tell me, Margaret?"

"They cheer our hearts, perfume the air with their sweetness; and many of them are useful in other ways."

"What does the sun do?"

"I know, papa," said little Lucy; "he warms the earth, and makes the plants grow; and he warms the water, and makes the cool showers fall."

"When does he do this?"

"At all times, papa."

"Now we have answered your question, *When* must we do good?"

"But he's a great big sun, and we are so little — not even stars, papa," said Lucy.

"Stop awhile, darling; we'll find a place even for little Sunbeam."

"Now comes my next question, papa: How?" said Alice.

"There is a beautiful answer to that in one of our texts, papa," said Allan: "'Not grudgingly, or of necessity; for God loveth a cheerful giver.'"

"That is not just what I mean," said Alice. "Perhaps the other question tells what I want better: In what way?"

"As the most good is done in bands or societies, I suppose that is what you are looking for, Alice?"

"Yes, papa; but I am more in the dark than ever."

"Think over the different societies at St. Barnabas'."

"There is the Dorcas Society, papa — we could not interfere with that; and then there is the Missionary Society — that is too hard to follow; then there is the Mothers' Meeting."

"Pet Alice conducting a Mothers' Meeting, ha! ha!" laughed brother Warren.

"I never thought of such a foolish thing, Warren: I was only naming the different things. Then there is the Mite Society — that won't do either; and there is the Sunday school — we are all too young to teach."

"Suppose I drop a word?" said Margaret. "We want to use our money and our time in some way to do good to the bodies and souls of poor, or sick, or ignorant people; is not that what you want, Alice?"

"Suppose, Alice," said her father, "that we pray most earnestly to have our hearts filled with the love of God: then we need not go searching about for ways to do good; for every breath of our existence will then be a spontaneous benediction."

"Now we must have a name," continued Alice. "There is the Gleaners — no, that won't do; for we are not that, nor the Mite Gatherers either."

"How will Young Disciples do?" asked Allan.

"Are we all really that?" asked Margaret. "That won't do either, I am afraid."

"What do you think of Sowers, or Workers, or Busy Bees?"

"I don't like these names either, Allan."

"How will Dewdrops do?" inquired Allan.

"It does not express what we want," answered Margaret.

"The Little Flock," "The Children of the Parsonage?"

"No — no," said Alice. "Just let me think: we want to help papa in his work among the poor, and needy, and sorrowing. I have it! 'The Pastor's Aid;' that's the name."

"Papa must be president, mamma vice-president," said Warren, "I secretary, Margaret treasurer, and all the rest managers."

12

"That's a new way, Warren, to elect one's self to office," said papa, laughing.

"It's altogether novel, papa, and we won't quarrel, shall we?"

"No — no," said all the voices; "Warren is the best secretary."

"Now, how shall we begin?" said Alice.

"Go about with your eyes open," answered mamma. "You may not see much at first; but if your hearts are in the work, there is not a day without its holy mission."

"We are to report at first once a week — on Saturday evening, just after worship," said Warren.

The parents were deeply interested in "The Pastor's Aid," but determined to give no more hints. Margaret and Alice were often seen now busily engaged in talking in the summer-house, but as yet have not accomplished any thing.

"Jacob is really sick," said Debby; "he needs some one to give him medicine and bathe his head with cool water: I can only run up now and then, poor fellow! I hate to leave him so much alone."

"Work for 'The Pastor's Aid,'" said Margaret. "I'll stay with him to-day. But stop — we were to go out with Mrs. Lacey this afternoon, to take that delightful ride. Well, I must give it up! you go, Alice!"

"I'll stay with him to-morrow," was the child's reply

And this was the first act of mercy performed by "The Pastor's Aid."

"'Not grudgingly, or of necessity,'" said Margaret, as she entered the room with a cheerful face, and took her seat by the sick man.

"You are very good, miss," said the invalid, as he felt the refreshment of the cool linen cloths upon his burning head.

Margaret saw the carriage drive off with the party, but kept down the feeling of regret, and resumed her seat by the sufferer, happy in the thought that she had resigned a pleasure for a duty.

The next day we find Alice in the sick man's room, and the parents smiled as they said to each other, "Work for 'The Pastor's Aid.'"

Next day, papa met Alice going out with her little basket.

"Which way, Alice?" said the pastor.

"To get some lemons for Jacob, papa. We are finding work."

"What are you about, Allan?" asked his father, seeing him busily employed with paper, twine, and scissors.

"Making some kites for the little Watsons. You know that they had such a good father: he is gone now; and I heard the boys say to each other, as they watched the kites upon the common, 'No kites now!' The father's gone, papa, but they shall have their kites."

For the afternoon, the orphans were soon made happy as the rest by Allan's act of kindness. This was all that they had to report the first Saturday evening:

"Twenty-five cents spent for poor Jacob, the sacrifice of two days' pleasure for his comfort, and the expenditure of twenty-five cents for the orphan boys."

Warren laughed heartily at the wonderful work of the Pastor's Aid; but the parents did not — for they looked deeper than did their son.

Margaret and Alice were out walking, when, by the road-side, they saw a poor, ragged child, without shoes or stockings, weeping bitterly.

"What is the matter, little girl?" inquired Margaret, in kind and sympathizing tones.

"My mother died last night: we have no way to bury her. I have no one to care for me, now that she is gone."

"What is your name?"

"Maggie Dodd," was the reply.

"Where do you live, Maggie?" inquired Margaret.

"If you will come with me, I will show you."

The two girls followed the desolate child to a wretched home in the most miserable part of Westbrook. The story was a true one, as the neighbors testified.

"Come home with us, Maggie," said Margaret Hastings, "and we will see what can be done."

Taking the little one by the hand, Margaret led her to the parsonage, and, taking her into the kitchen, begged Debby to give her a good meal, and then went into the sitting-room to consult mamma.

"We will find the grave-clothes, mamma," said Margaret; "but how can she be buried?"

"Mr. Robb, the sexton, will attend to it; he can get all that is necessary from the overseers of the poor. But what is to be done with the poor child?"

"She seems like a nice little thing, mamma, and the neighbors all give her a good character; we can give her clothes, and can't we get her a place?"

"We will try, Margaret. I heard Mrs. Lacey say, the other day, that she would like to bring up a little girl, for Ellen's time will soon be out."

The rest of the week was busily occupied with the poor orphan child. By the close of another, she was comfortably housed with Mrs. Lacey, and the Pastor's Aid had done a good service in this charitable work.

"Getting along, my dear," said papa, as the second report was read on Saturday night.

Maggie was placed in the Sunday school too, and the young girls always felt as if Maggie was in some sense their *protégée*. Work was multiplying now, for the cool weather was coming on, and we find the girls busy in knitting socks for the more destitute in the Sunday school, Warren and Allan hunting up shoes and cast-off clothing, and Edward and Lucy helping to buy flannel for the old people. There was no lack of occupation now, for the heart was in the work of the Pastor's Aid.

Late in the fall, a letter came from Nichol Lescure, stating that he was laid by with rheumatism, and would be housed all winter. Fortunately, he had got his supply of fuel under the shed, and provision enough to last

12 *

until spring; but he was in need of medicine, and **Nan**
of suitable clothing, for he had been unable to take her
down to Mrs. Hughes in time. If anything could be
sent soon, before the snow-storms commenced, Nan would
go down to the farm, and they would find a way to send
the box up the mountain.

"More work for the Pastor's Aid," said Warren.
"Now we shall have something worth doing; but our
funds are getting low. I'll ask Harry Seymour — he'll
give us something, and so will Dr. Arnold; but not a
cent will we get out of George: he is too selfish for
that."

His words proved true — the Arnolds contributed,
and so did Harry; but George had exhausted his
month's allowance — so he said, which no one believed.
The box was filled up — flannel for Nichol, warm clothes
for Nan, plenty of medicines and books selected from the
children's library, which they had read over and over
again.

"Won't Nan enjoy all this?" said Allan, as he saw
the books packed away in the box. And so the Pastor's
Aid progressed. establishing the household flock in
practical benevolence, but by no means forgetting their
accustomed contributions at St. Barnabas'. In about
two weeks, they received a grateful acknowledgment of
the arrival of the box, and a repeated charge not to
neglect poor Nan if the father should be called away:
"For she is a good girl to her old father," wrote

Nichol; "and if I am spared, she shall go back to Canada in the spring: but we are shut up now, for the snow is falling daily, and we shall soon be banked up for three or four months."

"That was a happy thought, Alice," said her father, when he had read the next report of the Pastor's Aid; "happy for the recipients, but most for the originators of this little working-band. May God continue to bless you in your work."

CHAPTER X.

"Even so, Father, for so it seemed good in Thy sight."

WE have an important subject to-day, my children," said the pastor. "Let us hear what you have found about the carnal mind."

"I have found most in the book of Romans, papa," said Margaret; "and first, 'For to be carnally minded is death, but to be spiritually minded is life and peace.'"

"And yours, Warren?"

"'Because the carnal mind is enmity against God; for it is not subject to the law of God, neither indeed can be.'"

"I have one, papa," added Allan: "'So then they that are in the flesh cannot please God.'"

"Let me hear yours, Alice."

"'That which is born of the flesh, is flesh; and that which is born of the spirit, is spirit.'"

"Will this do, papa?" said Edward: "'And you hath he quickened who were dead in trespasses and sins.'"

"Yes, my son, that is a very suitable passage. Now

140

remember, dear children, that this is a description of the nature which is brought with us into this world, and which must be spiritually changed ere we be made fit for the kingdom of heaven."

At the close of morning prayer, the father said: "The new horse is in the carriage, children — do not meddle with him, for we are unacquainted with his disposition yet; but I am inclined to think him very spirited."

There is mourning at the parsonage, for old Brownie is dead, the faithful creature that had drawn them for so many years.

Warren is impetuous and self-willed, daring in his nature, and, like all boys, fond of horses, and of displaying his strength and courage. He is standing at the gate, with Alice, his darling pet: she is a beautiful child, with deep blue eyes, and a profusion of golden curls; she is a sparkling little girl, very fond of brother Warren, who is proud of his lovely sister. They are admiring the new horse, who stands there pawing the ground, as though impatient to be off.

"Isn't he splendid, brother?" said the child. At that moment he gave a low whinny, turning his head toward the two.

"I do believe that he wants us to get in the carriage," said Warren; "suppose we do?"

"Would it be right, Warren?" said the child.

"I don't mean to drive off: I only want to see what he would say to us?" Lifting Alice in, he took his place on the driver's seat, and, taking the reins lightly in his hand, laid them on the horse's neck. The touch of the reins was enough for the spirited animal — he started off; and Warren tried to check him, but could not recover the reins, which had dropped from his hand, and were striking the animal's shanks repeatedly. Before Warren could regain possession of them he was in full gallop, and it was in vain to try to stop him.

Jacob heard the noise, and saw the danger; he followed the flying carriage, making a zigzag course, until, striking upon a large stump of a tree, Alice was dashed out of the carriage, and Jacob was just in time to save her from the hoofs of the animal.

Warren was in agony as he bent over the insensible child. "Is she dead, Jacob?" said the boy, wringing his hands.

"I think not, for the heart is beating; but we must get her home immediately;" and lifting the child in his arms, he hurried with her to the parsonage.

"Run on before, Master Warren," said the man, "and bring in Dr. Lacey."

Fleet as the wind, the boy soon reached home, and after having prepared the family for the sight of their sweet Alice, he hurried over to the doctor, who had not yet started on his morning tour. Upon examination, he pronounced the spine seriously injured, but could not tell the final result for weeks yet. Papa stood by with a troubled, reproachful face, as he looked at Warren.

"Don't reproach me, papa," said the boy. "I did not mean to drive off: we only took a seat in the carriage, to see how the horse would act; the reins fell around his feet, and that started him. I know what you would say, papa — we should not have got in; but don't reproach me — I am punished enough."

Weeks of great suffering followed this distressing accident, and Warren spent all his leisure time by the bedside of the sufferer, a most devoted and faithful nurse.

There is a consultation of eminent physicians, at the close of twelve weeks, and the sentence has gone forth: "Alice will never walk again."

Warren was in the entry, listening with fearful anxiety. He overheard the dreadful words, and clasping both hands to his throbbing head, he rushed away to his room, where he remained all day, pacing the floor in agony, or tossing upon the bed, a pitiable sight to behold. Repeated messages had been sent to him, but his door was fastened; at length his father knocked:

"Open the door, Warren: I have something to say to you, my son."

"Please, dear papa, spare me — not yet — I cannot see any one: I am not fit to see those whom I have so afflicted."

"By-and-by, my son, I will be back again." Toward evening the father returned. "This time I must come in, Warren." The boy arose and unlocked the door. With haggard face, and bloodshot eyes, he met

his father's pitying gaze. " Here is a cup of tea, Warren: you must take it—it will revive you ; and then you
must come to Alice : she is the only one that can com
fort you—sweet, patient child !"

" How can I look at her, papa? Have I not blighted
her young life, papa?—her sweet, young life? Alice!
Alice !" and the boy raised his clasped hands over his
burning head.

Dr. Hastings took the hands between his own, put
back the dark locks from his orow, and bathed his face
in cool water, laying iced cloths upon his head.

" So comforting, papa!" said Warren, as he laid down,
somewhat quieted. "How did she bear it, papa?"

" Almost like an angel, Warren ; she says, 'It is God's
will, I can bear it, papa ;' and ever since she has been
whispering words of peace to her mother and the rest.
Come, now, Warren, she wants to see you."

Leaning on his father's arm, the suffering boy went
slowly along the passage, until he reached the door of
his sister's room.

" Stop a minute, Warren — they are singing."

And the sweet voices within, in low, soothing strains,
sang the words of that beautiful hymn :

" Thy will be done."

They stopped, and Dr. Hastings opened the door.
Alice was lying on her bed, the most composed of all
that suffering group. Long confinement and suffering

had paled the roses on her cheek, but the lily tint was just as lovely, and the deep blue eyes turned to the door with such a look of love, as, smiling, she extended her arms, and said, "Dear, dear Warren, come to me;" and folding her arms around her brother, she pressed sweet kisses upon the boy's cheek and brow.

"You are weak, dear: come, lie down; I have a great deal to say, and the rest will leave us by ourselves." The door closed, and the two loving hearts were alone in their sorrow.

"Now, Warren, you must not grieve so: it is God's will, or I would not be lying here. You did not drive the animal — he started himself."

"Yes, sister, I know that; but I persuaded you to get in."

"Still, Warren, nothing happens without God's knowledge: you know the sparrow does not fall to the ground unless he knows it, and I know that we are better than the sparrows."

"But you are so young, Alice, and such a lively bird: how can you live shut up in the house all the time?"

"I shall not be, brother; Dr. Lacey says that I can have a carriage made, which can be drawn by the hand, and that I must go out every day. You will draw me, and so will Allan, and everybody at the parsonage; why, papa, mamma, and everybody would act horse for Alice."

"But are you to be always on the **bed**, Alice?"

13 K

"Not always, brother: papa is going to have a swing. ing couch made, on wheels, that can be moved about anywhere, with an arrangement for sitting up at any height, by hinges at the head-board. I am getting better now, and I can soon read, and sew, and draw; and I am to be down in the little room, next to the library, all day, and carried up at night."

Warren was sobbing again: the very sweetness agonized the boy. She laid her hand gently upon his brow, and whispered, "Don't cry so, dear Warren : we shall have many sweet hours together; and I am one of the Pastor's Aid yet. I shall not go to school any more, but Dr. Arnold will give me lessons twice a week, as soon as the doctor says that I am ready. All the meetings of the society will be in my room, Warren, and I can do more now than I used to."

"How is that, Alice?"

"I have been thinking a great deal about it, when alone. I can write little notes to children, and to poor people, and to sick people, and perhaps they may be willing to attend to a little girl's words, when they come from a suffering couch."

"Do you really feel happy, Alice?"

"Not yet, Warren, but contented. By-and-by, when I get used to my couch, then we shall have merry times, again ; we are not going to sigh and cry all the time."

This interview was a great comfort to the boy, and daily did he seek the sufferer's room, where gradually ne learned to bear this great sorrow patiently. In a few weeks more, the swinging couch arrived; cushioned and placed in the little room down stairs, Alice was laid upon it, and Warren rocked the cradle, for such it really was.

"You must learn the sweet cradle-song, brother, and when I am in pain, you shall sing it; I mean Gottschalk's; it is so soothing: go play it, Margaret; I can hear, if you open the parlor-door. Is not this delightful, Warren? Here I am in the midst of you all, close by mamma's sitting-room — so near papa that he can run in and get his twelve-o'clock lunch with me — in sight of the sweet orchard — in hearing of the singing birds. Mamma can sit here with her sewing, and Margaret can soothe me with her sweet music on the parlor organ. Then, in the afternoon, you can bring round my little carriage, and we can ride through the pleasant lanes, and I can enjoy life yet, Warren."

Alice spent much time now reading her Testament, and the Holy Spirit, with all His enlightening and sanctifying power, was her teacher. As soon as she was dressed in the morning, she would say, "Now, mamma, my little Testament — then leave me alone for half an hour; this is my sweetest hour until evening comes round again." Always present at morning prayer, she still took her part in the selection of the daily texts. Every member of the family vied with each other in attentions to the sweet child; and the lovely flowers, always

on her table by the side of her couch, gave daily proof
of the love bestowed upon Alice Hastings by the people
of St. Barnabas'. Smitten, indeed, in the early days of
bright, happy girlhood; but in this case truly did "patience have her perfect work."

Alice is growing in grace under the discipline of suffering. It is esteemed a privilege by many to sit by her
couch, and hear her tell, in her own touching way, about
the goodness of God, and all that is done to make her
happy; and many an impressive sermon is preached unconsciously in that little room of privation and trial.

But there is another visitation at the parsonage — the
little delicate lamb, baby Emily, suddenly taken from
the flock, and translated to the kingdom above. It is
the first empty chair in the family group; but with the
bereavement comes the comfort, for they feel that the
frail little blossom is sheltered in her Father's house
from the rude blasts of this lower world, and know that
they shall meet again.

CHAPTER XL.

ENGLESBY TERRACE.

" For the natural man receiveth not the things of the Spirit of God."

THERE is a fine site for a residence but a few rods from the parsonage, and the inmates of the latter have often wished that it might be occupied by some agreeable neighbor. It was the highest situation any-where near, and the fresh green of the grassy slope seemed exactly the spot for a beautiful lawn. There were many fine trees, too, on the hill, the property ex-tending back to the pretty creek bordering this part of Westbrook. One day, a carriage drove up to the hill, and a lady and young girl, accompanied by a gentleman, stepped out. Both were in deep mourning, and gave rise to some agreeable speculations among the young folks at the parsonage, as they walked around the premises, the gentleman measuring distances. In a few weeks, the workmen were there, breaking the ground, and Warren remarked:

"I think that we are going to have neighbors on the hill, papa: the workmen are already on the premises."

The children were deeply interested in watching the

progress of affairs, as the handsome brownstone house rose rapidly. In the meanwhile, one of the new order of ministers is about to take up his abode at Westbrook, bringing with him the fossils in which he imagines there is life. A number of the inhabitants are tainted with the defunct theology, and must have a chapel of their own, where they can enjoy High Ritualism, as they have it in the neighboring city.

The family at the parsonage somehow associate the new mansion on the hill and the embryo chapel to· gether, for a clergyman in peculiar garb is often seen walking around the grounds, conversing with the work-men, and frequently, with the lady in mourning, seems to be giving advice.

It is soon announced that the corner-stone of a new chapel will be laid about eight blocks from St. Barna-bas', to be called St. Gregory's, and the minister is the Rev. Hugh Moncrief.

The two buildings proceed until the cold weather obliges the workmen to stop until spring.

.   .   .   .

There is a letter from Mrs. Hughes at the Adirondack Iron Works, telling that Nichol Leseure is no more, and that poor Nan is at the Newcombe Farm, homeless and pennyless, asking, at the same time, if the former visitors at the mountains can do any thing for her.

Dr. Arnold is consulted.

"We cannot refuse the call, can we, sisters?" said the good man.

"I think not," was Mary Arnold's quick reply. "We could make such a girl very useful in our family, and it might be a great blessing to the poor child to bring her within reach of the Gospel."

"She shall come," said the brother, and, writing immediately, Mrs. Hughes replied that her husband was going on the following week to New York, and would be there on Thursday at the hotel-depot with the child, where he would wait for some one to take her to Westbrook.

Margaret and Alice were greatly interested in the prospect of a stranger added to the Westbrook circle.

"More work for the Aid, sister," said Alice. "We must hunt up something for Nan, for I suppose she will hardly look civilized here."

With the help of Mrs. Lacey and the ladies at Little Rugby, they gathered quite enough material for a decent outfit in a few days. Dr. Arnold was at the post on the day appointed, and poor Nan silently took his hand, bursting into tears; for the memory of the summer visitors had always been fraught with pleasant associations, and was now especially linked with her departed father.

"You have friends at Westbrook, Nan," said Dr. Arnold: "don't grieve too much — they are waiting for you."

Toward evening they arrived at Little Rugby, and the ladies wondered how they were going to make anything civilized out of such a wild, rough-looking child as the one brought to their fireside. Large and muscular for fourteen, with a brown, weather-beaten skin, and shaggy black hair, shrinking away from strangers, almost afraid to raise her eyes, which were the only redeeming features of her face; but when she did raise them for a moment, Margaret Arnold saw that they were large, lustrous, and full of feeling.

Dr. Arnold went over for Margaret after tea, and the soft dark eyes, with the low, sweet tones of voice that fell upon the ears of the orphan child, seemed at once to inspire her with confidence; for coming quietly to her side, she laid her hand in Margaret's, and seemed quite satisfied with her new friends.

"This is a subject for Alice," said Dr. Arnold. "Nan must go over on Saturday afternoon· I am sure that Alice will do her good."

Next morning she was early at the parsonage, and the two girls were soon busy, with the help of mamma, in devising ways of making Nan a little more presentable.

On the following day, Nan was present at family prayers, and listened very attentively to the instruction of the good pastor.

"What is our subject to-day, Margaret?"

"The duty of repentance, papa·; and this is my text:
· Then Peter said unto them, Repent, and be baptized

every one of you in the name of Jesus Christ for the remission of sins, and ye shall receive the gift of the Holy Ghost.' "

"I am ready for yours, Warren."

" ' I tell ye nay, but except ye repent, ye shall all likewise perish.' "

"What has Allan to say?"

" 'And the times of this ignorance God winked at, but now commandeth all men everywhere to repent.' "

"Has Alice any?"

" 'And they went out and preached that men should repent.' "

"I am waiting for Edward's?"

" 'Repent ye, for the kingdom of heaven is at hand.' "

"Now Sunbeam's?" said the pastor, with his smile for the little one.

" 'Repent ye, and believe the gospel.' "

"You have brought me excellent texts, my children, on a very important subject. Man is everywhere a sinner, and needs to repent before God; but true repentance is the gift of the Holy Spirit, and for this we must pray, that he would enable us to see our sins and to exercise that godly sorrow which needeth not to be repented of."

Nan looked around with a bewildered expression, for she wondered where they got all those g ' vords from; she was sure that she knew none.

Two days of altering and fitting, with Mrs. Lacey's help, did wonders; and when Nan made her appearance at Little Rugby at the close of the third day, the ladies scarcely could believe that there could have been such a transformation. The short, skimped, brown dress was exchanged for a dark de laine, made high in the neck, with a crimped ruffle, and a neat, white apron. Good boots and stockings had replaced those completely worn out ; and a straw hat, with black ribbon, placed upon hair neatly combed, and black and glossy now, gave quite a civilized appearance to the mountain girl.

"Are n't they good, Dr. Arnold?" said the girl, her dark eyes swimming in grateful tears.

"Yes, Nan; you have found friends now. Miss Margaret is one of the kindest and best; and Miss Alice —well! you 'll find out all about that, dear child, on Saturday afternoon."

The ladies at Little Rugby found Nan to be docile and willing, very anxious to repay her kind benefactors for what they had done for her, but utterly ignorant of all the customs of civilized life, so that they had much to teach — how to sit in a proper, feminine manner — what uses to make of her fingers — how to enter a room, and when not to enter — and how to take care of her person. But there was good progress; and what she once really learned, she was not apt to forget.

The appearance of Alice Hastings had made a deep impression upon the girl, for she had never conceived of anything so spiritual as the lovely child, who was now her teacher. Words from such a source came fraught to Nan with great power; and whenever she returned to Little Rugby from these interviews, she could relate all that had passed, and the ladies comforted Alice with the assurance that she had no more hopeful pupil than poor Nan Leseure.

But her first visit to St. Barnabas' was one not to be forgotten; for notwithstanding all the instruction of the ladies, concerning deportment in the house of God, she was so struck with wonder that she was an object of much amusement to the young folks near her. With eyes roving about, and mouth open, she watched the congregation and the minister; and when the organ struck up, Nan started to her feet with a bound, and, facing the organ, wondered what there was up in that high gallery. Nan had never been in the house of God before, and when Miss Mary tried to help her find the places in the Prayer Book, there was but little devotion in that day's service in the Arnold pew, for curiosity was so wide awake, that nothing could silence her whispered questions; but she tried in some degree to imitate the manner of the people rather too closely, for Miss Mary had told her to watch her neighbors, and follow their example, adding that she would know the meaning of everything hereafter. Unfortunately for the first lesson, there were strangers present on that morning at St. Barnabas', and Nan selected the most demonstrative in her first attempt at outward worship. Miss Mary observed persons smiling near her, and could scarcely restrain a smile herself, when she saw Nan imitating, in a wonderfully awkward manner, the bowings and genuflections of several ladies of the ritualistic order, not only in the Creed, but in all the Glorias, evidently satisfied with herself. The Hastings children had one glimpse, and the father was pained at the sight of Edward and Lucy, first glancing at Nan, and then covering their eyes in their efforts to hide their laughter, whispering every now and then at some new attempt at imitation. Miss Mary was careful, after that, how she told Nan to follow the example of her neighbors.

The winter passed rapidly away, for all were busy people, both at the parsonage and at Little Rugby. Alice was deeply interested in her *protégée*, for now she was full of questions, and drank in Scriptural knowledge with great avidity.

Early in the spring, the building on Englesby Terrace recommenced, and, by the first summer month, was completed. The young people at the parsonage asked permission of the workmen to go through the building, which they found to be an elegantly finished mansion, with all the conveniences of modern days. There was one room on the second floor, adjoining a large, front chamber, which most excited their curiosity, having a large bay-window, of the richest painted glass ; the walls also were illuminated and adorned with pictures of Scripture scenes. There was an especially fine painting of the Virgin, which overlooked something like a small altar, covered with a richly embroidered cloth, reaching to the floor; on each end of the altar were silver candlesticks, with a crucifix in the centre, and on one side lay the Prayer Book, the Book of Hours, and a copy of the *Directorium Anglicanum*, and a Bible.

"Can you tell me the lady's name?" said Margaret, to an upholsterer, passing through the room.

"I think it is Sherwood, a very wealthy lady from New York, who is coming here with her daughter to live."

"Is she a Roman Catholic?" inquired Warren.

"I believe not," said the man, smiling: "she is one of the ritualists; halfway to Rome, I should say."

The house was partially furnished, the halls and staircase adorned with large and elegant pictures set in niches, especially one of the Nativity and the Ascension. Flowers were blooming in the garden, for men had been at work there from early spring. It was evidently the home of affluence; but not of enlightened piety. So thought Margaret Hastings, as she turned homeward.

For several days longer, rich furniture was arriving, and the mansion was frequently visited by the lady in mourning.

One morning, at an early hour, Margaret perceived the lady, accompanied by a very young girl, in sable weeds also, walking in the grounds.

"I think that the strangers have come, mamma," said the young lady. "The younger one is a sweet-looking

14

girl of about fifteen, and seems very attentive to her
mother. I hope that we shall have agreeable neighbors."

Seclusion seemed, however, to be what the lady desired — seldom going out, except to ride, or to attend
upon the services at St. Gregory's.

Mrs. Sherwood was the widow of Howard Sherwood,
a wealthy merchant of New York, who at his death
left a princely fortune to his widow and child. They
had been a united, happy pair, and the bereavement had
so bowed down the widow's heart, that she had entirely
renounced the gay world in which she had formerly
moved, and turned her thoughts to preparation for
another world. Unfortunately, she had cast her lot
among the high ritualists of New York; but there
was too much of a longing desire to know the truth,
too much consciousness of estrangement from a holy
God, ever to be entirely satisfied with the glitter and
sensuous worship of St. Agapius'. To be sure, there was
emotion of a certain character during the processional
singing There was something of awe and superstitious
reverence when at the Holy Communion — she was
taught that she bowed in the presence of the real body
and blood of our Lord. She would have felt the same at
hearing the strains of Stabat Mater, or during the singing of the Miserere; but that was not spiritual worship.
She would have felt the same at an opera where dramatic performance sometimes partook of a religious
character; but neither was that spiritual worship.

Anxious to know the truth, Mrs. Sherwood read the Scriptures daily; and there she found justification by faith — the new birth, adoption, sanctification, and con· scious assurance of peace with God.   These were distant oases in the spiritual life never yet reached; for the mirage of the ritualistic desert constantly misled her thirsty search, only to tantalize her weary wanderings. But, under the guidance of the Rev. Hugh Moncrief, she still attended upon the daily service at St. Gregory's, for she knew nothing better.

Her daughter Agnes was a lovely girl of fifteen, most carefully trained in her mother's faith.   Imaginative, refined, talented, there was much in this sensuous wor- ship, these object-lessons of false doctrine, to fascinate a young and ardent nature, and Agnes was an enthusiastic devotee.

Taught that she was truly regenerated in the sacra· ment of baptism, at an early age she had been confirmed, and brought to the Holy Communion; and so the young creature thought herself a real Christian.

Agnes possessed many personal attractions — a grace- ful form, a clear olive skin, where the tints of the peach gave brightness to the dreamy dark eyes, a profusion of silky hair, dark as the raven's wing, and a smile whose fascination captivated all hearts.

We find her, one summer evening, walking near the parsonage grounds — the windows are open, and it is the hour of evening prayer.   Margaret Hastings is presid ing at the organ — the rich voices within are singing the sweet evening hymn:

> "Glory to thee, my God, this night,
> For all the blessings of the light:
> Keep me, O keep me, King of kings,
> Under thine own almighty wings."

Agnes is impressed by the solemn music, as it comes stealing through the windows, riveting her footsteps near the large tree at the gate of the parsonage. Then came the tones, but not the words, of the pastor's evening prayer. She is still leaning against the tree, when Margaret and Warren come out on the piazza, and, arm in arm, walk out into the orchard. Agnes walked slowly homeward, filled with the solemn thoughts of the music at the parsonage.

"I wish that you could have heard the sweet evening hymn at the parsonage, mamma," said the young girl; "it was so heavenly. I never heard anything that impressed me so much."

"They say that Mr. Hastings is one of the evangelicals, Agnes; and that means opposed to the views of the Holy Catholic Church."

"Then I suppose that I saw the son and daughter; she is about eighteen — such a lovely girl, and her brother equally interesting. I wish that they would call upon us, mamma."

"I dare say that they will, Agnes; but I don't care

for much intimacy; we don't think alike, and there would be no harmony in our religious views."

In a few days, Mrs. Hastings called upon her new neighbor. There was much in Mrs. Sherwood to attract — lady-like manners; a sweet, sad countenance, rendered still more interesting by her widow's dress; and evident refinement of taste.

"We have long wished for a neighbor on the hill," said the pastor's wife; "and I hope that you will not be a ceremonious visitor."

"I have lived a very secluded life since my husband's death," was the reply, "seldom going out, except to church; but I should be glad to see your family fre quently. Agnes was quite charmed with the peep that she had the other evening of your son and daughter."

"If you ever feel disposed to step in at St. Barnabas', you will always find a seat at No. 10, in the middle aisle, near the pulpit."

Mrs. Sherwood smiled as she replied: "I would return the courtesy by inviting you to No. 5, at St. Gregory's; but I suppose that Mrs. Hastings would not like her family to be seen among us ritualists."

"It is probable that we may accept your invitation occasionally," was the courteous reply; for Mrs. Hastings was too much of a Christian lady to indulge in free remarks on a visit to her new neighbor. A pleasant impression was left upon the minds of both ladies; and

14 *   L

Mrs. Sherwood took an early opportunity to return the visit.

Really pleased with all that she saw at the parsonage, she was especially impressed by the youthful sufferer, who lay so patiently on her couch, and who received the visitors with such a sweet, pleasant smile.

"How long have you been confined to your couch, my dear?"

"Two years," was the meek reply.

"I suppose that you look forward to your recovery, my dear, with great anxiety?"

Alice dropped her eyes as she replied: "I have no such prospect, Mrs. Sherwood. This is my couch as long as I live."

Tears suffused the eyes of both visitors, who could not reply.

"I am very happy, Mrs. Sherwood. I do not suffer much. I am surrounded by loving friends. I can sew, and read, and write, I can help the Pastor's Aid yet, can teach a class of little girls once a week; and have the hope of heaven at last, when all is over. Then I have such a father! Do you know my father, Mrs. Sherwood?" continued the child, fixing her eloquent eyes upon the lady's face.

"I have not the pleasure, Alice; but hope to know him soon."

"I have not told you the half of my blessings; but you 'll find them out by coming to see me often."

At the close of the visit, Mrs. Sherwood and Agnes both kissed the dear child; and, from that day, the lady sent frequent offerings of love to the invalid; sometimes a bunch of sweet flowers, at others a basket of rare fruit; sometimes a little sum for the Pastor's Aid, and occasionally a lovely picture for ner room.

CHAPTER XII.

CHRISTMAS AT ST. BARNABAS'.

"Glory to God in the highest, and on earth peace, and good-will towards men."

THE seasons come and go, with their sunshine and their shadow, and through their misty gates march out the immortals: this in the world of nature. In the kingdom of grace, the Church, too, has her seasons — marching closely in the footsteps of her glorious Master. For weeks the Advent trumpet has been calling to Christians to prepare their welcome for their Lord — in more exultant peals, as the Feast of the Nativity is drawing nigh.

It is now a winter evening at the parsonage. The snow is falling fast without; and the couch of the invalid is wheeled into the family parlor.

"Draw down the curtains, mamma," said Alice. "Please raise me up on high. I feel well to-night; and I have yet so much to do before Christmas. All my little girls must have a hood for the cold weather; and I can knit just as well at night as in the day-time."

164

The family are gathered around the fireside, for there is a low grate sending out its glowing light and heat.

"Isn't this pleasant, mamma?" said Alice. "Mamma and Margaret, Warren and Edward and Lucy."

Just then, the door opened, and, to the surprise of all present, in stepped the pastor, in wrapper and slippers, evidently prepared for an evening at home. Alice's bright eyes sparkled with delight, as she said:

"And dear papa, too! I wish that I could—" She checked herself, and added: "Come here, papa; let me kiss you on both your dear cheeks!" Drawing him down, she continued, "No lecture to-night? Are we to have you all to ourselves? Isn't that delightful!"

"No lecture, dear," replied papa; "and I rather think no visitor on such a night; and I am to have a concert here, at home."

Up jumped Warren; and, turning over the music book, he brought Margaret to the organ.

"Let us practise some of our Christmas hymns," said Alice. "It is coming on pretty fast."

"What first?" said Margaret, taking her seat at the instrument.

"'God Rest Ye, Merry Gentlemen,'" said Alice; and all the sweet voices joined in singing the several parts of that old hymn.

"Now, 'Three Kings of Orient,'" said Allan.

"Now for mine," said papa. "It is a great favorite among the ritualists; but, never mind, it is a sweet hymn, and we can enjoy it here in the parsonage parlor."

With full hearts and sweet expression the whole company sang "Jerusalem the Golden," Alice knitting busily all the while, and the family group wondering if anything more lovely in human shape had ever graced the earth. The faint color was returning to her cheek once more; the eyes were soft and lustrous again; a sweet look of saintly piety gave tenderness to the beauty which had once been so brilliant; the golden hair lay parted on the forehead, descending in waving curls around the fair young face.

In the midst of their enjoyment, a ring came to the hall-door.

"There, now! that is a visitor," said Warren. "I fear that our pleasant party will be broken up."

The hall-door opened, and the knocking of snow from the feet upon the entry carpet indicated a call. In a minute or two, the bright, sunny faces of Mrs. Lacey and Sarah peeped in at the parlor-door, the former with a basket in her hand.

"Let me take your hood and cloak," said Mrs. Hastings.

"I just imagined such a family party," said the visitor, "and I have brought some splendid bellflowers and English walnuts — just the thing for a winter fireside."

"Thank you, dear madam," said Warren, who had by this time changed his mind as to the intrusion.

Knitting in hand, the ladies were soon at home, and the music commenced again.

At the close of the entertainment, a very lively party gathered around the table, where they enjoyed the feast brought by good Mrs. Lacey.

"Show Mrs. Lacey my beautiful present," said Alice; and Margaret led the way into the little room, lighting the gas. The ladies were delighted by the sight of a melodeon that stood against the wall, and a picture of Christmas-eve that hung above it.

"That is the gift of Mrs. Sherwood, our new neighbor," said Mrs. Hastings. "She seems to have taken a great interest in Alice, and there is scarcely a day that she does not send something."

"What a pity that she is such a ritualist!" said Mrs. Lacey. "I hear that she even goes to secret confession to Mr. Moncrief."

"We must not believe all that we hear, Mrs. Lacey; though, according to her own account, she is a devoted ritualist."

"Is not that a lovely picture?" said the child, as they returned to the parlor. "I tell papa that I must have a party too on Christmas-eve."

"But you know, dear, that we don't have parties at the parsonage," replied the father; "for we can make no distinctions among the people."

"But I know that you will let me have such a one as I want, papa, where the Saviour himself would come, if he were on earth. Let me read you some of my passages;" and taking her little Testament from behind the pillow, she read:

"'When thou makest a dinner or a supper, call not thy friends, nor thy brethren, neither thy kinsmen, nor thy rich neighbors; lest they also bid thee again, and a recompense be made thee.

"'But when thou makest a feast, call the poor, the maimed, the lame, the blind;

"'And thou shalt be blessed; for they cannot recompense thee; for thou shalt be recompensed at the resurrection of the just.'

"Now I have been thinking of just such a party, and have hit upon a plan."

"Let us hear it, Alice," said Mrs. Lacey; "perhaps I can help you."

"I can find plenty of guests," said Alice, "among the poor communicants. There is old Aunty Miller, who is nearly blind; and there is Robert Jordan, who is lame and sick; and Matty Hoskins, so long a cripple; Jenny Thompson, poor and old; Daniel Horner, paralyzed; Letty Fenton and her grand-daughter, and my six little scholars: fourteen in all."

"How in the world are you to provide for so many, Alice?" inquired the father.

"I know," smiling. "I shall write to Mrs. Sherwood, and the Arnolds, to Miss White, and Miss Van Zandt. I know Mrs. Lacey will help me; and so will

Father Morgan, who will be glad to come to my party."

"It is a bright thought, my dear," said Mrs. Lacey, "and you may depend upon me for help."

Papa gave his consent, and the pleasant evening closed with a few words of prayer.

Mrs. Hastings went to the door with her visitors. It was snowing and drifting now with great violence.

"This is making work for us, Mr. Hastings," said the benevolent lady, "for such storms always bring suffering; so to-morrow I must on with my water-proof and over-shoes, and be off early to my district. Good night: God bless you all."

For the next four weeks, Alice was a busy, happy little creature. The ladies all sent their contributions, so that each guest should carry away something; then it was Alice Hastings' Christmas party, and all the people of St. Barnabas' were ready at any time to give her pleasure.

Christmas-eve is here. The two rooms adjoining are richly dressed with evergreens, which the sexton has brought in from the woods, and helped the young people to arrange. There are spicy cedar, shining laurel, holly, and ivy, with bright scarlet haws, and lovely flowers, sent by ladies from their conservatories, for dear Alice Hastings. The sweet child is dressed for the occasion in a warm, blue merino. Something of the former brightness rests upon her face. By the side of her couch

15

stands the table, on which are spread out her gifts for the guests.   Early in the evening, the hall-bell commenced ringing, and Warren handed in the guests.   " Happy Christmas ! " said Alice to each newcomer ; but it was with some sadness in the tones that the visitors echoed the wish to the young creature, stricken down so early in her bright existence.   When all had assembled, Margaret took her seat at the organ, and the whole party sang the old Christmas hymn :

"While shepherds watched their flocks by night."

Then they were invited out to the dining-room, whither Alice was conveyed too, enjoying the sight of the good supper spread out upon the table by the bounty of the good ladies of St. Barnabas'.   There were turkey, and cranberry-sauce, and ham, mashed potatoes and other nice vegetables, with mince-pies and plum-pudding in abundance.   Alice, perhaps, was the happiest of the whole party, for her own hands had done so much in spreading the board.   After supper, back again to her own room, where, reclining upon her couch, her own fair hands distributed the hoods, and handkerchiefs, and warm stockings, with a bag of bonbons and a Christmas book to each little girl.   Then papa came in, and talked so happily to the people about the blessed Saviour, whose advent they were so soon to celebrate.   Then several more sweet hymns and a prayer : then the guests came forward to take leave of the young girl.

"God bless you, Miss Alice!" said Aunty Miller, who was nearly blind.

"He does, Aunty, for I am very happy," was the low reply.

Then old Robert limped up to the couch, and said, "I shall remember you, Miss Alice, in the cold, winter days, when I wear this good, warm muffler."

"And I shall remember you, Robert, when I see the snow-storms, and shall be so happy."

Then each advanced one by one, to give and receive a parting blessing.

It were hard to say which pillow was most visited by happy thoughts that night; but it does seem as if Alice Hastings must have felt communion with the Christmas angels, as she looked out upon the silver moon, sailing through the clouds, with the peculiar brightness of the sharp winter atmosphere.

By early dawn, the Christmas chimes were ringing the joy-bells for the Feast of the Nativity, and as Alice lay awake, listening to their music, she called her sister. "Margaret, Margaret, wake up! Don't you hear sing. ing outside of the window?"

Margaret sprang suddenly from her bed, and there, out in the moonlight, stood a company of children, trained by the teachers of the Sunday school, and mar- shalled by Dr. Arnold. They sang several Christmas carols, after the fashion of old times, the children giving the choruses in grand style.

All were astir early in the morning, calling out from room to room the sweet salutation of "Happy Christmas!" After breakfast the family assembled for morning worship.

"Now, children, for the Christmas texts," said papa. "What idea should be most prominent at this season, in connection with our Lord?"

"That of his coming as our Saviour, papa," said Margaret, "and this is my text: 'And thou shalt call his name *Jesus:* for he shall save his people from their sins.'"

"What have you, Alice?"

"'For unto you is born this day, in the city of David, a Saviour, which is Christ the Lord.'"

"And yours, Warren?"

"'And the Word was made flesh, and dwelt among us.'"

"What have you, Allan?"

"'God was manifest in the flesh, justified in the Spirit, seen of angels, preached unto the Gentiles, believed on in the world, received up into glory,'"

"And what have you, Edward?"

"Just the same as sister Margaret," was the reply.

"And so have I," said Lucy.

"I perceive, dear children," said the pastor, "that your thoughts have all taken the same direction in searching for passages proclaiming the Lord Jesus as our Saviour. If there were but one, it would be sufficient for the heart of faith to rest upon. Let us never forget that 'He came to seek and save that which was lost;' and let us be very certain that he has really saved us."

After worship, the family met in the parlor to exchange their gifts of love, and at the usual hour assembled at church to celebrate the grand event in the history of Christianity. Dressed, according to the good old custom, in bright Christmas greens, everything wore a look of cheerful gratitude.

The joy-bells, the music, the prayers, the sermon were all full of the one grand theme of the Incarnation, and the blessings connected with that wondrous advent. While this religious celebration lasts, the world can never lose its hold of this starting-point in the history of its Redeemer. For more than eighteen hundred years the feast has been observed all over Christendom, and will probably roll on until that glorious day which ushers in the Second Advent of our Lord, amid the pomp and splendor of that day of triumph — the long expectation of the Christian Church all fulfilled.

On their return home, many gifts were found for the pastor's family, all more or less valuable, but all free-will offerings of love to the dear household, among which was a package for Margaret from Dr. Arnold.

"Why don't you open it, sister?" said Warren, with a look of mischief on his face.

15 *

Margaret blushed as she replied: "I will directly, brother."

Taking it to another part of the room, she found that it contained a beautiful copy of Longfellow's Poems, accompanied by a note, which she did not read now, but hastily put it into her pocket for a more quiet corner.

In the afternoon, the mothers' meeting assembled at the church, where the ladies distributed winter comforts among the grateful women.

Thus ended a happy Christmas-day at St. Barnabas', leaving behind it a warmer love to the Redeemer, more earnest longing for his blessed Second Advent.

CHAPTER XIII.

A SPIRITUAL HARVEST.

"And the Lord added to the Church daily such as should be saved."

BLESSED St. Barnabas'! standing as it were between earth and heaven with its messages of peace and love, its earnest ministry, its praying people, its spreading arms of benevolence, embracing all classes of human misery and guilt. Blessed sanctuary! where the dews of Heaven were constantly descending; for the Holy Spirit seemed ever to dwell more or less with this favored people. To cross its threshold was to take leave of earth, and stand almost in the vestibule of heaven.

This may seem an exaggerated description of a church militant, but it had its counterpart once in the recollection of some, in declining years now, who sat beneath just such a blessed, holy ministry. They will recognize the picture as they peruse these pages; for it is ever in the memory of one who now writes the history of St. Barnabas' and its sainted rector.

The ministry of Dr. Hastings was eminently one of prayer. Ever near the mercy-seat himself, he taught his people the true source of spiritual prosperity. Realizing the truth of such teachings, they loved to pray.

But he was a wise, judicious guide. Conscious that the praying members of a church are held up before the people as examp'es, he was careful to select the most intelligent and devotedly pious among the young men of St. Barnabas'; and these he trained. Chiefly candidates for the sacred ministry, they were supposed to be more fitted than others, whose lives were more in the world, for these public services.

There was a company of twelve or fifteen who conducted the Saturday night prayer-meeting, and who took turns in providing the conductors for a month at a time. They were notified of the same, and, it was presumed, made some preparation before the hour of prayer; consequently, there was no hurried approach to the mercy-seat — no crude words of mere repetition, often so irreverent in extempore prayer. The music, too, was in charge of the same committee, and the language of our beautiful service, so eminently spiritual and reverent, might always be felt mingling, subduing, elevating, in all these more social services. These meetings were held sometimes after the Friday night lecture; at eight o'clock in the morning, during the season of Lent; on especial fast-days appointed by the rector; and sometimes on Sunday afternoon, after service.

Dr. Hastings was not always present himself at these meetings, but kept a constant oversight, and was very careful quietly to put aside any whose lives did not accord with their high profession. If there were such cases, a private note, with a few passages of Scripture, came first, as a gentle admonition; and, where discipline was necessary, no public exhibition was ever dreamed of at St. Barnabas'. The sad erasure from the list of communicants was all that was known of any who disgraced their profession by unholy lives.

It was always esteemed a great privilege, when the state of his health permitted the rector to be present at the prayer-meetings, especially on Saturday evenings; and if only coming in with a slow and solemn step, after the services had commenced, every heart felt the preciousness of the few impressive words of exhortation that fell from his lips; or, at other times, seated at the reading-desk of the lecture-room, with closed eyes and heavenly aspect, in sweet, low tones, he would commence

"Come, Holy Spirit, heavenly dove,"

in which all would join, with earnest devotion in the time-honored hymn.

There were signs about the pastor now that often caused a sigh, as, with measured steps, he entered the house of prayer. Many remembered, in the years past, with what a buoyant tread he had gone in and out among his beloved people; but the feebleness had come so gradually that it had not hitherto alarmed his flock. Still he labored "in season and out of season," from

M

house to house, as well as in the sanctuary, for the good of souls.

Dr. Hastings was not a brilliant preacher, but he was eminently clear, earnest, impressive. There was solemnity in his calm, holy countenance, music in his rich tones, and that in his whole aspect which declared the fact that, as an ambassador for Christ, "he warned every man, and taught every man in all wisdom." He was never known to preach a sermon once upon ministerial superiority, or in any way to arrogate to himself a priestly distance between himself and his flock.

Dr. Hastings loved the souls of his people, and they loved their honored pastor. He lived in their midst the Christ-life, in all its saintly purity; and they venerated the representative for their Master's sake. In the abodes of the rich, or the cottages of the poor, love was the magnet which drew all hearts; and it would be hard to find a pastor of so few words, who wielded among his people such unbounded influence.

He was a burning and a shining light; a loving, faithful, diligent pastor, with sound common sense, so necessary in these degenerate days of tinselled Christianity. The one solemn word *eternity*, uttered in his own impressive manner, or the two, *repent, believe*, did infinitely more good than all the traditions of men, masked Episcopacy, or in other words, the foppish ritualism of modern days.

There were many blessed seasons of ingathering at St. Barnabas', and we are about to record one such rich spiritual harvest.

Dr. Hastings has become familiar with the stately steppings of the witness for his Lord and Master, as he draws near the flock, and frequently, after Friday evening lecture, invites any to meet their pastor in the vestry-room, who are anxious about the things that make for their everlasting peace.

On such occasions he was peculiarly happy in his choice of subjects, and always selected passages that were awakening, close, practical.

At this peculiar season, he delivered a course on the text: "I have a message from God unto thee;" dividing his hearers into classes, which he addressed separately — the serious countenances and the whispered words, as the silent company passed out of the lecture-room, gave evidence that the word had fallen upon good ground, ready for the Gospel seed.

Then came another course, from the words: "Is it well with thee?" which produced powerful impressions upon many hearts, especially the young.

A course of Sunday evening sermons were delivered at this time from the passage: "Run, speak to this young man;" and many a careless spirit was arrested in its worldliness by these awakening sermons.

In the midst of this season of revival, there came a notice of the Bishop's visitation, when he proposed to hold a confirmation at St. Barnabas'. Margaret and Allan Hastings are among the company who gather with the praying band in the vestry-room after evening lecture. The sister saw the lingering, hesitating step of her brother; and although she was herself a professing Christian, she felt that her encouragement might have much to do with Allan's decision, and so she whispered: " Come, Allan, I will go with you; papa will be so glad."

The father glanced toward his son with a look of tender interest, and in the few words addressed to the company gathered around him, his remarks were especially directed to cases like his; for he knew the character of his boy.

Next day, we find him knocking at the door of his father's study.

" Come in," said the pastor's voice, for he imagined who was there.

"Sit down, Allan, close by my side, and tell me all that you have to say," said the father.

" It seems so little, papa — it is just to say that the notice on Sunday seemed addressed to me. And ever since, the words of your sermon have followed me all the week: 'The Master is come, and calleth for thee : ' I am ready, papa; can I come?"

" A very few questions will decide, Allan. You have been carefully taught the theory of the Gospel plan, have you any of its experience? "

"I know that I am by nature a sinner, papa; I feel that very often: I know that I need a Saviour, and I believe that I have taken him for my own. I have heard so constantly about our dear Lord, that sometimes I am afraid that mere habit may influence me; but then I know that I want to give my whole heart to Him, who gave His life for me: may I come?"

The father laid his hand upon Allan's head in blessing, as he knelt by his side, saying: "Let us pray."

And there, in this silent study, he poured out a full heart before God, his Father, for a blessing on his darling son.

They rose from their knees. The father passed his arm around Allan's waist, and pressing a warm kiss upon the downy cheek, said:

"Not only my dear son, but a brother now, a brother in the Lord. May your path be that of the shining light, Allan!"

Alice has heard of the Bishop's visitation, and of Allan's decision, and has sent for papa to come to her couch

"Will you leave us alone, Margaret?" said the invalid, as the door opened, admitting her father.

"Come, sit down close by my side, dear papa," said the child; "for I have much to say to you. Margaret has told me about Allan, and I am so glad. I wish that I might be one of that company, papa. Am I too young to own that I love the Lord?"

16

"Not too young to be a Christian, Alice. If you have truly repented of your sins, and believe with your whole heart in the Lord Jesus; if you have truly renounced the service of the world, the flesh, and the devil, and, by God's help, intend to lead a new life, come, renew your baptismal vow, and give yourself openly away to the Saviour, who died for you."

"I think that I can say 'Yes' to every one of those conditions, papa. One thing I am sure of, and that is, that I truly love the precious Saviour, and want to be His forever and ever; but there are many things I don't understand yet; many things that seem to mark the old Christians of the New Testament, that I don't know anything about."

The pastor smiled, as he replied:

"Remember, my love, that you are not one of the old Christians of the New Testament, only a babe in Christ. First, then, you must lisp the words, and totter with the feeble steps of infancy; then with the stronger gait of youth, then with the firm tread of a mature and steadfast Christian. God knows our feeble frame, Alice, and does not look for the fruits of ripened faith in the mere babe in Christ."

"All that I want to know then, papa, is, am I really a babe in Christ?"

"Yes, Alice; if you have a child's faith, a child's love, a child's obedience, then you are a Christian child."

"Then I may come, papa, and own my dear Saviour before the world?"

"Come, and welcome, my child. Jesus is ready to receive just such as you."

"If we could only see dear Warren among the candidates, papa, how happy we should be l"

"Yes, Alice; but God has different ways by which to bring to himself the souls that Jesus has redeemed. We must pray and trust, my love; and now let us seek our Father's face."

Alice closed her eyes and folded her hands so meekly, while the pastor poured out his heart in lively gratitude for the spiritual mercies thus far bestowed upon his household, and in earnest prayer for those who still stood aloof from the Saviour.

The day of confirmation has arrived; and on the afternoon of the sacred Sabbath, a solemn crowd have assembled at St. Barnabas'. The aged Bishop, with his silver hair, his saintly face glowing with benevolence, and the tottering steps of age, is seated in the chair, looking at the large company of candidates who are seated in the front pews. It is a solemn, impressive scene, for all ages are represented in that group: old age, middle life, and fresh, ardent youth are there. There are about fifty ready to consecrate their all to Jesus; for there are none there who imagine that to know the Creed, the Lord's Prayer, and the Ten Com-

mandments, by itself, entitles them to the name of
Christian.

Every heart is touched at the sight of Alice Hastings,
drawn up the aisle by her brother Warren near the
chancel. She is dressed in pure white, and a holy expression of saintly devotion rests upon her lovely countenance. Warren is just about to turn away, to take
his seat among the worshippers, when Alice whispered:

"Will ye also go away, Warren?"

"I am not ready, Alice."

The boy entered the pew, and it was with a serious
face that he listened to the solemn sermon from the good
old Bishop, who was his father's uncle. Then came the
singing of two verses from the hymn, sacred in the
memory of thousands:

> "O happy day, that stays my choice
> On thee, my Saviour, and my God:
> Well may this glowing heart rejoice
> And tell thy goodness all abroad."

While these words were sung, the candidates slowly
and solemnly approached the chancel, and then the confirmation service proceeded, with its simple, impressive
language, its earnest, fervent prayer. When the
Bishop stepped down the aisle to lay his hands upon
the sweet invalid in the carriage, many voices joined
audibly in the fervent Amen uttered by the pastor and
Father Morgan, who was present on this occasion.

After all were confirmed, then came the loving words of the faithful pastor, reminding them what a solemn vow they had just made in the presence of Almighty God. Nearly all were his own spiritual children, and as he spoke to them of the trials and temptations that would beset them on their journey to the heavenly city, he commended them to the warm love and sympathy of their fellow-Christians, who had travelled in the pilgrim's road for so many years before them; but most of all did he point them to the guidance, the love, and the example of their blessed Saviour.

Then, at the close of the services, while the last verses of the sweet hymn were sung, with solemn step the candidates returned to their pews.

The Methodist and Presbyterian ministers were present, for they highly esteemed the good rector of St. Barnabas', and as they passed out, stopped by the side of the carriage, to give their blessing and the hand of Christian fellowship to the young disciple. Mrs. Sherwood and Agnes, too, were there, deeply impressed by the solemn service that, at St. Barnabas', *meant so much.*

Warren, too, has had many serious thoughts throughout this holy day; but the proud heart is not ready to submit to the reign of the Lord Jesus yet. The sight of his saintly sister deeply affected him: "But then," he argued, "Alice has nothing else. The bright world of fame is before me, and beckons me forward. I dare say that I shall become a Christian some day, but not **yet.'**

16 *

Edward and Lucy had their own artless talk, when they were alone. "Did n't Alice look holy, Edward," said Lucy, "when the Bishop laid his hands upon her head? I am sure that she is one of Jesus' lambs. When I am a little older, I 'll ask papa if I may not be confirmed."

"I wonder why Warren was not among them," said Edward. "I suppose that he 's too proud to own that he is a sinner, before all the people."

"I hope that he will be a good Christian yet, Edward, for it would be a dreadful thing for any at Westbrook Parsonage not to be a servant of the Lord."

The good Bishop remained until next day, and, assembled in the parlor, he addressed words full of holy unction to the new candidates at the parsonage; for there were four in that household — Debby and Jane belonging to the company.

Warren remembered the words of Alice, and lay long awake, thinking of the tender expostulation, and wondering if it were possible that there might be eternal separation in the world to come — *not from Jesus*, for he had not learned to love him — but from the dear, precious ones at home.

Very carefully were the new disciples instructed in their duty, and posts of usefulness assigned to each, according to their ability. There were no isolated Christians at St. Barnabas', but at once they were brought acquainted with each other, and a few private words from the pastor directed especial care over some particular case, in need of sympathy and encouragement. Truly it was a band dwelling together in unity, and very sweet and comforting were the pastor's remarks, at the familiar lecture, on the week following, from the words: " I. have no greater joy than to hear that my children walk in the truth." Comfort, guidance, encouragement were in the precious message. Inspired by these heavenly teachings, Christian love was here in its highest exercise; and here it might be sung from full hearts —

> "Blest is the tie that binds
>   Our hearts in Christian love;
> The fellowship of kindred minds
>   Is like to that above.
> Before our Father's throne
>   We pour united prayers;
> Our fears, our hopes, our aims are one,
>   Our comforts and our cares."

Then followed a course of rich instruction from the words: "Speak to the children of Israel that they go forward." Here it was that a broad line of distinction was drawn between the children of the world and the children of God; and though the spirit of true benevolence was inculcated toward all men, none thought of joining hands with the world of the ungodly, for higher, holier joys were to be found on this mount of privilege; and the favored members of St. Barnabas' could at all times answer to the seductions of the world, "I have a great work to do, therefore I cannot come down."

Unbounded was the influence of the meek and lowly pastor of St. Barnabas'. The vigor of youth had passed away, but the ripened graces of the Spirit spread a halo of peace over the saintly face, and imparted a depth of tone to the musical voice of Dr. Hastings. In every department his influence was felt; in the field of benevolence, where the people were always ready to respond to his calls, in the field of activity, where a hive of busy workers were always at work. Mr. Moncrief wondered how it was, for he knew much of the power of St. Barnabas'.

"Here," said he, "am I preaching and teaching, making everything attractive, holding up the divine power of the ministry, teaching the difference between priest and people, showing that disobedience to us is disloyalty to God, and what do I see? — just a few disposed to work, but no heart is in their services; when here is this feeble man, with his faltering step, his pallid face, his failing health, wielding a power second to none. He wants means to carry out some grand scheme of benevolence — he speaks a few plain, practical words, and at once the people respond by thousands; he wants workers, and at once come forward a willing band. How is it? For he is one of the humblest and most unpretending of men."

Here is the great secret. Study it, Rector of St. Gregory's, and all others of like spirit.

Dr. Hastings keeps himself in the background,

comes with no priestly arrogance, no high and lofty claims; but, holding forth his Master's claims, presenting his Master's image, preaching his Master's Gospel, he is beloved for the Master's sake. and thus he wields a power all unsought, tor tne peopie uf St. Barnabas have "learned to esteem *him* highly in love for *his* work's sake."

CHAPTER XIV.

ALICE.

"And a certain woman named Lydia, a seller of purple, of the city of Thyatira, which worshipped God, heard us; whose heart the Lord opened, that she *attended to the things which were spoken of Paul.*"

ALICE HASTINGS' disease has taken a new form, for now she is subject to hours of extreme suffering, when spasms rack her delicate frame.

At such times, a darkened room, a quiet couch, and whispered words of holy prayer send Warren rushing from the house, pacing up and down the students' walk at Little Rugby, or along the shady banks of the creek. He generally stays until the paroxysm is over. He can scarcely bear the saintly patience of the gentle sufferer, as she presses his hand, on his return, between her own, and whispers:

"Better, Warren. Jesus comforts me. He was with me all the time. What should I do without Him now? He sends nothing but what we are able to bear. Come, sit down by me a little while, and read me some sweet hymns."

Warren took his seat, and Alice pointed out what she wanted.

190

It generally took several days for her to recover from these attacks, and Warren was devoted in his attentions.

"You may open the shutters now, Warren," said the sister, "and let in the sweet fragrance of the flowers."

The boy obeyed, and pushing aside the curtain, Alice said with a smile:

"These days of suffering prepare the way for great enjoyment, Warren; for I don't believe that any of you can know how sweet the flowers seem after hours of pain."

"Do you think that you can ride to-morrow, Alice?" said the brother.

"I think not to-morrow, but next day, for my back is quite sore to-day. I have a great deal to do among my friends, Warren; for it has been some time now since I have been among them. Father Morgan is so good, and keeps me all the time supplied with books, and the tracts, and money."

In a few days Alice is ready for her ride. and, in her soft white hood and wrapper, she looks almost like one taking leave of earth, so pale, so pure, so heavenly is the sweet face.

Warren lifted the transparent little hand and kissed it; and drawing him down close, she said:

"Dear brother Warren, how good you are!"

"Which way, Alice?" said the brother.

"Along the border of the creek, and then home by

the way of Aunty Miller's. I have something to give her."

Propped up by pillows, Alice looked around upon the fair face of nature with a serene and holy joy, for it was a bright, balmy day; and her talk to Warren was that of a cheerful child. Passing down a small street that led to the creek, Alice was shocked by the language of a man walking just behind her carriage.

"Tell him to come here, Warren," said the sister.

"He may abuse you, Alice."

"No, he could not do that, brother."

Warren stepped up to the man.

"There is a helpless child in that carriage, who wants to speak to you, my friend."

The man, surprised, stepped forward, evidently impressed by the sight of the saintly face that met his gaze.

She extended her hand. He seemed almost to shrink from touching its purity.

"You see, my friend," said the young girl, "that I cannot walk, but I am very happy. I want to ask you a few questions. Have you the use of your limbs — your eyes? Have you good health?"

"What makes you ask me these questions, little miss? But I answer that I am neither lame, nor blind, nor sick."

"Do you know who gives you all these blessings?" continued Alice.

The man hung his head as he replied, "I suppose that you would tell me that God has done it."

"Yes, my friend; and yet, just now, you were cursing that holy, blessed Name. Oh, how you hurt me! Don't commit such wickedness again. Remember, my friend, that we must all die, and after death comes the judgment."

"I suppose that you are the minister's daughter," said the man. "I've heard about you before; and I'm ashamed that you should have heard me swear."

"It is God that you have offended, my friend. Think of that — not poor little Alice Hastings."

"It is a very bad habit, miss, I know, and I'll try to break it up."

"Here is a tract," said Alice. "Will you promise me to read it?"

"That I will," said the man; "and maybe I'll do better. I thank you, miss, for caring for a poor fellow like me."

"Good-by, my friend. If you want to see me, call at Westbrook Parsonage. But give me your name and address before you go."

The little carriage passed on, and the man stood looking after it.

"That's what they call a little missionary, I suppose," said the man. "A fellow must listen to such a one as that."

Passing quietly along, many a pleasant greeting was

extended to the child, for she was generally known in Westbrook.

Coming in sight of the creek, a sound of loud and angry voices struck upon their ears.

"Look there, brother!" said Alice. "Do part those wicked boys! See how they are fighting."

They were little fellows, and Warren soon succeeded in holding them apart. Both were crying with anger, and stood viewing each other with a fierce expression. Turning for a moment, they were attracted by the sight of the pale occupant of the carriage.

"Come here, boys," said Alice; "I have something to say to you. Are you any relation to each other?"

"We are brothers," said one.

"Why, then, do you quarrel?" inquired the child.

"Jim threw my kite into the creek," said one.

"And Sam tried to tear my hair out," said the other.

"Do you know what the Bible says, boys? 'Little children, love one another.'"

"A fellow can't love one that tries to hurt him all the time."

"But you need not strike back again, Sam, need you? If, when Jim is angry, you try to be kind, he would soon become ashamed. Just try now, and see if he is not ready to make up."

Jim was beginning to relent, for he had heard much of Alice's conversation with his brother, and was deeply moved by the gentle words from such an afflicted sufferer

"Come here, Jim," said Alice. ' Are you sorry for throwing away Sam's kite?"

He hung his head a moment, and replied: "I did it when I was angry, miss; but I am very sorry now, and will give him mine in the place of it, when we get home."

"Do you hear that, Sam?" said Alice "Now, you must be friends, boys; and remember how much happier you are, when you love each other."

The boys stepped forward and shook hands, while Alice gave to each a tract on brotherly love. Taking their names and address, she bade them good morning; and passed on along the shady creek. She was growing more cheerful every step of the way; for her loving spirit shed its brightness over tree and bush, over sky and water, all reflecting a glow within the placid bosom.

Plucking wild flowers that grew by the wayside, and enjoying the song of the birds, they turned at last into the little street where the blind woman lived. Aunty Miller was sitting at the door with her knitting, for, blind as she was, she was quite expert at this.

"How do you do, aunty?" said the young girl.

"Is that you, Miss Alice? I wondered what had become of you."

"I have been very sick, aunty; but am better now. How are you getting along?"

" God is very good, Miss Alice. With help from the church-alms, the kindness of friends, and my knitting,

I have all that I need, and a little mite to give every Sabbath day."

"I have brought you some good little books, aunty: I know that you can't read them; but Becky Taylor has promised to come every Saturday, after my class is over, and read to you."

"God bless you, Miss Alice; with all your suffering, you never forget us poor people."

"That is my happiness, aunty: but I must go now; I have several more to see. Good-by."

Going on still farther — some gentle words at Robert Jordan's, with a book that she had promised; a visit to Matty Hoskins, the cripple, and a few delicacies with Letty Fenton closed the ministry of that day. Very quiet and unobtrusive had it been: but if angels do minister to living saints, doubtless some walked by the coach of Alice Hastings all that summer day. Coming home through the more frequented streets, Mrs. Lacey met the carriage, and, opening a little basket that she carried, dropped a few ripe peaches in her lap, and pressed a warm kiss upon the soft cheek. Mrs. Sherwood saw who was coming, and at the gate she too met the invalid with a bouquet of the sweetest flowers.

By this time, Alice was bright as a lark; and when she entered the house, Margaret hastened to her, and taking off the hood, said: "Why, really, Alice, you have brought back some pale roses on your cheek, dear Your ride has done you good."

"It has been such a happy morning, sister; for I find that I can do some work for the Pastor's Aid yet; but I am a little tired now. Please give me a biscuit and a glass of milk; and then I'll take a short nap before dinner."

It is fine weather, and Alice spends much time out of doors in the pleasant orchard, either knitting or sewing, while one of the family reads to her from some entertaining or useful book. It is a very inviting picture, and many a visitor drops in to chat awhile with the interesting invalid, who, propped up in her couch under the green shade of the low, spreading trees, enjoys these seasons of social intercourse.

Mamma keeps an eye upon the company, and when she thinks Alice is growing weary, sends out a little lunch, or warns them that it is time to rest.

She is very much interested in the pigeons that build their nests in the tower of St. Barnabas', and Warren and she have succeeded in taming the little creatures so well, that they flock around the couch as soon as they see it brought out in the orchard, to get their supply of corn, cooing around Alice, and many of them lighting upon her hand or on the head-board of her couch. She has named many of them, and it is an entertaining sight to passers-by to watch their gentle movements with their young friend.

Alice is thirteen, now, and we meet her on the morning of this day at family prayers.

17 *

"We have an interesting subject for our texts to-day," said the pastor. "I hope that you are all well prepared; · for nothing is more important in the whole range of Christian doctrine than the subject of faith."

"I have mine, papa," said Margaret: "'Faith is the substance of things hoped for, the evidence of things not seen.'"

"What have you, Allan?"

"'Without faith it is impossible to please God.'"

"And yours, Warren?"

"'The just shall live by faith.'"

"What has Alice on the subject?"

"'For we walk by faith, not by sight.'"

"And what has Edward?"

"'By grace ye are saved through faith.'"

"I am waiting for Lucy's?"

"'And He said to the woman, Thy faith hath saved thee; go in peace.'"

"You have brought excellent passages, my children," said the pastor, "showing what faith is, and how absolutely indispensable it is in the work of our salvation. For every step of our way to the heavenly city is in the march of faith — called upon to reach after joys which 'eye hath not seen, nor ear heard, neither have entered into the heart of man;' so that we have constant need to pray, 'Lord, increase our faith!'

After worship, the family offered their congratulations to Alice upon her birthday, all coming with their love-gifts, however small.

It is generally known among the people of St. Barnabas', and all day other gifts of love arrive, to show that she is remembered. Mrs. Sherwood sends a beautiful picture of Easter morning, and Mrs. Lacey a picture of the family at the parsonage.

"How lovely this picture is!" said Alice. "How did Mrs. Lacey know that I would rather have it than anything else? Both shall hang in my little room where I can see them all day long."

In the afternoon, Alice received her young friends out in the orchard, where they enjoyed an hour in childish games — Alice looking on with great pleasure, checking Edward and Lucy whenever she saw the least appearance of selfishness; but all in such a quiet way, that no one but the children knew what she whispered in their ear, when she called them to her side to give her gentle hints.

"Let the guests choose the games, always, Edward," whispered Alice; "even if you don't like them."

"I can't bear 'Pussy wants a corner;' it is such a baby-play."

"Never mind, Edward; don't you see how the little ones like it? It pleases them, and that ought to please you, brother."

At the close of the afternoon, assembled in the parlor, the children partook of some refreshments. And kissing sweet Alice Hastings, all went home very happy, each having something to tell of her pleasant ways.

But rainy days shut Alice up in the house, and then she is busy with her correspondence, for she is very fond of sending her little notes around. She has not forgotten Jim and Sam McGowan, the little boys that quarrelled. We find them now and then at the parsonage, and in regular attendance at the Sunday school of St. Barnabas : therefore are they in the list remembered in the prayers of Alice Hastings.

"What is the use, Alice, of spending your time over that worthless sot, Dan Galway?" said Warren.

"He answers my notes, always, brother; and says that he has nearly given up the habit of swearing, ever since that day that we met upon the road."

Aunty Miller waits too for the little notes that Becky Taylor reads to her, and Robert Jordan says that they always come to him like dew after a hot day.

Nan Leseure comes in for her share, and Miss Mary says that the wild mountain-girl is softening daily under the gentle influence of Alice Hastings. Truly the pale invalid is an important member of the Pastor's Aid, with her gentle words, her little notes, her holy prayers, her sweet example.

Mrs. Sherwood is drawn to the parsonage frequently by the sufferer, and never comes without her offering of fruit or flowers, or other delicacies. We find her thus domesticated one morning, by the side of the couch of the invalid; both she and Mrs. Hastings occupied with needle-work. There is still a look of fixed despondency on the face of the visitor; for she has not yet found the peace of the blessed Gospel: but she is learning to talk more freely to her neighbor upon the great subject that interests them both.

"How is it, Mrs. Hastings," said the lady, "that you seem to dwell in such an atmosphere of peace? I have been so long searching for the true Church of Christ; and now that I have found it, I am still without a sure hope of heaven, my frames of mind are ever so variable."

"It will ever be so, my dear madam," said the pastor's wife, "so long as you depend upon frames and emotions for your comforts. While we are in this mortal body, subject to all its infirmities which cloud our earthly joys, and surrounded by so much in the outer world to disturb our peace, it would be a sad thing, indeed, if there were no unchanging rock — no harbor of peace where our little bark might ride at anchor: such an unchanging rock, such a harbor of peace we find in Christ only; so long as we keep our eye upon Him, the soul is at peace "

"But I dare not come to this infinitely holy Saviour; He is so far removed out of mortal sight, so high, so distant, that I shrink from an approach which to me seems so presumptuous, and therefore I have been taught that, in compassion to our infirmities, God hath instituted an order upon the earth, to mediate between our souls and God. But here, too, I find a difficulty: these priests are themselves fallible men, and though I believe that there is such an order in the Church, even that does not impart the peace that you enjoy."

Alice had been listening all the while to this conversation, with great interest, and in an interval of silence, said, "I wish that you could talk to my papa, Mrs Sherwood; he could comfort you, and make the way so plain: he says that it is not the Church that saves us, it is Jesus—Jesus only. His is such a grand, large Church, Mrs. Sherwood—the Holy Catholic Church, that we profess to believe in, every Sunday—the whole body of true believers throughout this great, large world. I do love to say those beautiful words, for it seems as if we were stretching out our arms so wide, to embrace all who love our Master."

"It is a beautiful faith," said Mrs. Sherwood; "but I have been told that it is a great error—a mere delusion; and that all not regularly ordained are in a state of schism; if so, then we commit a sin in fraternizing with such."

"Monstrous!" said Mrs. Hastings; "denouncing—rejecting those whom the Lord has blessed."

"I want to know the truth, Mrs. Hastings," replied her visitor, "but there are great difficulties in my way."

The family at the parsonage were greatly interested in

their visitor, and Alice said, as she closed the door, " We will pray, mamma, that God would lead her to our precious Saviour—then she will be happy."

Agnes, too, is a frequent visitor, for there is so much in that favored household to attract. We find her, one morning, seated with Margaret, by the couch of the invalid, Agnes engaged on a piece of very rich embroidery.

"What are you doing?" said Alice. "That is very beautiful work."

"I am embroidering an altar cloth," replied the young lady.

" An altar cloth," replied Alice; "what for ?"

" For the altar at St. Gregory's," replied Agnes.

"Why, have you an altar," inquired Alice; "papa says that ours is a table. It seems very strange to have two names for the one thing, in the same church: why do you call it an altar?"

" Mr. Moncrief says that is the proper name, for there is the place of sacrifice, and there is the sacrificing priest."

"What sacrifice, Agnes?" inquired Margaret Hastings.

"The sacrifice of our Lord Jesus Christ," replied Agnes.

"We are taught that our Lord was offered *once* for all upon Calvary," replied Margaret.

"And we are taught that whenever the Holy Commu

nion is administered, at the time of consecration, the
Lord himself, in some mysterious manner, swift as a
lightning flash, descends from heaven, and enters bodily
into the holy elements; and because the Lord himself is
there, we worship the elements — hence the altar decorations, altar lights, incense, flowers, processions, facing
the east, and reverential bowings."

"And do you believe all that, Agnes?" said Margaret,
with a look of surprise upon her eloquent face.

"I do, and much more, too — that is the reason for the
use of priestly vestments."

"I have heard a great deal of talk, lately, about an
alb, and a chasuble, about a tunicle, and dalmatic, in
our Protestant Episcopal Church," said Margaret. "Will
you show me, Agnes, in our Book of Common Prayer,
where they are authorized?"

Agnes looked slightly confused as she replied, "I do
not think that they will be found there; but we use an
English book, called the *Directorium Anglicanum,* and
the Priest's Prayer Book."

"What right have we, Protestant Episcopalians, to
use such books; have we not an authorized service-
book?"

"*That* does not *forbid* the use of such, our minister
says."

"That argument would bring in a flood of anything
that the fancy of man could invent."

"We don't like the word 'Protestant Episcopal,'"

said Agnes; "we prefer the word 'Catholic,' and want to bring back the good old days of the ancient Church."

Alice lay very silent for awhile, her eloquent eyes fixed upon the face of Agnes Sherwood, with a tender, sorrowful expression, as she said: "Do these foolish things bring Jesus nearer, Agnes? When you go to the communion of our Lord, does it seem as if He spoke the words of peace?"

"I never felt that, Alice, for the thought that the Lord himself was so near, that I was actually feeding upon his body, inspires me with fear and trembling, not with love."

"Only listen to our Saviour's precious words, Agnes," said the youthful Christian: "'Come unto me, all ye that travail and are heavy laden, and I will refresh you.' Jesus means what he says, and if we come in faith He will bless us."

"I have no such feelings, Alice; Mr. Moncrief says that such familiarity is presumptuous."

"Our Lord seemed to encourage the most intimate and affectionate relations between himself and his disciples, when he was on earth," said Margaret; "and He is the same yesterday, to-day, and forever — partaking of the hospitalities of Lazarus and his sisters — eating even with publicans and sinners, and allowing John to recline upon his bosom. Surely, this compassionate Redeemer is no less loving and faithful now."

18

"I wish that I could feel so," said Agnes, "but I dare not. Clouds of mystery surround the Saviour that I am taught to worship."

"What a pity," said Alice; "you lose so much! I can tell him anything, and I know that He is touched with the feelings of my infirmities; and though I am a sinful child, it was for exactly such that He came."

CHAPTER XV.

EMMAUS.

"Did not our hearts burn within us, when he talked with us by the way?"

THERE is to be a convocation of the brethren at St. Barnabas', and it is a season of unusual interest, for not only are the members expected, but large numbers of clergymen, called together by the peculiar exigencies of the Church of their affections. Mr. Morgan is the first, for he is anxious to know how so many are to be provided for. Debby has become accustomed to the ways of the good man, by this time; and therefore, as a matter of course, puts away five pairs of chickens, two fine hams, two large tongues, a pot of fresh butter, and a large basket of eggs.

"Will that do, Debby?" said the visitor.

" How many do you expect at the parsonage?"

"Four clergymen, I think; but there will be company at every meal, and I will see that all is right. You 'll let me know just what you want, Debby; for these are my children, you know."

The pastor has vacated his room, and Margaret hers; and arrangements are made also at Dr. Lacey's, and

207

among the people generally, for the entertainment of the strangers.

Two clergymen, with carpet bag in hand, are already coming up the garden walk.

"I am so glad that we are to have Mr. Thayer and Dr. Nelson," said Margaret; "they are so different, and yet I like them both so much."

By this time the clergymen were in the parlor, warmly greeted by the rector, and perceiving Alice in the little room adjoining, Mr. Thayer hastened out, and taking the little hand, said: "And how is my little Alice, now? Though, I see that you are growing tall, my dear."

"I am pretty well, now, Mr. Thayer, though I have suffered very much since you were here last."

"You keep close to the Saviour, Alice, I hope; then your trials seem so much less."

"That is all my comfort. I am so glad that so many of our Lord's ministers are coming. I can't go to church, only on communion-days, and that not always. But won't you have one of the meetings here, that I may attend?"

"I dare say that we shall, Alice, for these rooms would accommodate a large number."

Late in the evening, George Vincent, a young minister, one of Father Morgan's *protégés*, joined the company.

"We have come together for solemn work," said Dr. Nelson; "in the midst of a sharp conflict in religious thought. I own that I feel despondent, for so rapid is the progress of the defection in our beloved Church, and so lax the discipline on one side, that I fear we have but little to hope for in the way of relief to brethren whose consciences are burdened with a weight of responsibility."

"We need heavenly wisdom and divine charity," said Mr. Thayer, "to guide us in our deliberations; for there is so much in the movement to excite our indignation, that, ere we are aware of it, we may be impelled by the spirit that our Master rebuked in the disciples of old, who were for calling down fire from heaven to consume offenders."

"It appears to me that the new developments are mere matters of taste," said George Vincent; "only an efflo- rescent ceremonial."

"A ceremonial teaching corrupt doctrine," said Dr. Hastings; "object-lessons in the Church that we love. If we could believe that these were mere matters of taste, then we might look with pity and surprise upon pageants and postures, on perfumes and scenic decorations; but they should create alarm, for the great leading minds avow that they are intended to teach doctrines."

"You take the right view, my son," said Father Mor- gan. "Ritualism is the fruit of Tractarianism. New- man and Pusey knew what they were about, when they so carefully indoctrinated the teachers, and trained a band by a process of reasoning; for one says: 'Without dogma, ritualism is an illusion — ritual is the visible expression of divine truth—the surest way to teach the Catholic faith, is by the Catholic ritual."

"They exhibit profound knowledge of the weakness of human nature, when they address the senses," said Dr. Nelson; "for through these avenues, the most powerful impressions are made. The central point of Ritualism is the same as Tractarianism—the real presence, in the communion of the Church—and so by every mode, they paint it to the eye. It may be well to quote one of their own leaders, who writes:

"'It may be well at this time to restate that great doctrine which is the groundwork of the whole theory and practice of church-worship — the true doctrine of the Eucharistic Sacrifice; and because that doctrine of the real bodily presence is believed by the ritualists, we have lights upon the communion table, incense, "advanced" music; vestments of strange patterns and gorgeous coloring, changing with the seasons; reverences toward the place where the Presence is supposed to be, and bowings and prostrations as acts of adoration.'"

"Truly this object-teaching should alarm all true Protestant brethren," said Father Morgan; "but really sometimes it appears only ridiculous, when we see the lengths to which they travel to defend their folly. Only the other day, I read an attempt to prove that the Apostle Paul must have worn vestments, when he sent for the *cloak* that he had left at Troas."

A general laugh followed this speech, at the bare idea

of rigging the grand Apostle in the millinery and foppishness of ritualism.

"By-the-by," said the quaint old man, "do you know, brethren, that I have found names for all of you?"

"Let us hear them," said Dr. Hastings.

"I call you, Timothy, my son; Thayer, is John, the beloved disciple; Dr. Nelson is our Luther; Vincent is doubting Thomas; and you must give me my name, brethren."

Dr. Nelson smiled and replied: "Zealous, warm-hearted Peter."

"Yes, that will do," said the old man; "but one thing, let us all be called by the name of our Master, only."

There is a ring at the hall-bell, and Bishop Lysle is introduced, most welcome to the group at the parsonage. He is rather small, with a calm blue eye, thinnish brown hair, and by no means of an imposing presence, and is to preach the opening sermon of the convocation.

Blessed and holy was the communion of saints in that parsonage parlor, one of those stopping-places in the Christian pilgrimage, where the weary may rest awhile from their toils and conflicts, and commune together of the blessed future in store for those who truly love God.

"A little taste of heaven, papa," said Alice, as he bade her good night; "so many of God's dear servants all together, such as we shall dwell with forever."

"Yes, Alice, only without fault or blemish, clad in

our Master's image: let us press on, darling, to our heavenly inheritance."

" ' Where eye hath not seen, nor ear heard, neither have entered into the heart of man, the things which God hath prepared for them that love Him.' Good night, dear papa."

Assembled next morning around the family altar, Bishop Lysle presided, pleased that a cardinal doctrine of Christianity formed the subject of the family texts — that of justification by faith.

" A doctrine hated by the high ritualists," said the Bishop; " for one of the writers of that school styles it ' that most anti-missionary and anti-Christian of dogmas.' But we are taught to consider it the rock on which the soul can find its only sure resting-place. Now let me hear some of the texts."

Margaret spoke first : " ' Therefore, being justified by faith, we have peace with God, through our Lord Jesus Christ.' "

" This is mine," said Warren: " ' Being justified freely by his grace, through the redemption that is in Christ Jesus.' "

" I am ready for Allan's."

" ' Knowing that a man is not justified by the works of the law, but by the faith of Jesus Christ, even we have believed in Jesus Christ, that we might be justified by the faith of Christ, not by the works of the law: for by the works of the law shall no flesh be justified.' "

"Has Alice a passage on the subject?"

"'And by him, all that believe are justified from **all** things, from which ye could not be justified by the **law** of Moses.'"

"I have one, Bishop," said Edward, who saw that he was closing the Bible: "'Much more then, being now justified by his blood, we shall be saved from wrath through him.'"

"I have a very nice text," said little Lucy, with a timid voice: "'But ye are justified in the name of the Lord Jesus, and by the Spirit of God.'"

"Blessed are ye, my dear children," said the good Bishop, "to be so constantly and faithfully taught these precious truths of the Bible: impressed by the Spirit of God, though assaulted on every side, the gates of hell shall not prevail against it."

In language glowing with love and strong in faith, the Bishop commended the household to the care of the Good Shepherd, confident that he would fulfil his promises to the children of the righteous.

Assembled in the lecture-room, there was an hour of blessed intercourse with heaven before the public service in the church, where Bishop Melville, in his own impressive manner, addressed the brethren :

"Let us know where we stand, my brethren, far advanced in the nineteenth century — eminently in the latter day of the Gospel dispensation, when we are told that there shall be a great falling away from the faith

in the Church of God.   There is much to alarm true
Christians, for the very foundations of our hope are attacked, and the Church that we love undermined by
miners and sappers, who are seeking to weaken the sup-
ports of the Protestant faith.   Let there be no divisions
among us, but as one man let us stand firmly shoulder
to shoulder, in defence of the Gospel.   There is need of
great wisdom in every movement, for we are standing, as
it were, on the borders of the Red Sea, as did the Israel-
ites of old.   They were in danger, too, beset by foes on
every hand, but they did not rush into the sea without
orders; when Moses gave the word of command, they
marched, and the waters divided on either side, making
a safe passage for the mighty host.   God will fight for
his own Church now, brethren; let us listen for our
Moses' voice—watch for his dividing staff—and we, too,
shall pass through our Red Sea in safety."

Every eye was fixed upon the tall and dignified form
of the venerable speaker, for Bishop Melville was venerable now—silver hairs crowning his broad, expansive
brow; and as the clear, sonorous tones rang out their
trumpet notes, many in that listening throng could not
but compare him to the Moses of ancient days.   After
solemn prayer and another hymn, Mr. Thayer arose—
always a welcome speaker—with his heavenly wisdom,
his loving spirit: "Let us beware, dear brethren, of
harsh judgment in dealing with the propagators of error,
in these troubled days.   While we do not give place—

no, not for one hour—to the adversary, let us remember that all are not to be equally condemned. With some, it is very likely a mere æstheticism; with others, an exaggeration of forms which our Church appoints, but which it has carefully restricted, who have not yet realized to what these innovations may lead, and from which they will honestly shrink. Toward such, let us exercise 'the charity which hopeth all things;' but with those who avow their purpose to unprotestantize our beloved Church, we must not, cannot hold communion. We can weep over their unfaithfulness to ordination vows—can pray for their recovery from the snare of the tempter; but the right-hand of fellowship must be extended only to those who contend for the faith once delivered to the saints." Deep impressions were made by both of these speakers, and earnest were the prayers put up by that company of the faithful sons of the Protestant Episcopal Church.

Gathered in the church of St. Barnabas, a listening crowd hung upon the words of Bishop Lysle, with an impressive silence that might be felt. With the zeal of a true apostle, he placed the decisions of Councils and ancient Fathers just where they belonged. We will give an extract from his bold and faithful sermon:

"Why make our appeal to Councils and Fathers, to patristic, or mediæval, or modern definitions, when we have veritably infallible guidance—the guidance of the men upon whose heads rested the cloven flames at Pen-

tecost, and whose names are on the foundation-stones of
the New Jerusalem? The Apostles, the *only* unerring
guides and governors of the Church, live as perpetual
witnesses to the truth. They speak now, as they spoke
of old, with decision and clearness. We can consult
them with greater convenience than could their own
contemporaries. For they are not now dispersed over
the earth. Their testimony is combined and complete.
Points which they have not settled, never will be settled
under the present dispensation; and where they have
spoken, there is no appeal. An eminent divine, identified with the movement that has for so many years dis-
tracted the Church of England, avows his readiness to
defend ' the real objective presence, the Eucharistic sacrifice, and the adoration of our Lord truly present under
the Eucharistic symbols, as being the teaching of the
whole Catholic Church *from* the time of the Apostles.'
He does not defend it as the teaching of the *Apostles*
themselves. Then we say, even if the claim could be sub-
stantiated, to what does it amount? The whole Catholic Church, from the first century to the twentieth, cannot establish a doctrine unrevealed in Scripture, respect-
ing which the Apostles are silent, or which contradicts
their teaching. *This is our rock*, from which nothing
can move us. The Church is built upon the foundation
of the Apostles and Prophets, Jesus Christ himself being
the chief corner-stone, and our confidence is firm and
unwavering, that by them no important question is

unanswered — no vital truth undiscovered — no divine requirement left in obscurity and doubt."

Loyal sons of the *Protestant* Episcopal Church listened to this stirring, able sermon, with hearts deeply moved, and joined, with renewed devotion, in singing the beautiful hymn:

> "I love thy kingdom, Lord,
> The house of thine abode,
> The Church our blest Redeemer saved
> With his own precious blood.
>
> "I love thy Church, O God,
> Her walls before thee stand,
> Dear as the apple of thine eye,
> And graven on thy hand.
>
> "If e'er my heart forget
> Her welfare or her woe,
> Let every joy this heart forsake,
> And every grief o'erflow.
>
> "For her my tears shall fall;
> For her my prayers ascend;
> To her my cares and toils be given,
> Till toils and cares shall end."

Truly there was no need of surpliced singing-boys at St. Barnabas' on that occasion, for the earnest volume of responsive worship that filled the church from the clergy assembled, gave full evidence of the majestic power of our service, when the people join heartily in its different

19

parts; for they were all inspired on that day by the example of the fifty clergymen in their midst.

The venerable Bishop Miles read the Communion Service in his own solemn manner, and tears started in many eyes, as the trembling tones of his voice fell upon their ears, for they seemed to say that his ministry of holiness and love would soon close upon earth.

Two days were spent together in holy consultation, and the last evening had arrived. A large number had assembled in the parlor of the parsonage, where they communed together for the last time of the things of the kingdom of our blessed Lord.

Margaret Hastings presided at the organ, and sweet strains of sacred music filled not only the room where they had assembled, but swelling upon the air, had stolen out through the windows, enticing Agnes Sherwood into the garden of the parsonage, and almost unperceived into the presence of the worshippers.

Fresh vows of fidelity, deeper consecration to the Master's service, prayers which could never be forgotten, and exhortations that stirred every heart followed each other until a late hour in the evening, and at the close, all standing, sang the sweet hymn:

> "Blest is the tie that binds
> Our hearts in Christian love;
> The fellowship of kindred minds
> Is like to that above."

' Surely the Master was in our midst," said Father Morgan, " for did not our hearts burn within us, while He talked with us by the way ? It is not easy to break up such a meeting ; but we must say farewell now."

As one by one shook the parting hand and uttered the parting blessing, Father Morgan followed George Vincent out into the hall, and, with one arm over his shoulder, and the other grasping his hand, said in earnest, loving tones : " God bless and keep you, my son, for I fear that you are on the borders of temptation, or why do I hear of you so often at St. Gregory's ? "

" I cannot see so much to disapprove, Father Morgan, for you will own that there was much in the ancient church to admire, and much in the modern to deplore."

" Listen to an old man's warning, my son, and beware how you are beguiled from the simplicity that is in Christ. Keep close to the blessed word of God — close to the Holy Spirit of God: let no sophistry beguile you from that safe, that blessed path ; but come what may, George Vincent, I am your true friend at all times. Good-by. God bless and keep you."

Father Morgan returned to the parlor to bid farewell to several of the brethren who yet remained.

" We shall meet, I trust, at the Anniversaries in New York," said the old man, " but we will not see George Vincent there, or among us here again ; he is among the ritualists, I fear."

" His is a poetic, sensitive nature," said Mr. Thayer,

"and may be led aside by the music and display; but if the root of the matter is in him, he will come back to us."

"It has been a precious season," said Dr. Hastings; "for the Lord has been in our midst blessing his ser-. vants: may it be seen in our work hereafter!"

The gate has closed upon the last member; but a deep impression has been made by the visitation—Margaret, Allan, and Alice partaking largely of the blessing, and Warren too much impressed by the realities of true piety to make any remarks.

"What a holy benediction they have left among us!" said Alice, as the last one bade farewell. "It seemed, all the time, just like the walk of the disciples on the way to Emmaus."

"And so it was, my dear," said the father; "for we all realized that Jesus was in our midst."

"Now we know, papa, what the disciples meant when they asked that question."

"What question, Alice?"

"'Did not our hearts burn within us, while he talked with us by the way?'"

CHAPTER XVI.

SHACKLES *versus* FREEDOM.

"Beloved, believe not every spirit; but try the spirits whether they are of God."

WARREN is eighteen, quite prepared for college, and the idea of a first separation in the household is beginning to sadden the spirits of its members, especially of Alice; for she is so tenderly beloved by her elder brother. But the world is beckoning Warren away from Westbrook, for his ambition is pointing to the metropolis: there he hopes to realize the dreams of the Adirondacks — fame being his idol yet. The time of separation has come at length, and tender emotions are filling the young heart with sorrowful images. He is passing through the green orchard, where he has spent so many happy hours; and sitting down a moment in the summer-house, the soft cooing of the pigeons in the church tower are drawing tears from the boy's eyes, who, looking around for fear of observation, proudly dashes them away; but it is hard to keep them back, as he thinks how long it may be ere he sits with Alice under the green trees, calling her gentle pets around her. Now he is in the room under the gable in search of his trunk, when the sight of the old pictures of Lady Anne and Sir Charles brings back the days of childhood, which Warren feels will never come again.

Strange that such simple things should stir these human hearts so deeply! But all Warren's emotions now are sorrowful, for he is not leaving an ordinary home. He is paying his last visit to Little Rugby, and, with Dr. Arnold's arm around his waist, he is pacing the students' walk with his beloved preceptor.

"You are going into new scenes, among new faces, Warren," said his friend. "Do you ever think of the snares of college life?"

"Yes, Dr. Arnold, for some; but I go for study, for improvement, and every thing will bend to that one object."

"I allude to the snares spread around you by new companions."

"I am not likely to be entrapped by the dissolute, Dr. Arnold: my pride will keep me aloof from them."

"Neither am I afraid of that, Warren; but you worship intellect, and will be drawn to that, even though it is openly arrayed against the truth."

Warren smiled as he replied: "You know that I was always fond of a tilt with sharp intellects, and have a passion for mental broadswords yet. I can never make friends with shallow-brained fops; and if I meet with superior minds, must choose such companionship"

"They are dangerous, Warren, especially to such as you. If I could only feel that you were settled in your religious faith, I should not feel so many misgivings."

"I don't think that there is much to fear in my case, doctor; for although I have often been tormented with skeptical doubts, there is such a host of evidence at the dear parsonage and Little Rugby, that the chambers of my brain are pretty well filled with able defenders of the truth. There is my honored father, a living epistle himself; my beloved mother, with her saintly life; my sister Margaret, good, precious Allan, and my darling Alice. Why, Dr. Arnold, these blessed faces and their holy words are with my memory always — the trouble is somewhere else."

"Yes, Warren, it is in the carnal mind, everywhere the same antagonist of spiritual piety. But I shall remember you, my boy, every night, in my most earnest prayers."

"You will let me hear from you, Dr. Arnold," said the boy; "for," pointing to Little Rugby, "go where I may, that will be my Alma Mater still."

Just then, Nan came running out with a needle-book made by her own hands, to offer to the young man. It was roughly made, for she was only just learning to sew; but Warren appreciated the motive, and thanked the girl heartily for her little gift.

An hour's loving counsel and prayer was spent in the

study with the good pastor, and then Alice sent for her brother.

"How shall I do without you, Warren?" said the sister, as she folded the dear hand within her own. "But I know that it is for your good to go away, and I try to be contented; but I shall think of you every morning and evening in my prayers, Warren. If I only knew that you were a Christian, parting would not be so sad, for then I should know that God was taking care of you: but out of Christ He is a consuming fire."

"I am not such a terrible sinner, dear little sis. God is very good and merciful, and he will not deal hardly with one who wants to do right."

"I know what the Bible says, Warren: 'Except a man be born again, he cannot see the kingdom of God.'"

It is the last morning at the parsonage, and the subject is the doctrine of the Holy Spirit. "What have you upon the subject, Margaret?" inquired her father.

"'If ye, then, being evil, know how to give good gifts unto your children, how much more shall your heavenly Father give the Holy Spirit to them that ask him?'"

Warren is repeating his last text for many months, perhaps never again to join in the holy service; he feels it as he utters slowly, "'Which things also we speak, not in the words which man's wisdom teacheth, but which the Holy Ghost teacheth, comparing spiritual things with spiritual.'"

Allan, too, has his: "'But God hath revealed them unto us by his Spirit; for the Spirit searcheth all things, yea, the deep things of God.'"

Alice, with sweet, low tones, repeats the blessed words as though she knew their power "'Likewise the Spirit also helpeth our infirmities; for we know not what we should pray for as we ought; but the Spirit itself maketh intercession for us with groanings which cannot be uttered.'"

Edward follows with his: "'For as many as are led by the Spirit of God, they are the sons of God.'"

"I have a prayer," said Lucy. "'Create in me a clean heart, O God, and take not thy Holy Spirit from me.'"

"Blessed, precious doctrine!" said the pastor. "What should we be in this dark, benighted world, without the light divine? Let us pray that each member of our dear household may receive in its fulness the holy gift."

It is a cold, drizzly morning, and Warren feels its dreariness, as passing out of the blessed parsonage, he is slowly walking down the garden path, in company with Allan and his father, having left the other members in the house, watching his retreating footsteps with tearful eyes. Drip—drip—drip fall the raindrops, not only in the garden path, but on the heart in harmony now with their melancholy measure.

"God bless you, Warren, my son," said the pastor,

P

taking his leave at the gate. "Let me leave a text with you: 'Grieve not the Holy Spirit of God.'"

Warren is gone, and the last farewell is spoken at the cars by Allan, who is waiting to catch the last glimpse as the train rushes by, and the hand waving out of the window is answered by one that is dashing tears away from the dark-blue eyes.

Warren is fairly settled at college, now, much respected by all the faculty, for he is a fine scholar, has a brilliant intellect, high principles, and a warm, impulsive nature, that gathers friends around him ; but there is still the same repulsion from spiritual piety, for he imagines that it imposes unnatural restraints upon the free spirit, and fetters his manliness by its shackles ; then his aims are all directed to the distant temple of fame, and he fears that many of its requirements would clog his footsteps up the dizzy height.

There is a debating society among the students, and Warren is one of the most gifted among its members, always defending the opposite side of all questions, and taking great delight in demolishing what he terms the barricades of old-fogyism, to let in the sunlight of philosophy and science ; exercising the power of his logic on what is still unsettled in his own mind.

After being at college for some months, there comes along a travelling evangelist — a burning, fiery preacher, who has obtained permission to preach to the students. Having a fine, flexible voice, a startling, awakening manner, an expressive eye, and great command of language, he exercises a powerful influence over the young, in his short visitations.   But few sober-minded Christians desire the return of Brother Hellings, for, generally, what seemed for awhile to be the result of the Spirit's power, proved itself to have been wildfire, burning up the spiritual pastures.   But a first visitation always creates a stir, and his violent declamations and alarming appeals, accompanied by a certain sort of machinery, awaken terror and a slavish kind of repentance.   He is in the habit of proposing certain tests, by which hearers shall express their decision on the great subject of religion, calling on them to " come out upon the Lord's side," and to show that by arising — denouncing those who remain seated. Many are wrought upon by these measures, but not Warren Hastings, whose strongest feelings of repulsion were aroused by these violent appeals.   One evening, influenced by this aversion, he arose and left the lecture-room, and as he walked slowly down the aisle, the preacher called out: " There goes a poor sinner, straight to —— ; pray for him, brethren."

Warren turned round, and fixed an indignant gaze upon the speaker, and then passed to his room, more skeptical, more hardened than ever.

Several of his young companions were led hastily to connect themselves with Christian churches, but, after the lapse of a few weeks, returned to their former course of life, excepting three.   Very unfortunate that Warren

Hastings should have passed through such a season, for, mingled with the wildfire, there had been genuine visitations of the Spirit, for warm-hearted Christians had implored his presence; and Warren, in repelling the excesses of fanaticism, may have grieved the Holy Spirit of God.

Alice frequently writes to her brother, and thus tries to keep alive in his bosom the impressions of his childhood's home. She has his picture in her room, among her treasures, and counts the months at first, and now the weeks, ere she shall see the dear original.

Warren is at home at length, and Alice tells him to stand off, that she may look at the tall young man by her side. "Why, brother, you are taller than papa, I do believe. How very much you have grown!"

"And so do you, little sis. Not much stouter, darling, but certainly taller. But papa looks very frail, Alice: how is he now?"

"Not often well, Warren; but you never hear complaints from our dear father. But what kind of a minister was that at the college, brother, that made such a stir?"

"One of the ranting order, Alice, that could never have any effect upon me. I listened, sister, and thought of the sermon on the mount, and finding no resemblance, I turned away disgusted; but I met him in the street, one day after that, and I wish that papa could have heard him send me to perdition: so much for Brother Hellings.

"What about that debating society, Warren? I hope that they do not attack the blessed Bible."

"It is a society that does its own thinking, Alice. I suppose that papa and Dr. Arnold would sometimes be shocked to hear some of the debates; but though I like the excitement of argument, it does not follow that I adopt all their notions: still, I must own, that freedom from mental shackles is very agreeable. I shall come out right, yet, Alice, but every step of the way must be thoroughly examined."

Alice looked troubled, and said meekly: "I don't understand all that you say, Warren, but I wish that you knew how blessed it is to feel the precious words: 'Lord, I believe; help thou my unbelief.'"

Warren stooped down to kiss the saintly face, saying: "Darling little sis, don't be troubled about brother Warren, when the defences of the parsonage are all around him."

He is to spend part of his vacation in New York, with Uncle Richard, his mother's youngest brother: accordingly we find him domesticated with the Warren household. The females are devoted members of St. Agapius'; his aunts, Gertrude and Helen, no longer young, spend their days in a round of religious observances, dwarfing, not developing the Christian life. Warren has promised to go with them to church on the following Sunday.

"There is nothing in the external or internal appear-

20

ance of St. Agapius' unlike other Episcopal churches, until you come to the chancel. This is decidedly Romish in all its arrangements. In fact, there is no difference to be distinguished. First, there are three steps to the altar. This altar is the same in size and form as that of the Church of Rome; it is covered with a dark-colored cloth, with a large cross embroidered on it; the top is covered with red velvet and fringe. On it is the altar-service, on a stand similar to that used in the Mass, and something very like a pyx, a box, it seemed to me, covered with a dark cloth, and emblazoned with a cross. Behind this altar is a screen, with a deep ledge, and on this ledge, and directly back of the altar, is a large silver cross. This cross is flanked by two gilt vases, which seemed to me to contain artificial flowers. On either side of the vases are two very tall candle-sticks, with candles; and on each side of these, three other candlesticks and candles, much smaller.

"At half-past ten, a man in a surplice placed himself at the organ. A hymn was started, and taken up by boys' voices in the vestry-room. Soon the sound became more audible, and lo! there issued from the vestry, first a small boy, in a cassock and surplice, bearing a large wooden cross, I should think about six feet long; then followed some dozen little boys, with folded hands; then a few men, all in short surplices and cassocks, and finally, the ministers; one in a white robe, which reached to about the knees, with a black cassock beneath; and the other with a white garment, of about the same length, but tied about the waist with a cord; both wore black scarfs. The procession moved slowly up to the altar, singing — I know not what. The singers filed off to their sedilia; the head priest knelt at the rail, with a little boy on either side, and directly behind him knelt the other priest. This latter then commenced to intone the Litany. Directly after the Litany, the head priest arose, and, for the first time, turning toward the people, said that the Fourth Selection of Psalms would be sung. Then the two priests retired. A young acolyte entered, and proceeded to light the eight candles, and, after bowing to the altar, retired. The two priests returned, and now the celebrant wore a white robe, reaching a little below the knee, and apparently covering a black cassock — over the white robe, a cape or cloak, of dark color, embroidered before and behind with a white cross. With folded hands, and on either side a small, surpliced boy, he entered the chancel, and, mounting the steps, stood before the altar, and, of course, with his back to the people, and reverently bowed to the altar: so did the boys, and so did the second priest, who stood on his right, two steps below, and who had changed his stole, so that now it was passed over his left shoulder and under his right arm.

"The chief minister then commenced the ante-communion service, turning his face to the people when he read the Commandments, and then immediately back

again to his former position, where he remained, while
the second priest read the Epistle on the right and the
Gospel on the left of the altar.   After the Gospel, the
Nicene Creed was sung, all facing the altar.   At the
words, 'I look for the resurrection of the dead,' the
priests, boys, choir, and many in the congregation
crossed themselves.   The junior priest preached a sermon.   He distinctly told them that the only way to rid
themselves of unbelief and doubt was the Holy Catholic
Church; and if they inquired what was the Catholic
Church, he would give them three tests — Universality,
Antiquity, and Consent.   Not a word of Christ as the
way, the truth, and the life.   Nothing but implicit faith
in Holy Mother Church.   A more thoroughly Romish
discourse cannot be imagined.

" After this sad exhibition of a distorted Gospel, the
mummery recommenced.   The alms were then collected,
and then the little boys brought the cup and wine from
the credence table.   There was no 'fair white linen
cloth' on the table, as the rubric plainly directs.   The
wine and bread being upon the altar, the little boys
brought to the priest water and a napkin, with which
he washed his hands.   Then was intoned the prayer for
the Church Militant, after which the second priest, facing
the congregation, read the invitation ; and at the words,
'with the Father,' &c., he wheeled about and faced the
altar.   At the Confession, both priests prostrated themselves before the altar, almost to the floor.   In pro-

nouncing the declaration of absolution, the head priest made the sign of the cross. The service then proceeded as usual to the prayer of consecration. Standing before the altar, the priest began the prayer of consecration in a very subdued voice. When he came to the words, 'Take, eat: this is my body,' he paused, changed his voice and said them in a whisper; then paused again; then bowed his head, and then actually elevated the bread, and the people bowed their heads. The same thing was done with the cup; it was elevated, and the people bowed again. Then once more prostrating themselves before the altar, the priest communed. After this, he delivered the bread — not to his assistant, nor to the other minister at the rails, as the rubric directs — but to the two little boys; actually putting the bread into their mouths and pouring in the wine. Then he gave the elements to the clergymen at the rails. The two celebrants then faced the people, one elevating the bread and the other the cup, as high as their eyes. The priest who delivered the bread, first made a sign of the cross with it to each communicant. The one who bore the cup did not deliver it at all to the communicant, but poured the wine into his mouth. While this was going on, the organist was performing a voluntary. After all had communed, the head priest proceeded to consume all the bread that was left and to drink the wine. The little boys then brought him two small silver pitchers, and as he held the cup alternately poured what I sup-

20 *

posed to have been water, for the priest thereupon shook
the cup, after the manner of Rome, and drank the contents.   This was done three times, and the cup was returned to the table, covered with a black cloth, and by
the boy removed to the side-table.   In dismissing the
people, the sign of the cross was used; after which, the
procession moved slowly out — the cross-bearer first, the
boys next, the priests last, singing, as when they came
in, and bowing to the altar as they passed." *

And now let us inquire, is this indeed our Protestant
Episcopal Church?   Are these things to be tolerated
within it?   Have they any countenance in the laws of
the Church?   Without law and against law, shall they
be neglected as harmless absurdities?   Or shall they be
put down as pernicious superstitions?

Warren looked and listened, an expression of intense
contempt resting upon his face, while he contrasted the
mummeries of St. Agapius' with the dignified and reverential worship at St. Barnabas', wondering how any one
could offer such a service of incense, flowers, lights, atti-
tudes, and vestments to the great and glorious God, who
fills the universe with his presence, and requires from
man the prostration of his spirit, and not the mere will-
worship of the body.

"Is that Protestant worship, Aunt Gertrude?" said
Warren, when they met at the dinner-table.

* Quoted literally from a clergyman's description of public worship
in an Episcopal church.

"That is Catholic worship, Warren; we do not own the name of Protestant."

"And you really believe that these childish mummeries are acceptable to the great and holy God.?"

"Why not, Warren? they all have a deep and sacred meaning, all connected with some doctrine of the Holy Catholic Church."

"Oh, yes, I perceive that the one central idea of God's especial presence at what you term the altar, is the reason of all that bowing and wheeling round, and genuflections innumerable."

"You have the idea exactly, Warren; that is what we really believe: hence the altar, the lights, the vestments."

Warren started to his feet, and throwing up his hand, said excitedly: "This is the way you make infidels. Men of free, expansive intellects are not to be trammelled with such baby-shows in the house of God. Rather would I follow Colenso in his rationalism, than be bound soul, fast in such shackles of superstitious mummery!"

"You shock me, Warren," said his grandma, "to speak so freely of the mysteries of our holy religion — don't let me hear it again, I beseech you."

Unfortunate again that Warren Hastings should have been thrown into such an atmosphere of puerile Christianity, with all his doubts and questions, and unsettled faith. First, into the region of fanaticism at college, and now into the cloisters of superstition. Verily the bayonets of unbelief were bristling now on every parapet of the citadel.

The ladies are alone after dinner.

"Was not that shocking, sister?" said Gertrude Warren. "1 do believe that our nephew is an infidel."

He too is alone at night, and the morning texts one by one come over his waking dreams, as his thoughts fly back to the dear parsonage and the epistles written there.

"I can never be an infidel," said Warren, "so long as I remember the powerful preaching of that home circle; but I can never be the slave of superstition, nor the puppet of fanaticism."

Under the influence of powerful habit, Warren repeated the Lord's Prayer, and even the time-honored "Now I lay me down to sleep," ere he closed his eyes in slumber.

Strange that such a captious nature should yet retain so much of the spirit of a child.

A mother's love had fashioned the shield of these few simple words of trust and love, and as Warren repeated them so far from home, other hearts at the parsonage were remembering him in their nightly prayers.

He cannot always restrain the expressions of contempt which are daily awakened by the employments of his aunts, who spend much of their precious time in embroidering priests' vestments and church decorations.

"Where is the priests' millinery-shop, Aunt Gertrude?" said her nephew, one morning; "I should really like to have a peep; for last Sunday, at church, I heard a young lady say, ' What a love of an opera-cloak that would be!' and only think! she was speaking of the priest's alb."

" I wish that you would not indulge in such profane talk, Warren," said his aunt; "you really have no reverence in your composition."

"I own that I have not a whit, Aunt Gertrude, for alb and maniple; for dalmatic and tunic; for chasuble and gremial and chirothecæ; but I have for the great and holy God, who must look upon these things with supreme contempt at folly like theirs."

Repelled by the excesses at St. Agapius', Warren is led about by Uncle Richard among his own acquaintances, where he meets congenial minds, and rejoices in what he esteems freedom from religious shackles. He has met too with his schoolmates — Harry and George Seymour — rapidly reaching the end of their ambition; occupying apartments at the Metropolitan, the one driving a splendid carriage and pair, moving in the higher circles of Upper-Tendom, wearing on his young face marks of fast living ; and the other already dabbling in stocks and preparing to enter the arena with the bulls and bears of Wall Street as soon as he is of age: both bearing marks of discontent and ennui; for they are feeding on the ashes of worldliness ; and when did that ever satisfy the cravings of an immortal spirit?

Warren is at home again, with accounts of St.
Agapius' that sometimes amuse, but most generally
sadden the good pastor of St. Barnabas'. Warren can
scarcely analyze his present emotions, there are so many
of the seeds of divine truth floating about in the intellect.
But should convictions of personal transgression once
disturb the present security, then will he learn to welcome the only remedy for a sin-sick soul.

He is at college again, and the household at St. Barnabas' return to their usual avocations — not, however,
with the same tranquil spirit of repose; for there are
marks of debility about Dr. Hastings that cause the
loving hearts there to send up to heaven many a silent
prayer for restoration.

CHAPTER XVII.

THE MISSION OVER THE HILL.

"To the poor is the Gospel preached."

THREE miles from Westbrook there is luite a growing settlement at the Iron Foundery ; but there are
no means of grace within reach, and on Sundays, the
men are lounging about the porches of the little drink
ing-shops; the women gossiping from house to house in
dirty, slatternly dress, and the children roving where they
please, undisciplined, untamed, untaught. Dr. Arnold
had discovered this in one of his rides with Margaret
Hastings ; for it is generally understood, now, that the
pastor's daughter is likely to be the life-companion of
the master of Little Rugby.

Very tender and holy is the affection bestowed upon
Margaret by the good man, and very sweet and reveren
tial that cherished in her heart of hearts for Richard
Arnold, two qualities insuring happiness in the marriage
relation.

"Let us stop a moment," said Dr. Arnold, in one of
these rides ; and calling a little white-haired boy to the
side of the carriage, he said: "Have you any school
here, my little man ?"

"Nara one," said the boy.

"Can any of you read?"

"Jest a few, sir; but the fellows don't care — it's first rate to run about all day. We go a-fishing and a-bird's-nesting — and something else sometimes, when the hens lay a good lot."

"Do you like pretty pictures?"

"First rate. Have you got any?"

"Yes, plenty of them, my little friend; and if you'll just get together your little friends next Sunday about two o'clock, under that big tree, we'll come and bring you plenty."

"We'll be there — never fear, sir."

The carriage drove off, and Dr. Arnold said: "Here is plenty of work for the Pastor's Aid — we must take possession at once. Will you come, Margaret?"

"Gladly," was the reply. "I should like to labor among these ignorant people. Let us see, how many can we count upon? There are Allan, Archie Murray, Sarah Lacey, and you and I — there are five at once."

"Sister Mary will come too, for she has no engagement on Sunday afternoon."

Alice was delighted to hear of the new work.

"I cannot go, sister," said the young girl; "but I can help too. I can pray at home that God would bless you, and I can help make clothing for the poor things when the cold weather comes. It shall be under the care of the Pastor's Aid, Margaret; and I know that it will do good among the people."

"Dr. Arnold thought of it first, Alice, for he is always looking out for work in the Master's cause. I hope that it won't be too much for him; teaching all the week — Bible-class Sunday morning, and now this added work: but he says ' it is better to wear out than to rust out.'" And tears filled Margaret's eyes as she continued: "Don't let us talk of that, Alice."

Sunday came, and Margaret and the Doctor first went alone to spy out the field. Stopping at the appointed place, the little white-haired boy and two others only were in waiting.

"Not very encouraging," said Margaret, as she alighted from the carriage.

Followed by the Doctor, who placed two camp-stools under the tree, she took her seat on one, and, while her companion was fastening the horse, entered into conversation with little Dick, for that was his name.

Then Dr. Arnold, accompanied by Margaret's sweet voice, began to sing the words of a hymn, and from several points they perceived the rude children approaching, attracted by the music.

By this time, about ten had gathered under the large tree, and Dr. Arnold unfolded his roll of pictures, large and showy, with abundant matter of instruction — the children all held in mute attention as he talked to them in such deep, impressive tones of voice.

21   Q

At the close he gave to each astonished child one of the bright pictures.

"Is this mine to keep?" said little Dick.

"And mine, too?" said another, and another.

"Yes, my little friends; and if you'll come next Sunday, we will bring some more."

"That we will!" cried out every voice.

And so the work grew around them.

"Sometimes it may rain, boys," said the teacher, "and I think we must have a room now;" for about twenty were in regular attendance.

"We like the green trees best," said the children. "We don't want to be shut up in a hot room."

On making inquiries, it was found that there was a long room in the second story of one of the buildings formerly used by the workmen, but now unoccupied.

It was very gloomy now; and, being filled with lumber and dirt, Margaret shrank back at first from such an uninviting place.

"We can make it bright and cheerful," said the Doctor; "it has plenty of windows: remove the lumber, bring in plenty of soap, water, and whitewash, and some good Sunday-school furniture, and we'll scarcely know the place. The main thing, now, is to secure the room. I'll come up to-morrow, after school, and see Mr. Stone: the rest will be easy enough."

The room was found to be at his disposal, rent free. Margaret and Sarah Lacey came up to oversee the cleaning ; Dr. Arnold followed with a few forms, chairs, and tables that had just been removed from the Sunday-school room of St. Barnabas', to make room for new ones, and the work went gayly on : the only objection was, that the entrance was from a staircase outside of the building.

By Sunday afternoon, a cheerful company of twenty-five children took possession of the room, and Allan, Archie Murray, Sarah Lacey, and Mary Arnold joined the laborers.

The school continued to increase, and Dr. Hastings opened a Thursday-night service for the people. So much had their children improved under the care of their faithful teachers, that the parents were ready to seek some of the benefits of the mission. It was telling upon the neighborhood, in the cleanliness and orderly deportment of the children, the neatness and industry of the mothers, and the increasing desire of many to hear the precious Gospel; for good news of salvation, through a crucified Redeemer, did Dr. Hastings carry weekly to the people.

It is considered a branch of the Pastor's Aid; and sending its reports monthly to the parsonage, Alice feels herself one of its members, aiding by her prayers, her little notes, and the labor of her hands.

Father Morgan is ready with his means to aid the good work; but Mrs. Sherwood cannot step out of the hard shell of ritualism, for she says candidly that she has heard that teachers of other sects labor there, and she cannot think it right to aid irregular proceedings.

It is the blessed hour of morning prayer at the parsonage, where the daily manna falls from heaven around the dwelling. It has been a singularly happy, unbroken family, for they have, as yet, lost but one little lamb from the household circle; but the changing seasons now come fraught with whispering voices to every loving heart, which, as yet, they scarcely breathe to each other. There are marks about the beloved pastor of St. Barnabas', too plain to be mistaken — with every autumn, an increase of cough, debility, and waste of flesh, that are not repaired when the spring birds sing on the trees around the dwelling. Very, very slow is the change; but the faithful pastor labors on with an eye to the great account, and a heart fixed on heaven.

The Sherwoods are intimate at the parsonage; for although so different in religious faith, there are many mutual points of attraction. There are no young companions that suit Agnes so well as the Hastings children. Allan and she are especially congenial, for they both love music, poetry, and flowers, and these tastes are abundantly gratified at Englesby Terrace. Then, she is such a dutiful, affectionate child to her widowed mother, so generous in her charities, and gentle in her manners, that she has endeared herself to every member of the family at the parsonage. But she has been absent now two days, and Margaret has stepped over to inquire the

reason. The servant met her at the door, with the in-
telligence that Agnes was very sick with fever, that
seemed daily on the increase, and the mother was beginning to feel greatly alarmed.

From day to day there is no improvement; and Mrs.
Hastings spends much of her time with the afflicted
mother, sitting up at night, and comforting her with her
sympathy and her prayers. Sweet Agnes Sherwood is
very ill, her young life hanging upon a slender thread.
Dr. Hastings is a daily visitor, and although Agnes is
herself unconscious, his holy, heavenly prayers are such
a source of strength and comfort to the mother! Mr.
Moncrief is faithful, too; but in this hour of heavy trial,
she needs the strong arm of Christ himself to lean upon,
and this she feels always after a visit from Dr. Hastings.

Agnes is spared to their prayers, and the mother is
bound now to the family at the parsonage with enduring
ties, which time can never break.

"It was a great comfort," said the mother, "to know
that Agnes had been confirmed so early — was a regular
communicant, and a member of the true Church of
Christ; for I was sure that if she were removed from
earth, it would be to go home to heaven."

"Not on this account, my dear friend," said Dr. Hastings; "for many a deluded soul may have travelled exactly such a road, and have no well-grounded hope of
heaven: not that I would imply such a thing with regard

21 *

to your precious child, who seems to have a simple trust in Jesus, that He will never disappoint."

Agnes had a good constitution, and recovered rapidly. It was a happy day when, leaning upon Margaret's arm, she was once more in the midst of the family circ'e at the parsonage.

"We shall have our pleasant rambles again," said Allan. "You don't know, Agnes, how I have missed you, in these long weeks of anxiety. I have been learning some new music on purpose for you."

"Let me hear it, Allan," said the young girl.

"The old times are back again," said Alice; "how thankful we should be!"

Early next morning, Agnes was taking her usual walk: passing by the parsonage, the sweet sound of the morning hymn held her spell-bound for a moment; and then quietly stepping in, she joined the family at their daily worship. A slight moving on the part of Margaret left a chair between herself and Allan, which Agnes took, listening with great interest to the repetition of the daily texts.

Turning to the visitor, the pastor said, "Our subject to-day, Agnes, is the fruits of the Spirit. Margaret will give me her text."

"'But the fruit of the Spirit is love, joy, peace, long-suffering, gentleness, goodness, faith, meekness, temperance: against such there is no law.'"

Allan is ready with his:

"'For the fruit of the Spirit is in all goodness and righteousness and truth.'"

"I have one, papa," said Alice: "'For they that are after the flesh, do mind the things of the flesh; but they that are after the Spirit, the things of the Spirit.'"

Edward is repeating his:

"'For ye have not received the spirit of bondage again to fear; but ye have received the Spirit of adoption, whereby we cry Abba, Father.'"

"Now I am ready for Lucy's."

"'The Spirit itself beareth witness with our spirit, that we are the children of God.'"

"Now you see, my dear children," said the pastor, "that all these passages refer to something going on in the soul, between itself and its God; not connected *here* with ordinances, although, when they are used in faith, conveying great blessings, the act that appropriates them being faith in the believer; the agent that gives them any efficacy, the Spirit of God."

The words were interrupted by a fit of coughing, a sharp pang seizing every heart as they listened to the warning voice.

Agnes pondered the words of that morning service attentively, and as she walked home she thought how different were the two systems of doctrine at St. Gregory's and St. Barnabas'. Which was in accordance with God's word? she was mentally asking daily.

Mr. Moncrief is not able to preach more than once a day for a short time, and much to Dr. Hastings surprise, he is invited to fill the pulpit in the afternoon.

"Shall I go or not?" inquired the pastor of himself. "If I go, it may be regarded as thinking lightly of the practices there; but then I can preach the simple Gospel to people who hear about nothing but the Church."

The invitation was accepted, and we find Dr. Hastings in the midst of ritualism — the processional music, praying to the east, bowing in the Glorias, strange vestments, lights and incense, all so offensive to his pure Protestant principles; but he preached a glorious sermon, justification by faith only being his subject — and preached it boldly at St. Gregory's. Dr. Hastings was painfully impressed by the whole service, and in the vestry-room affectionately entered his solemn protest. Laying his hand upon Mr. Moncrief's shoulder, he said: "It was hard to realize that the new additions heaped upon our old majestic forms could possibly be the same."

"We don't wish them to continue the same," replied the rector; "we are growing weary of the bold and vulgar exhibitions of Protestant individualism, real Puritanism, and are going to restore the good old Catholic faith through the Catholic ritual."

"You will not stop there," continued the good pastor; "whatever endangers the doctrine of justification by faith leads direct to Rome."

"I must own that I prefer Rome to Geneva," replied

Mr. Moncrief. "I know of no regeneration but that in baptism, and rejoice in the doctrine of the presence in the Holy Eucharist as the very food that the soul craves."

"What then becomes of the Articles in our Book of Common Prayer?"

"There is our trouble," said the ritualist; "if they were only out of the way, we could march on with rapid strides."

"This generation will not see that calamity," said Dr. Hastings. "The work baptized in the blood of Cranmer, Latimer, and Ridley is not so easily overthrown. There is a sturdy band of true and faithful Protestants left yet, to defend the faith of the Reformers."

"They destroyed a great deal that was excellent in my opinion," said Mr. Moncrief.

Dr. Hastings fixed his calm blue eye upon the speaker's face, and asked solemnly: "Have you ever, upon bended knee, asked sincerely for the light of the Holy Spirit, that you may know the truth as it is in Jesus?"

"The Church is my interpreter of Catholic truth," was the reply.

"Through what channels, my friend?"

"Through the fathers of the ancient Church from the days of the Apostles."

"Why not go farther back, my brother, back to the Apostles themselves?—for on them alone sat the cloven tongues at Pentecost."

"We cannot agree, I see that," said the ritualist; "our systems are too wide apart."

"The days of trouble are coming, I fear," said Dr. Hastings. "Freedom cannot always be confined to one wing of the Church that we love; and if there is not corresponding relaxation of canon law for us, as well as for you, other relief must come to burdened consciences."

"What relief, Dr. Hastings?"

"Either reform, or separate organization — the saddest remedy that an arrogant course would lay upon us."

"May our Master defend us from schism!" said Mr. Moncrief.

"We should leave the schismatics behind us; for they have already divided our beloved Church in spirit. But may God defend the right! I can trust Him. Good day, Mr. Moncrief."

He extended his hand.

"Good day, Dr. Hastings. I thank you for your candor and your courtesy."

CHAPTER XVIII.

A VEIL AT ST. GREGORY'S.

They have taken away my Lord, and I know not where they have laid him."

AGNES has often invited members of the parsonage family to accompany her to church; but, hitherto, none have availed themselves of the invitation.

There are to be some new ceremonies at St. Gregory's on Good Friday, and Allan has obtained permission to go, for once.

The chancel railings are draped in black, also the pulpit and the lectern. The altar is covered with sable; and running round the upper edge is a silver fringe. In front, on this dark ground, is represented the crown of thorns, in the centre of which are three nails, typical of those with which our Redeemer was fastened to the wood of the cross

The chandeliers are enveloped in black cloth; and over the large chancel-window, back of the altar, there is a covering of sable, and on this a large cross, made of purple stuff, extending the whole length and breadth.

Morning service commenced at nine o'cl ck, the Rev.

Messrs. Moncrief and Charlier officiating ministers, the former habited in a black chasuble, fringed with silver. At half-past twelve o'clock commenced the service, called the Three Hours' Agony, celebrated but once before in New York, similar to the service in Catholic countries, and certainly found nowhere in our Book of Common Prayer.

There was a procession of priests and acolytes, a cross-bearer, incense swingers, solemn music, darkness, and all the accompaniments of a Romish service — in fact, a complete drama.

Allan is shocked at this exhibition; and, walking home in silence, Agnes said, at length :

" Well, Allan, was it not impressive ?"

" It was a real drama, Agnes — our dear Lord's sufferings the subject."

" Why do you object, Allan ?"

" First and foremost, we have no such service in our Prayer Book ; and it is altogether Romish."

Mrs. Sherwood has seen so much of pure spiritual piety at the parsonage that she is beginning to crave something better than these object-lessons in this sensuous worship. She is deeply convinced of sin, and gilded altars, smoking incense, flowers, lights, and processional music meet no want of an awakened soul. She is conscious of a need that she cannot define ; for there is a veil at St. Gregory's between her spirit and the blessed Jesus, hiding His preciousness from the true penitent.

We find her frequently in Mr. Moncrief's study, who directs her not to the Bible, but to the *Directorium Anglicanum*, to the Book of Hours, and daily partaking of the Holy Eucharist; but Mrs. Sherwood is seeking peace with God, and such counsel does not meet her case.

She reads of peace with God, of a full assurance of faith, of joy in believing, of a sense of adoption: she has neither. And so she gropes on in darkness, although she is living in the light of the nineteenth century — all dim and shadowy to her, obscured by the misty veil at St. Gregory's.

She has gone once or twice to the lecture-room at St. Barnabas', always returning with a deeper consciousness that there is a void yet unfilled in her aching heart. Then she becomes more abundant in charity, more self-denying, and imposes more restraints upon herself; but she is groping still, and carries about a face still shrouded in sadness; for "they have taken away her Lord, and she knows not where they have laid Him"— almost as much entombed to her as when buried in the sepulchre of Joseph of Arimathea.

"Sir, we would see Jesus," is the dumb language of her spirit — a supplication all unanswered at St. Gregory's.

She is seeking for free access to a throne of grace; and the smoke of swinging incense and a face directed to what is styled an altar is the answer of that pulpit.

22

She needs a Mediator between earth and heaven, and the vestments that mark the divine character of an earthly priesthood are held up before her. The soul is lifting beseeching eyes to heaven for a sacrifice that will forever atone for sin, and the Holy Eucharist, with all its ancient superstitions of altar, priest, and daily sacrifice, is spread before the convicted spirit. But neither altar, nor priest, nor swinging incense can satisfy a soul that is athirst for Jesus in His precious offices; and so she goes with spirit yet bowed down, scarcely knowing that they have taken away her Lord—not yet convinced that she will never find Him here.

How many immortal souls may be uttering in their silent chambers "We would see Jesus," receiving just such answers from their spiritual guides! Solemn responsibility in those ordained to make known the preciousness of a Saviour's love, who thus hide the Master behind a veil of superstition !

But Good Friday has passed away, and we will describe still farther the "steps forward" at St. Gregory's, quoted from one present on such an occasion, in the great American metropolis of ritualism, on Easter day :

"The candles that had been put out at the Tenebræ of Good Friday were relighted, and the church shone with the brightness of the Easter festival. The service commenced at a quarter before ten, and continued for nearly four hours. At about half-past ten, one of the

altar-boys entered with a long taper, and lit the can
dles that flanked the altar on either side. These being
lit, the strains of distant music were heard, swelling
gradually on the ear as the procession entered the vestry
door — first the cross-bearer, in purple and white; then
two acolytes, with huge candles of colored wax, and
dressed in crimson and white; then another little altar-
boy, swinging clouds of incense from a silver censer;
then the banner-bearers — the first banner having the
figure of the patron saint, his head encircled with the
halo of martyrdom, (he was the martyr sacrificed on
British soil,) the other being the banner of the Holy
Sacrament, on which was painted the sacred ritualistic
emblems : finally came the officiating priests. As the
procession, with its candles, banners, incense, and
cross, ascended the chancel steps, and made its reverence to the altar, the scene was quite brilliant and
imposing.

"The ante-communion service was then proceeded
with, the music being from Mozart's Twelfth Mass, and,
truth compels us to say, very badly sung. Except frequent genuflections and crossings, and the obeisance at
the statement of the incarnation ("and was made Man")
in the Creed, the service did not differ materially from
the ordinary usage of the Episcopal Church. At the
reading of the Gospel, however, a variation occurred.
The Epistle having been read on the Epistle side of the
altar, the priests crossed to the left, or Gospel side, and

Father Niles taking his place on the topmost step, the assisting priest standing on the next step below, held the book on a level with his own eyes and supported against his forehead, and from this the officiating priest read; while the little boys held their tall tapers on either side of the reader, and the censer-bearer swung incense toward the group.

"Then came the sermon, prefaced by the preacher crossing himself and commending the exercise to the Divine guidance by the words, 'In the name of the Father, and of the Son, and of the Holy Ghost, Amen,' and the congregation did likewise. The sermon was upon the resurrection of the body, and the preacher — Father Worrell — of course took the ultra Church view of the subject, and maintained the resurrection of the very particles of our present actual fleshly bodies, supporting his doctrine with the usual texts and well-known arguments. Two significant sentences were those in which the preacher cautioned his hearers to 'beware of those blustering private judgments for which the things of God are never too profound,' and in which he made reference to 'her who bare the Holy Child, peerless among created beings.'

"The discourse was not long, and was succeeded by the communion service, Father Niles being the celebrant. He was robed in a black under-robe, over which was worn the alb, a white garment reaching to the knee, and finished by a deep lace border. Over this was worn a rich white chasuble, bordered with gold braid, and worked with crimson. The mode of administering the communion differs from the ordinary practice of the Church in that a consecrated wafer is used in place of the bread. With this the priest first crosses the communicant against the forehead, and then places the wafer in his mouth."

. Truly St. Gregory's is on the Appian Way. What must be thought of our Church discipline, which can bring to trial offenders against canon law on one side, and tolerate practices like these in the *Protestant* Episcopal Church!

Have we no law for *these?* — no law by which to banish and drive away from the Church all erroneous and strange doctrines contrary to God's word? Surely — surely we have. Surely the Church of Cranmer and Ridley and Latimer will not surrender one inch of the triumphs of that day of reformation.

But to return to Agnes. She is almost daily at the parsonage now; for she knows how tenderly the good pastor and his wife waited upon her in her hours of sickness. Frequently we find her by the side of Alice in her excursions out of doors, Allan drawing the carriage; sometimes by the borders of the creek, in the more quiet streets, or up and down the shady orchard; frequently stepping in at the hour of morning prayer, for Agnes finds that it is good to be there. She is seated among them to-day, when they are discussing the subject of the new birth.

Margaret is ready with her text

"'And he said, Verily I say un to you, Except ye be converted and become as little children, ye shall not enter into the kingdom of heaven.'"

"I have a good one," said Allan: "'Jesus answered and said unto him, Verily, verily, I say unto thee, Except a man be born again, he cannot see the kingdom of God.'"

"Have you any passages describing the evidences of the new birth?"

"I have, papa," said Alice: "'Whosoever believeth that Jesus is the Christ, is born of God: and every one that loveth him that begat, loveth him also that is begotten of him.'"

"I have given several to Edward and Lucy. Repeat yours, Edward."

"'For whatsoever is born of God overcometh the world: and this is the victory that overcometh the world, even our faith.'"

"This is mine, papa," said Lucy: "'Beloved, let us love one another: for love is of God; and every one that loveth, is born of God, and knoweth God.'"

"You see, my dear children, that these passages refer to a spiritual change which must pass upon our moral nature, ere we are meet for an inheritance with the saints in light, the great agent of which is the Holy

Spirit, and faith the instrument by which we receive the promised blessing."

Many a seed of divine truth is thus dropped in the hearing of Alice Sherwood.

After the service, we find the two rambling together along the banks of the creek, for Alice is not well enough to accompany them to-day, and very sweet and holy is the intercourse between these young persons.

Agnes is seventeen now, small and delicately formed, the character of her beauty touching rather than brilliant; for there is a world of feeling in the soft dark eyes veiled by the drooping lash. There is such a similarity of taste in reference to music, poetry, and the beauties of the world in which they live, that Agnes is beginning to tell her thoughts freely to Allan, who is daily acquiring more influence over the young lady.

They are communing thus to-day.

"How is it, Allan, that I feel so differently toward Dr. Hastings from what I do to Mr. Moncrief; he is really my pastor, but I cannot talk to him as I can to Dr. Hastings."

"I suppose, Agnes, that it arises from the difference in their claims; one comes to you as a minister of the Lord Jesus, a shepherd, a guide, a father; and the other as a priest, to administer the holy mysteries and to absolve you from sin."

"I stand in awe of Mr. Moncrief, and could never come to him with soul-confidence; but I venerate and

love Dr. Hastings, and see in him the marks of a true
minister of our Lord and Saviour. Both cannot be
true, so wide apart in their teachings. Which am I to
follow?"

"Whichever leads to Jesus, Agnes: pray for guidance,
keep close to the Bible, give up reading the books of
the ritualists—they will lead you into the paths of a sen
suous religion, certainly not taught by the Apostles."

CHAPTER XIX.

WINGS AT ST. BARNABAS'.

"Now the God of hope fill you with all joy and peace in believing, that ye may abound in hope, through the power of the Holy Ghost."

IT is the favored hour of Friday-evening lecture at St. Barnabas', a service largely attended in the lecture-room. The pastor is in the reading-desk in his black gown; for it is the custom of Dr. Hastings to be thus clad at the familiar lecture. There is a growing look of deeper spirituality upon the pale, thoughtful countenance, a more solemn light from the blue eyes, a more tender sweetness around the large mouth, and a few scattered locks of light-brown hair crown the broad, expansive brow. His slow and measured movements indicate weakness; but none who listen to the rich melody of the deep, musical voice, can fully realize that the slender frame from which it proceeds can be so very frail.

The service opens with the words of the sweet hymn, sung always to the same tune:

"Far from my thoughts, vain world, begone!
    Let my religious hours alone:
    From flesh and sense I would be free,
    And hold communion, Lord, with thee"—

the pastor sitting with closed eyes, joining in the solemn hymn.

Then came the evening service, so impressive in its simplicity, and then the familiar lecture, full of a pastor's tenderness and an ambassador's faithfulness — Jesus Christ and Him crucified, the great subject of his ministry; His offices, His example, His teachings, His holy life, His atoning death, his one absorbing theme. These heavenly doctrines he pressed upon his people's hearts with all a father's love: this the language of his whole ministry at St. Barnabas', as it is his text to-night:

"For whether we be beside ourselves, it is to God: or whether we be sober, it is for your cause.

"For the love of Christ constraineth us; because we thus judge, that if one died for all, then were all dead.

"Now then we are ambassadors for Christ; as though God did beseech you by us, we pray you in Christ's stead, be ye reconciled to God."

A silence that might be felt rested upon the congregation. There had been a solemn, weeping listener there, who had realized the constraining power of such Gospel preaching, as Jesus, and He only, was held up as the sinner's hope. The message had fallen upon her heart with a sweetness that she had never known before. No mummery of the services of a defunct theology was there; no embroidered vestments, no processional music, but sweet devotional hymns, in which she could join, and the simple evening prayer, that she had been accus-

tomed to before the days of object-lessons. Conscious
that she had found wings on which to soar to heaven, no
earthly priest could henceforth delude her spirit.

No thick veil of excessive ritualism is here to hide
the Lord from the believer's vision; no mirage to entice
her footsteps into a mere desert; but an open Bible, free
access to the Great High-Priest, where she may draw
near even to the Holy of Holies with perfect confidence,
to plead the merits of the one Great Advocate. She has
been borne upward, as it were on angels' wings, at St.
Barnabas', and none of the worshippers knew with what
sweet tears of holy joy the figure in the mourning dress
joined in the hymn:

> "Jesus, Saviour of my soul,
>   Let me to thy bosom fly,
> While the waves of trouble roll,
>   While the tempest still is high
> Hide me, O my Saviour, hide,
>   Till the storm of life is past;
> Safe into the heaven guide;
>   O receive my soul at last."

Here was spiritual, not sensuous worship. No object-
lessons here, for here were no objects of sense to discern.
The things of *sense* only can be taught by the objects of
sense. Not so the immortal spirit — that must be sanctified by contact with spirit of a like essence: the things
of the Spirit can be discerned only by the spirit.

After the closing hymn, the usual invitation was

given to any desiring religious counsel to meet their pastor in the vestry-room; and observing several turn their footsteps that way, Mrs. Sherwood followed. A bright smile of welcome flitted over Dr. Hastings' face as he saw who so meekly took her seat among the little flock. A few faithful words of individual counsel, a fervent, loving prayer closed the service that had completely severed Mrs. Sherwood from a ritualistic ministry.

Next morning, we find her at Dr. Hastings' study, with the history of her heart struggles.

"The law has pursued me with its glittering sword for years," said the lady; "and all this while I have been taught to rest in everything but Jesus."

"That is what might be expected from sacramental theology," replied the pastor. "The sacraments were never intended to originate emotion; they feed the Christian's faith when rightly received. As in the Lord's Supper, the food is spiritual, and as the soul, in a state of nature, is spiritually dead, it follows that a dead soul must be endued with spiritual life before it can feed upon heavenly nourishment."

"This is all new," said Mrs. Sherwood. "If the sacraments do not impart spiritual life, what does?"

"The Holy Spirit, which is given in answer to believing prayer."

"I feel, Dr. Hastings, as if I had to begin my Christian life all over again: it has all been so unsatisfying."

"It is all expressed in these simple words," was the reply:

'In my hand no price I bring;
Simply to thy cross I cling'—

close to that blessed Saviour every step of your way: keep your eyes ever upon Him, and he will reveal himself to you as a pardoning, loving Saviour."

With the docile spirit of a child, she bowed before the mercy-seat, while the good pastor committed her case to the teaching of the blessed Spirit.

Father Morgan is on a visit to the parsonage, his spirit sorely troubled by the progress of ritualism in the Church of his affections.

"Here is something for the press," said the old gentleman, taking out a small manuscript. "Shall I read Father Morgan's Vision?"

Seating himself near the couch of the invalid, he wiped his spectacles, unrolled his manuscript, smoothed its wrinkles, and then commenced:

"Methought that I was sitting in the church of St. ——, one of the fossil churches of the nineteenth century, musing over the defections of these latter days. In my waking dreams, this is what I saw:—The congregation were assembled at morning prayer. Seated in a side-pew, where I could see the entrance, methought three shadowy forms moved slowly up the aisle, clad in the loose, flowing robes worn in the days of our Lord, girt about the loins, and with uncovered heads. Though

23

clearly defined, they were singularly transparent, and 1 felt that we were in the presence of the spirits of another world.

"They glided up the aisle, entered the chancel-rails, and took their seats within, evidently unseen by the two ministers, who proceeded, with their genuflections and their droning voices, in the service of God. One, smaller than the rest, and much less imposing in appearance, stepped forward, and raising his shadowy hand to heaven, called out in solemn tones, that startled every hearer:

"'Listen! listen! I come with a message from heaven to you, degenerate Christians of the nineteenth century.'

"Methought that now these forms were visible, for many started to their feet fully aroused, as the impressive voice continued:

"'What mean you, Christians of the latter days, by these forms of Judaism? Having begun in the Spirit, are ye going back to the flesh?'

"I knew him now: it was Paul, the great Apostle to the Gentiles.

"'Is this spiritual worship?—this outward service of posture, and vestment, and processions. What mean ye, ambassadors of the Lord Jesus? (who seemed now to shrink before him.) Do you call this the Church of the Apostles, left upon earth to defend the faith once delivered to the saints? What was that ancient, simple faith for which so many died? Hear it, degenerate sons! Justification by faith, sanctification by the Spirit, a life of holiness, the resurrection of the body, and the life of the world to come: this is Apostolic doctrine!

"'Preaching the word from house to house, laboring for immortal souls, giving of alms, and brotherly love: this is Apostolic doctrine. How much of all that is left in this apology for a Christian church — this bowing multitude before the idol that their priests have made? I say to you now, what I said to the men of Athens, "I perceive that in all things ye are too superstitious;" for I find what you call an altar here, on which you claim to sacrifice, an unknown god. The time is short, the dispensation is closing; the sifting-time is coming, when the tares shall all be burned up, and nothing left but the pure wheat to be gathered into the garner.'

"Every eye was fixed, every voice was hushed. Me thought that the two ministers were ashy pale as they listened. The Apostle of the Gentiles had uttered his warning; and then methought that the second arose. The face was heavenly; the dark-brown hair lay in wavy locks around his shoulders; the voice was sweet, and full of love; the glance tender and holy. This was he who leaned upon Jesus' bosom; and, in words of love, he spoke:

"'I am he that in the Isle of Patmos received the revelations from heaven — the brother and companion still of all true believers. Much of that divine revelation has been fulfilled; the most solemn judgments yet remain, when the Lord Jesus shall descend from heaven, to consume every form of opposition to His kingdom by the brightness of His coming. A shadow of that apostasy is here, and shadows are born of realities. Beware lest, beguiled by the great deceiver, you lose the substance of Christianity while pursuing its counterfeit. I come to warn the true flock of our dear Master; for, mixed up with all the varying sects of Christendom, we find that little flock. Come out, come out, true followers of the Lamb, from every form of opposition to the true spiritual Church of our precious Master; for "Behold, he cometh with clouds; and every eye shall see him. He which testifieth these things saith, Surely I come quickly; Amen. Even so come, Lord Jesus. The grace of our Lord Jesus Christ be with all who truly love the Lord. Amen."'

"Methought that, amid silence deep and profound, the seer of Patmos sat down; and then arose the third. Tall, commanding, with a glowing eye, in ringing tones he spoke. It was Peter; free from human passions now, for he had dwelt in the presence of the Lord for eighteen centuries:

"'Beware of the seducing spirits of the latter days, who may come clad in forms of beauty, but only to lead away from the true faith of the Gospel of the Son of God. Remember where it is found in its purity — in that upper room in Jerusalem, where the cloven tongues sat upon the chosen few. Go back to them for the blessed Gospel. Keep close to their teaching. Whatever departs from the spirit of their holy doctrine or practice is of man, and not of God. We leave our warning! It will be heeded by the true flock only ; for the Saviour's sheep know His voice and follow Him.

"'But, beloved, be not ignorant of this one thing, that one day is with the Lord as a thousand years, and a thousand years as one day.

"'But the day of the Lord will come as a thief in the night, in the which the heavens shall pass away with a great noise, and the elements shall melt with fervent heat; the earth also, and the works that are therein, shall be burnt up.

"'Seeing, then, that all these things shall be dissolved, what manner of persons ought ye to be in all holy conversation and godliness.'

"Awestruck, the people listened. Then the three arose, saying:

"'We shall meet again. Farewell, farewell!'

"Then methought that slowly they ascended to the roof, which seemed to open, disclosing a band of angelic spirits ; and then, amid strains of heavenly music filling the whole church, they disappeared.

"Thus ended my vision at St. ——. Doubtless could these holy Apostles return to earth, just such would be their testimony to the defection of these latter days."

Mrs. Sherwood had been among the listeners deeply impressed by the notes of warning. She was sitting daily now at Jesus' feet, and was learning, under the teachings of Dr. Hastings, the blessedness of joy and peace in believing

23 *

CHAPTER XX.

EASTER MORNING.

"But now is Christ risen from the dead, and become the first-fruits of them that slept.

"For since by man came death, by man came also the resurrection of the dead."

TWO new worshippers are added to the family group at the parsonage; Mrs. Sherwood and Agnes esteeming it a great privilege to join that little band who meet morning and evening at the mercy-seat.

She has removed her altar and its coverings, her flowers, and her crucifix, and all other symbols of her former faith.

A simple table takes the place of the altar, on which are laid her Bible and Prayer Book — these, with a kneeling-stool before the table, are all that remain of objects of sense. But there is another altar there, now, where she holds spiritual communion with the Great High-Priest of our profession. No Book of Hours, no *Directorium Anglicanum*, is there.

She has escaped the shackles of ritualism, and in her holy freedom uses her great wealth in schemes for the good of the Church and benevolence to man; for she has found the Holy Catholic Church for which she has searched so long. When she repeats that article of the Creed now, she can extend her arms very wide, to embrace all who love our Lord Jesus Christ; for although, in its outward organization, she still prefers the *Protestant* Episcopal Church, she recognizes the great multitude of true believers throughout the world as members of the church of the first-born, whom she hopes to dwell with in the church of the resurrection. She is especially attached to the good rector of St. Barnabas', for he is her spiritual father in Gospel bonds, and is anxious to do something to show her gratitude.

The congregation has grown so rapidly that a transept is necessary, and Mrs. Sherwood gives largely of her means for that purpose; at the same time begging to replace the old bell by a chime of bells. The offer is accepted, and the work goes on bravely. Mr. Moncrief is much grieved by the loss of his wealthy parishioner; but her choice is a matter of conscience, and there is no redress.

Agnes, too, is with her mother heart and hand, for she was gradually prepared for such a step, by intimate intercourse with the young people of the parsonage.

Mrs. Sherwood has no scruples now about aiding the mission over the hill, and, seeing that the field is ripe, and the mission growing, offers to build a chapel herself, calling it St. John's.

Agnes and her mother engage heartily in the work

as teachers, and walking in the fear of the Lord, and in the comfort of the Holy Ghost, are very happy.

In the meanwhile, Father Morgan has heard of the defection of his former *protégé*, George Vincent, for he is avowedly now with the ritualists. He remembers the Gospel precept, and obeys: "Moreover, if thy brother shall trespass against thee, go and tell him his fault between thee and him alone; if he shall hear thee, thou hast gained thy brother."

We therefore find the faithful Christian in the study of the young minister, surrounded by pictures of the fathers, the writings of mediæval days, and on the back of a chair several articles of clerical costume unknown in the service of our Book of Common Prayer.

"Have I heard aright, my young brother — are you really with the retrocessionists?"

"I am with those, Father Morgan, who wish to restore the ancient faith of the Holy Catholic Church."

"So am I, my young brother, only farther back than you. I am for bringing back apostolic, not mediæval faith: but what do you see in your new faith to prefer to the old paths of the Reformers?"

"A worship full of meaning, a revival of verities long buried."

"Do you experience any more of peace and joy in these appeals to the senses, George, than in former days?"

"There is certainly more solemnity, more awe, more of reverence."

"I think that if you will analyze your emotions, you will find that they are of the same character that you would experience in the concert-room, at an opera, or any other merely dramatic representation."

"I think not, Father Morgan; for in none of these places do we ever hear of a truth so mysterious, so awe-inspiring as the central doctrine of the Holy Catholic Church, that of the real presence in the Eucharist."

"All overthrown long ago, George, by giant minds who died to seal their faith. I cannot believe that you will always be led away by these fables. Your poetic nature has been your snare; that, joined with a want of watchfulness and prayer in these days of trial, has tempted you away from the simplicity that is in Christ."

"I thank you for your interest, father," said the young man; "but thus far I am satisfied."

Thus ended the conference, Father Morgan having discharged a Christian duty, and George Vincent still joined to his new idols.

The addition to St. Barnabas' is completed, an assistant minister engaged, and the chime of bells hung in the old tower. It is Easter morning — a bright and beautiful day; and assembled in the parlor of the parsonage, the texts of that day are on the glorious subject of the resurrection. Margaret is ready with her text:

"'For as in Adam all die, even so in Christ shall all be made alive.

"'But every man in his own order; Christ the first-fruits; afterward they that are Christ's, at his coming.'"

Alice said, "I have the blessed Saviour's words: 'Jesus said unto her, I am the resurrection and the life: he that believeth in me, though he were dead, yet shall he live.'"

"I have also the Master's words," added Allan: "'Marvel not at this: for the hour is coming, in the which all that are in the graves shall hear his voice,

"'And shall come forth; they that have done good; unto the resurrection of life; and they that have done evil, unto the resurrection of damnation.'"

"I have a text," said Edward: "'And have hope towards God, which they themselves also allow, that there shall be a resurrection of the dead, both of the just and the unjust.'"

"This is mine," said Lucy: "'For the Lord himself shall descend from heaven with a shout, with the voice of the archangel, and with the trump of God: and the dead in Christ shall rise first.'"

"We must not overlook the glorious texts in the fifteenth chapter of Corinthians," said Dr. Hastings:

"'Behold, I show you a mystery: we shall not all sleep, but we shall be changed,

"'In a moment, in the twinkling of an eye, at the last

trump: for the trumpet shall sound, and the dead shall be raised incorruptible, and we shall be changed.

"'For this corruptible must put on incorruption, and this mortal must put on immortality.

"'So when this corruptible shall have put on incorruption, and this mortal shall have put on immortality, then shall be brought to pass the saying that is written, Death is swallowed up in victory.'"

Dr. Hastings closed the Bible, and sitting silent for a moment, said:

"Stupendous joy! Blessed, glorious hope! Let us thank God on this Easter morning."

In words of fervent, holy prayer he committed the dear household to the keeping of the blessed Redeemer, and then all joined in singing the Easter hymn:

"Christ, the Lord, is risen to-day,
　　Sons of men and angels say:
　　Raise your joys and triumphs high,
　　Sing, ye heavens, and earth reply.

"Love's redeeming work is done,
　　Fought the fight; the victory won:
　　Jesus' agony is o'er,
　　Darkness veils the earth no more."

Just then the new chime of bells struck up their joyful peals, echoed on this Easter morning from city to city, from hamlet to hamlet, from hill to mountain-top, through valley and shady dell, over the waves of mighty rivers, throughout Christendom. Could a human ear catch all those echoing peals, stirring the ripples of the air with such joyful tidings, what a grand chorus of magnificent joy-bells would transport the soul with the yearly tidings that "Christ has risen," and, because He has risen, that we shall rise also.

Assembled at St. Barnabas', there was the usual celebration of the Easter festival, with one of Dr. Hastings' most stirring and eloquent sermons. There was no processional singing, no embroidered vestments, no brilliant lights; but there was music worthy of the day, a sermon that pictured the glorious kingdom that was coming, holding out expectations big with immortality, and services that trembled on the lips of thousands, bursting forth at last in one grand chorus of exultation on both continents.

It was Mrs. Sherwood's first Easter-day at St. Barnabas'; and blessed indeed was the communion of saints at the table of our Lord on that holy day.

"It was a precious day, Dr. Hastings," said the lady. "So different from former occasions, where the awe that filled my mind at the bare idea of receiving the real body and blood of our Lord utterly banished the idea of love; but to-day it seemed as if I could hear my Lord and Master speaking to my soul in tones so full of love and compassion that my whole being was bathed in that fountain of love."

. Mrs. Sherwood is a very happy Christian, her views

of the exceeding love of Christ deepening each day **of her** mortal life — from her own blessed experience now **able** to tell to the children of the mission how precio**us** that dear Saviour should be to lost and ruined sinner**s.**

The little chapel on the hill is completed, and **Mrs.** Sherwood is very active among the people. Agnes, too, **has** found her work here, not employing her time now in embroidering magnificent robes for the priesthood, but in making garments for the poor and needy — in visiting the sick and afflicted, instructing the ignorant, and cultivating the talents which God has given her, for the happiness of those with whom she dwells.

Warren is still at college, expecting to graduate in another year, and then to read law with Uncle Richard in New York.

Alice, on her couch of privation, is still one of the most useful of the family chain of the Pastor's Aid; happy in the ability yet to write her notes and letters wherever she hopes that they may do any good. Warren is the recipient of the largest number, and many a silent hour is spent alone in his room, conning over their precious contents.

Dear little epistles! full of a sister's love, but fuller of a Saviour's.

"It is all real here!" said Warren, as he laid one just received away in his writing-desk. "Sweet, precious Alice! how little of earthly dross is left in that frail frame!'

24

Warren sighed at the thought, for the rapid ripening of her Christian character always came fraught to him with the idea of translation — and how could he do without that beloved sister? More powerful than Warren dreamed were these little missives; dropping, seed by seed, the precious germs of truth, watched by the God of all grace, though hidden long beneath a soil hardened by procrastination and semi-unbelief.

CHAPTER XXI.

BECKONING FINGERS.

"And the prayer of faith shall save the sick."

SHADOWS are thickening at the parsonage, for Dr. Hastings' health is seriously affected; a constant hacking cough, debility, waste of strength — until at length he is obliged to suspend his labors; for he is alarmingly ill.

For several weeks his physicians are anxious, doubtful as to the result. The deepest anxiety is manifested by his affectionate flock, trembling, watching, praying. At length a praying band made his case the subject of special prayer — and at that very hour the crisis of his disease was passed. The work of recovery was slow, until, by permission of Dr. Lacey, he appeared once more among his people.

It was in a meeting for prayer, when unexpectedly their beloved pastor stood once more in their midst. The pallid countenance, the faltering footsteps, the solemn, thrilling tones of his voice held the audience spell-bound, as he acknowledged the hand of God in his restoration, and returned thanks for the love that had watched over him, and the prayers that had brought him in their midst once more.

But Dr. Hastings was not deceived: notwithstanding this favorable respite, he saw the beckoning fingers, he heard the whispered words, "Come up higher," and day by day he walked now in sight of heaven.

Nor was his faithful wife deceived: she, too, saw the beckoning fingers, and heard the whispered warning; but she stilled the beating of her heart, and brushed back the scalding tears, that she might minister to his comfort and happiness, so long as he lingered on the shores of time.

Dr. Lacey says that absolute rest for one year is indispensable, and a voyage to Europe is decided upon. His people would do anything to lengthen out his valuable life; and furnish means to send him abroad, and supply his pulpit in his absence.

Every day, some love gifts reach the parsonage. Wrappers for the sea, and for the land; slippers and scarfs, furs and caps — a dressing-case thoroughly furnished, and a writing-case equally complete. Hampers of delicacies, stores of all kinds for an invalid — in fine, there was nothing lacking for the sick pastor, who had worn out his life in their service.

Father Morgan sends Allan with him as a companion, at his own expense. "For," said the good man, "I would never dream of allowing my Edward to go on such a voyage, alone;" for although Dr. Hastings has overstepped the boundaries of middle life, he is "Edward" yet to Father Morgan in the domestic circle.

"Have you everything, my son?" said the good man as he examined the comforts provided for him.

"More than I need," replied the pastor, with moistened eyes. "I have so much of everything, that I can supply other invalids, if we have them on board; an that is really pleasant. God bless my precious people!"

It is the last day at the parsonage. Father Morgan, Dr. Arnold, Mrs. Sherwood, and Agnes are present at morning prayer, and so is Warren, who has been sent for to come home. It is a melting season, for who knows whether the same attached circle will ever meet again at the parsonage?

"We have an impressive subject for our morning texts," said the pastor; "the future state of the righteous and the wicked, or, in other words, heaven and hell."

"This is my passage," said Margaret: "'And these shall go away into everlasting punishment: but the righteous into life eternal'"

"I have mine, papa," said Warren: "'And many of them that sleep in the dust of the earth shall awake; some to everlasting life, and some to shame and everlasting contempt.'"

Turning to Alice with a very tender look, he said: "I am waiting for yours, my daughter."

"'For our light affliction, which is but for a moment,

24 *

worketh for us a far more exceeding and eternal weight of glory.' And the other, papa: 'The wicked shall be turned into hell, and all the nations that forget God.'"

"Allan, my son, where is yours?"

"'For we know that if our earthly house of this tabernacle were dissolved, we have a building of God, a house not made with hands, eternal in the heavens.' And the other text: 'And fear not them which kill the body, but are not able to kill the soul; but rather fear him which is able to destroy both soul and body in hell.'"

"This is mine, papa," said Edward: "'Knowing in yourselves that ye have in heaven a better and enduring substance.' And the other: 'And in hell he lifted up his eyes, being in torments, and seeth Abraham afar off, and Lazarus in his bosom.'"

Then Lucy read hers: "'And I give unto them eternal life, and they shall never perish, neither shall any man pluck them out of my hand.' And the passage for the wicked: 'Who shall be punished with everlasting destruction from the presence of the Lord, and from the glory of his power.'"

"These texts are rich and full, my children," said the pastor, "declaring in strong language the doctrine of a future life. May we be sure that our footsteps are treading in the narrow way that leads to heaven! Now let us pray."

In earnest, loving words, the father committed his household to the covenant-keeping care of God his

Saviour; but those last words were few, for his heart was full. In silence he took leave of his own family; and then, turning to Mrs. Sherwood, he said:

" Your kindness will be remembered, dear friend; for your box contains most valuable comforts."

And then pressing Dr. Arnold's hand, he said

" You will look after these dear ones, for my sake."

He is passing down the garden-path now, accompanied by Allan and Father Morgan; for the latter is to see him safely on board the steamer. It is early spring; and stopping at the gate, he turned to take a last look at the dear orchard, and to inhale the perfume of the sweet apple-blossoms, that will always bring back the memory of the parsonage.

He is gone; and it is a dreary day in the household, for the pastor is its light and joy. The weary month dragged on, for they were looking for letters now. A short one from Allan announces their arrival — papa not very well; will write in a few days. A longer one, to Margaret and Alice, comes in a few weeks:

" I am very busy in seeing sights now. Papa does not always go; but I have plenty of friends ready to take me everywhere. Last Sunday I went to the cathedral: very solemn and imposing, but no processional singing. The choristers entered quietly, took their seats reverently, without any show; but the service was very impressive. I wonder how our American ritualists would like that? We are staying now at the residence of minister of the Church of England — one of the choice spirits of the day; and dear papa and Dr. L—— do so enjoy their intercourse in talking over the things of the kingdom, for they are kindred spirits, with like views of almost everything. Papa is certainly better. Everything is done for his comfort. His cough is not so troublesome; his flesh and strength are increasing; but he does not attempt any labor. Assure Dr. Lacey that I will always protect him from importunity. In a few days we are going on a short tour to the Lakes, in company with Dr. L—— and his son George, a very nice youth, with whom I am quite intimate.

"I do not entirely neglect my studies, for papa keeps a watch upon that. How is dear, precious Alice? Do write me a long letter. And Warren, too, dear fellow! I wish that I could see his bright face, and hear his firm step once more! And Dr. Arnold, dear, valued friend! I suppose that Margaret and he take the walks on the creek, and up and down the students' path at Little Rugby, yet. Some of these days, I look for nothing else but a flitting from the dear old parsonage of our elder sister to that ball of science. Well, Heaven bless our darling Margaret! If she is to leave us, I would rather that it should be with Dr. Arnold than any one else. Now, don't blush, sister dear!

"I suppose that you see Agnes every day. I fancy her daily visits to the couch of Alice, smell her sweet flowers, and imagine her little baskets of fruit. I wish that I could just have one peep at the sweet face — one grasp of the little l and. When the pictures come, can't you contrive, in some way, to send me hers? She need not know it; but, if she gives you any, you can spare me one. My best — my warmest love to dear mamma! How lonely she must be without our father! Kisses to all the household circle, and a good, hearty shake of the hand to good old Debby and Jane. I could write pages more ; but the carriage is at the door to take us out to dinner. Farewell, my precious sisters! Write soon and fully to your loving brother,   ALLAN."

Over and over again did they read this free, affectionate epistle, and soon despatched the journal that they kept of daily life at the parsonage, that the two absent ones might enjoy the blessedness of their distant home.

Father Morgan is almost a weekly visitor now; and Dr. Arnold, too, takes abundant advantage of the pastor's last request — transacting their business and seeing that everything is comfortable around them.

The winter is remarkably cold ; and it gives them joy to know that dear papa is spending it in the balmy climate of the South of France. Although improving, still beckoning fingers from the heavenly turrets are calling him home. Of that his dear companion is well assured by the increased spirituality of his letters, from which we give an extract:

"Just as near to heaven, dearest, when I write from

Pau, as from the study at Westbrook; for very precious is my communion with our dear Lord in this distant land. I have learned to resign myself and you, and our beloved children, all entirely into His hands, willing that He should do with us just as seemeth right to Him.

"We have had a blessed life together, with no ripple to disturb our perfect harmony, and with the hope of spending our eternity in the presence of our Lord and Master. We can bless Him, Emily, for this hitherto happy life; and if it is His will to call me over the river first, you will learn to say, 'Even so, Father.' Time and its sorrows are very short; eternity, with its blessedness, none of us can measure.

"My health is much better, so that I anticipate a return to my labors among my beloved people; but still this worn-out frame cannot last many years, and we must learn to contemplate the possibility of separation. When we realize that every step of our way is appointed by our Master, all that we have to do from day to day is to take our pilgrim-staff in hand, and march gladly where He appoints.

"Allan has been a great comfort. So thoughtful, so devoted, so spiritual; his thoughts all turning seriously to the ministry of our blessed Lord. He is twenty now, and will be ready to enter the seminary when we *return*. How sweet that word looks! You may see it realized in the spring, if the Lord wills it so. I am glad to hear what you say of Margaret — truly our 'pearl,' as her name indicates. The attachment between our daughter and Dr. Arnold has my full approval. As an earnest Christian, I do not know his equal. May God bless them both!

"And precious Alice! God is leading her by another way home to heaven — our sweet lily of the valley, sending out her fragrance all around her lowly path. Her letters are so comforting! Doubtless there will be many in her crown of glory that the dear girl dreams not of now, for she has been a blessed member of the Pastor's Aid. How well I remember the day when she came to me with her puzzled face, wondering 'How, when, where she could do some good? — she, a little girl!' She has learned, dearest — has she not? — in the school of the Redeemer. What a blessed Teacher we have!

"And dear, captious Warren! I have many hopes of him; for I am pretty sure that the intellect is well fortified on the subject of religion, notwithstanding his questions and criticisms. It is the heart that needs renewal: that is the citadel of opposition. What a stalwart Christian he will make! I am glad to hear such a good account of Edward, for Dr. Arnold's commendation means a great deal. And Lucy, too — our sunbeam; tell her that I am delighted with her school reports. My best love and a pastor's blessing to Agnes and her mother, and to the Laceys especially. May God have you all in His holy keeping until we meet again, prays your affectionate husband,

"EDWARD HASTINGS."

The winter has passed away. Dr. Hastings is much better; and after a short passage across the Atlantic, we find him in the spring safely landed at New York, where Father Morgan is ready to meet him. A swift journey brings him in sight of the dear parsonage, after an absence of twelve months.

They are at the gate now, and the perfume of the apple-blossoms fills their hearts with silent joy, for it comes from the dear old orchard. A quick raising of the parlor shades, a rush into the hall, and in another moment Dr. Hastings is in the midst of his overjoyed family — mamma and Margaret clasping each arm, Alice shedding quiet, happy tears, and Warren dashing moisture from his eyes too — all so blessed in this reunion.

"You look so much better, papa," said Margaret. "Almost well, I hope!"

"I am better, much stronger, my cough relieved, and ready for work once more."

Warren has graduated with high honors; Edward and Lucy have grown so much; but Alice, their sweet lily of the valley, looks so much more frail than when he went away.

"She suffers much more," said the mother in answer to the questioning look; "but," in a whisper, "so patient, Edward! it almost breaks the heart to see her, sometimes."

Mrs. Sherwood has seen the carriage, and, with Agnes, is at the parsonage to welcome the travellers. A bright, swift blush suffused the lovely face of the younger, as she welcomed Allan home again.

"It has been such a long absence, Agnes," said the youth aside to the young girl; "but we will have the walks again — only for a little while, however; for I am to go to the seminary in the fall."

"For how long, Allan?"

"For two years, and then I shall be ready for the ministry of the Lord Jesus."

Father Morgan has miserable accounts to give of the progress of ritualism in the Church that he loves.

"Would you believe it, Edward, that they have celebrated the feast of Corpus Christi in our Protestant Episcopal Church?"

"The steps forward are very rapid, Father," answered the pastor.

"Never say that again, Edward: they are all steps backward, my son, to the mediæval days; those days of superstition."

"Is there nothing to check these proceedings, Father Morgan?"

"Not in this diocese, Edward; they seem to have it all their own way; but it cannot be so always — there is a deep undercurrent setting in another channel."

The sight of the dear pastor in the pulpit of St. Barnabas' once more, was indeed an occasion of rejoicing to his flock, testifying their joy in the sweet chimes that pealed forth on the first Sunday morning, from the

25   T

church-tower.   Arriving on Saturday, it was not generally known on that day; but as the people met at tne
church-door, the joyful news spread rapidly, and it was
understood, now, why the church-bells rang out sucn
joyful peals.   It was a blessed day to Dr. Hastings, for
he loved his holy work, and the sight of these familiar
faces, all looking so happy, woke a new throb of gratitude in the pastor's heart.   Still, in his hours of retirement, the beckoning fingers and the whispering voices
quieted the pulses of hope; and in quiet resignation to
the will of God, he pursued his blessed work of saving
souls.

Agnes Sherwood is eighteen, and is about to celebrate
her birthday at Englesby Terrace.   The parlors are
thrown open, beautifully decorated with flowers, and
Agnes, in her dress of soft, thin muslin, is ready to receive
her guests.   Her only ornaments, lovely white flowers in
her glossy black hair, and a set of jet and pearls, the
birthday gift of her mother.   The Hastings family, the
Laceys, and the Arnolds are the only invited guests.
Alice is brought on her couch, for it is one of her best
days; she enjoys the music and the social intercourse,
and is ready with her pretty gift of an embroidered
toilet-cushion, the work of her own hands.   A beautiful
basket of flowers, arranged by Margaret and Allan, is
placed in the centre of the supper-table.   Agnes' harp,
Margaret's piano, Warren and Allan's flute, and the
trained voices of all, make enchanting music; and the
parents of the young people are quietly enjoying the

sight of their happiness. Mrs. Sherwood and the good pastor are sitting apart from the rest, engaged in pleasant chat.

"Does it please you, Dr. Hastings, to see the growing attachment out there?" pointing to Allan and Agnes, who were plucking some flowers in the conservatory.

"They seem very happy in each other's society, my friend," was the reply; "and I see no reason for checking it, if you do not."

"I could have wished no better choice," said the mother; "for Allan is everything that one could wish."

"Only a poor clergyman's son, madam: a very unequal match for Agnes Sherwood."

"I desire nothing but what I find in Allan," said the mother; "but really we are in a hurry settling affairs for them," she continued, "when nothing has been said to me by either upon the subject."

Supper is announced, and gathered around a table spread abundantly with delicacies, the well-assorted guests spent a happy hour; at the close, each one taking away the bouquet found at the place assigned.

Once more in the drawing-room, a side-door opened, disclosing Agnes' class of little girls from the mission on the hill, all made very happy by a neat outfit for the autumn, and a good supper. After they had all partaken, the children were entertained by some of the sweet music, and, in their turn, sang a very pretty hymn, accompanied by Miss Agnes on the piano.

It had been indeed a happy birthday, with no draw-
back but the pastor's delicate health, and Alice Hast-
tings' exceedingly frail appearance.

In a day or two after the party, Warren took leave
of the dear ones once more, to settle in New York, where
he was to read law with his Uncle Richard.

"You will be quite in your element, brother," said
Alice; "plenty of argument, and you know that is your
delight."

"I shall miss you, pet," was the reply; "but just
keep a journal for me, and send it every Saturday, and
then I shall know all that goes on here at the dear old
parsonage."

"I will, dear, whenever I am able."

"Don't hurt yourself on my account, Alice; but
whenever you can, remember me, so far away from
home."

"Not so far, Warren; you can run down in a few
hours."

"Yes, I know; but I must be diligent. I can spend
Sunday with you sometimes. But, Alice, I want to
whisper a word: what do you think of Agnes, for a
sister?"

"Think, Warren! I should be so happy — but do
you think it is really so?"

"I think that is the road good old Allan is travelling, and she would just suit for a minister's wife

But, good-by, pet. Now take care of yourself, for my sake."

Warren is gone, to prepare for life in the great metropolis — Allan is going in a few weeks to the seminary, and so the family circle is dwindling slowly. The beckoning fingers still calling home the beloved pastor. seen only by himself.

25 *

CHAPTER XXII.

"CHARGE, CHESTER, CHARGE! ON, STANLEY, ON!"

"Beloved, when I gave all diligence to write unto you of the common salvation, it was needful for me to write unto you, and exhort you that ye should earnestly contend for the faith which was once delivered to the saints."

ALLAN is ready for departure to the seminary, and Agnes is looking forward to a long separation; and then their pilgrim steps will travel side by side in the service of their dear Lord.

Father Morgan is at the expense of his theological education, and, after a tender leave-taking, accompanies his ward, that he may see him in comfortable quarters, and well provided with all that he needs.

Returning home by the way of New York, the good man has tarried a few days in the metropolis, and writes home to Dr. Hastings :

"Yesterday, I dropped in a moment at St. Agapius', for I had heard that Vincent was one of the assistants, and wished to know the truth. It was indeed with feelings of real sorrow that I beheld our young friend habited in the tawdry millinery of that school, partaking in its services.

294

"He does not look happy, Edward; and I hope in his case, that when the novelty has passed away, he will re turn to the old paths.   I was present, too, at the public reprimand of one of our most zealous young preachers of the truth as it is in Jesus; and I can assure you that my heart burned within me when I remembered the shameful innovations at St. Agapius' all unnoticed, and the alleged irregularity of this young servant of the Lord so publicly reproved.   If his was a violation of canon law, let others be brought before the proper tribu- nals, too : let there be justice, uniformity in the services of our *Protestant Episcopal Church;* but where are the presenters of such ?   Have we no laws to reach them ? If we have not, let us make them speedily, or we are gone as a protesting branch of the Church of Christ.

"I stepped in at one of their meetings, and felt my cheeks burn at the congratulations exchanged upon the progress of their mummeries.   The whole burden of the speeches, 'Try, try, try; write, write, write; watch, watch, watch; preach, preach, preach.'

"We Americans must have show in everything: hence it must be brought into the Church of God, that the higher classes may worship God in a manner different from our humbler brethren.   The sappers are getting bolder every day, advocating sisterhoods, confession, etc., etc.; and yet a strait-laced severity is dealt out to violators of questions of discipline, while the sappers and miners, who are undermining the faith of the Church, work on unchecked. *Iron canon-law* for the teachers of a simple Gospel, but a quiet opening of many little secret doors for the ritualists, that the '*blessed calm*' of the Church may be maintained — that '*holy equipoise*' which leans all on one side. '*Open the little doors quietly, be careful that there is no creaking,*' say the leaders; '*but keep them open.*'

"Edward Hastings, my dear son, there never was, there never can be a blessed calm, when the true faith left us by inspired Apostles is openly or secretly attacked. We have three classes to contend with: one, and that a large class, who say, 'Let them alone, the evil will cure itself,' a system tried since the days of Pusey and Newman, and we see its fruits. Then another smaller class, who are led by the attractions of the ritual, a poetic, sentimental company, who do not see the specious poison infused through this outward show. A third and more daring class are the openly avowed ritualists, who advocate a return to the practices of the mediæval days, with all their false doctrines. This is what we have to contend with, and God defend the right.

"I have just read Bishop Melville's address upon the subject of 'Processional Singing by Surpliced Choirs,' demolishing the last plank, I think; and Dr. Harris' noble sermon on the subject of 'Christian Worship not Symbolical,' calculated to enlighten the minds of the masses of our people. Let us have sermons, tracts, books, prayers, action, in our beloved Church. We know that our Lord has His little flock everywhere throughout the world; and to such he says, ' Lo, I am with you always, unto the end of the world.' Let that be our joy, our comfort in these days of abounding error and deep trial.

"Will you send to the Secretary of the Convention, and call a meeting of the clergy? We have failed once before the General Convention, but we must knock again. With a father's love to all the dear family at Westbrook, I am yours in Christian bonds,

"ALLAN MORGAN "

Father Morgan has not given up George Vincent, and cannot leave New York without paying him a visit. He is received cordially; for the young man cannot forget the kindness of his old friend.

" And so I see you among the ritualists," said the aged minister, laying his hand upon his shoulder. " Are you happy, George?"

" I enjoy the reverence in the worship at St. Agapius', Father Morgan."

" Reverence for what, George? Exploded practices? for showy, tinselled decorations, in the place of spiritual worship? I trust that the day will come when you will see your folly."

" You will acknowledge, Father Morgan, that there is solemnity in the services."

" I make no such admission, George; for I presume that the same emotions fill the mind in an opera-house or a concert-room; for, only the other day, I heard **a** gentleman say, 'I was in a strange city on Sunday, and entered, not a *theatre*, not an *opera-house*, not a *concert-room*, but a *Protestant Episcopal Church.*' This was the way that it struck a stranger."

"When was there ever a more gorgeous ceremonial than in the Jewish temple? and that was of God's own devising," said the young man.

"We are not Jews, but Christians, George; and think what a miserable sham these modern ritualists give us of that grand and divinely-ordered ritual? Where is the ever burning fire upon the altar first kindled from heaven? Where the ark of the covenant and the cherubim of glory overshadowing the mercy-seat, and the Urim and Thummim, and the indwelling Shechinah? Is this pitiful mimicry a substitute for the Aaronic priesthood? — these tawdry vestments the garments of glory and beauty? — this bowing and bending and crossing before a gaping crowd — is this the solemn and reverent ministration of anointed Aaron and his sons? No, no, my son! That grandeur all has passed away, never to be restored; for we have the glorious Gospel, the grandeur of the new dispensation which the Jewish ritual typified. May God reveal its glory to you, my dear son, ere you are completely Romanized. But, farewell now   I must be going. God defend our Reformed Church!"

With a heart bowed down in sorrow, Father Morgan

returned to Westbrook. and waited for the gathering of the clergy.

Dr. Nelson, with his stalwart Protestantism; Mr. Thayer, with his loving spirit; Dr. Hastings, with his calm, well-balanced mind; Father Morgan, with his Scriptural knowledge and lively faith — all were there, and many other faithful sons of the *Protestant* Episcopal Church, guided by these leaders. Father Morgan, the oldest of the brethren, is chairman of the meeting, and, in his own impressive manner, made known its object:

"We need not disguise the fact, dear brethren, that we have the battle of the Reformation to fight over again. We are in the midst of tumult, but not of our making. It commenced across the water. With whom? With Cecil, Venn, McNeill? or with Pusey, Newman, and Keble? With William Wilberforce, or Archdeacon Wilberforce? In our land, with the sainted Bishops Moore, Meade, and Griswold? or with Doctors D——, M——, V——? It is easy to answer these questions. The disturbers of our peace are in harmony with Rome, the old disturbers of the flock of Christ; and we must prepare for the conflict. It is not merely the foppery of ritualism that we are to withstand, for that, sometimes, is simply ridiculous; but we are called to withstand the *doctrines* that they inculcate, so utterly at variance with the teachings of the Reformation. Nor is it men that we are to attack; for there are several types among the advocates of the exploded theology —

the conservative, who sometimes, by their timidity, strengthen the enemy; the decided, open, out-and-out ritualist, who avows the design of unprotestantizing the Church; and the poetic, the sentimental, led away by the sensuous display.

"We must meet them all with calm, firm, unflinching determination to give not one inch of ground to Popery; for this it is, and not quite so much disguised as formerly. But it must be in a spirit of love that we contend, with not one uncharitable speech, not one attack upon human motives; for God only can deal with these secret movers of human action."

Then arose Mr. Thayer, with his loving, heavenly temper in full exercise:

"Brethren, I came here directly from the mercy-seat; for when human passions are stirred so deeply, it behooves us to keep very near the Master, lest we offend against the law of love. We see yet through a glass darkly, but our Lord and Master face to face. To Him, then, let us leave the motives of our brethren, and love their immortal spirits still, remembering that for them, as well as us, our Master died. But the doctrines which they would teach," and here his fine eye kindled, "let us not tolerate for one moment, in any shape, open or disguised, if they touch with the slightest finger one of the bulwarks of the Reformation."

Then rose Dr. Nelson:

"I own myself rebuked by the speech of Brother

Thayer; for very much of human feeling has been mingled with my protest against ritualism. I thank him for his Christian counsel, and trust that we may all have grace to follow it. Let there be union among us in one thing — opposition to any approach to Romanism in our reformed Church. Let us stand by our Articles, and labor and pray and wait for the day when offices and articles shall mutually explain each other. We are on the borders of our Red Sea, brethren. Let us watch for the word of command which bids us go over."

Every eye was now turned upon Dr. Hastings, who, with a very solemn look, arose:

"It may not be long, dear brethren, that I sit among you in your councils; for there are beckoning fingers daily around my path, that point upward to a land where strife and discord are words unknown. But while I tarry here, let me add my word. We believe that in all ages of the world God has stood by His own Church, to defend her from her enemies. Let us do our duty; give not one inch to the adversary. Remain firm and true to the great principles of the Reformation, and then 'stand still, and see the salvation of God;' for He will save us. It may not be in the way that we suppose, but He is with His own, and will bring the little flock safely through. And here let me quote, dear brethren, the words of a beloved bishop of our Church, in the very camp of ritualism. It is such a beautiful picture of what we long for, that I would bring it to your memory:

26

'A bright vision has oft risen before my mind of a Church, pure and primitive, combining the early organization, zeal, and love, with the freshness, energy, and progressiveness of the times; gathering from past ages experience, wisdom, and liturgic treasures, while discarding utterly all corrupt additions, and cleansing the temple from all profane intrusions. Conservative, without being narrow and bigoted; liberal, without being lax; a true interpreter of Holy Writ, and yet referring all men, not to her own interpretations, but to the living oracles; rebuking with power, worldliness and wickedness, sympathizing with all that is good and heaven-born; a rallying point for those who are weary of sectarian strife; a candlestick of the Lord, whose radiance should illumine our cities and forests, our mountains and plains. Is such an ideal never to be realized? Is it but a dream and a cloud-picture?'"

Dr. Hastings sat down amid a silence so deep that for a few minutes none seemed disposed to break it.

Then spoke Father Morgan:

"That was a charming picture, brethren, but, I fear, not very soon to be realized. We must go through the wilderness to reach our Canaan. The action of the last General Convention disappointed us, but there may be great changes ere the next.

"In the days of the great Reformation, God raised up His Luther to do His work. In the midst of that day of darkness and corruption that giant mind strode on, striking with his sturdy hammer on the anvil — striking boldly, steadily. Out flashed the fiery Gospel, consuming the *débris* of ages. Where is our Luther now? Corruptions in the Church are multiplying. Will this falling away culminate, at length, in such a mass of superstition and anti-Christian doctrine that it may require the fires of the Second Advent to purify the Church?

"Is this the great apostasy spoken of in the New Testament? Will there be another Luther? Or will Christ Himself consume every anti-Christian system of idolatry by the whirlwind of fire at His coming? These are solemn questions, brethren. God only can answer them. Let us be found at our posts, contending against Antichrist in every form — working, praying, trusting."

Every true son of the Episcopal Church was deeply stirred, and a committee appointed to collect facts from time to time, to keep minutes, and, at the proper season, to appeal once more to the General Convention, asking at least for liberty in the interpretation of our canons, and uniformity in the conducting of our services; begging, at the same time, for a revision of those terms which *seem* to favor the doctrines of the ritualists.

Solemn prayer closed the meeting; and after the adjournment, Father Morgan said:

"Stop a minute, brethren, lest we forget that aggression upon the enemy of our Church is duty now. Let me repeat the words of Dr. McNeill, of Liverpool, to two Bishops of the Church of England on a **similar** occasion." And here the old man raised his arm **to** heaven, while his eye glowed with youthful fire, and his voice, in tones that thrilled every one, called out: "Charge, Chester, charge! On, Stanley, on! till we rout the last foe of the Reformation."

It had been a trumpet-call, indeed; for, gathering around the speaker, hands clasped with fervor, eyes glistening with feeling, and voices, deep and full, replied: "We are ready to follow the Master in the defence of his Gospel, God being our helper." And every voice repeated solemnly, "Amen. **Amen!**"

CHAPTER XXIII.

MUFFLED BELLS.

"But I would not have you to be ignorant, brethren, concerning them which are asleep, that ye sorrow not, even as others which have no hope.

"For if we believe that Jesus died and rose again, even so them also which sleep in Jesus will God bring with him."

FADING slowly, surely, the beloved rector of St. Barnabas' was passing away from his people. The summer of his return was full of hope, but not to himself. The autumn came, with its whispered warnings, its falling leaves, its sighing winds around the parsonage. Every heart felt the approach of a sorrowful presence. But it came in the form of an angel; for, with the sorrow came the healing, and they told their tale of grief not yet to each other, but to their Lord and Master, each one for him or herself; and so they walked peacefully in the path that He had marked out.

The winter came, with its sharp, fierce breath; and the pastor seldom went out to church now at night. The Sunday-school teachers, "a part of his own family," as he called them, assembled once a month at the parsonage, and the choir weekly. Very precious were these gatherings now; for the nameless fears of approaching separation agitated every bosom.

Dr. Hastings had fine musical tastes, composing sacred music himself, and took his seat at the organ at all these meetings of the choir. It was so sweet to feel that all who composed that band indulged the same hopes of a blessed resurrection, when they should sing in the glorious kingdom the song of Moses and the Lamb; for every member of the choir was a communicant of the church. It is still his blessed privilege to conduct the services of family prayer; and we will join them once more, perhaps for the last time this side of heaven.

"Our subject to-day, my daughter?" said the pastor.

And Margaret replied: "The second coming of our Lord; and this is my text: 'For this we say unto you by the word of the Lord, that we which are alive, and remain unto the coming of the Lord, shall not prevent them which are asleep. For the Lord himself shall descend from heaven with a shout, with the voice of the archangel, and with the trump of God: and the dead in Christ shall rise first. Then we which are alive and remain, shall be caught up together with them in the clouds, to meet the Lord in the air: and so shall we ever be with the Lord.'"

"What have you, Alice?"

"'Behold, he cometh with clouds, and every eye shall see him, and they also which pierced him: and all kindreds of the earth shall wail because of him.'"

'This is mine, papa," said Edward: "'And his feet shall stand in that day upon the Mount of Olives, which is before Jerusalem in the east; and the Mount of Olives shall cleave in the midst thereof towards the east, and toward the west, and there shall be a very great valley: and half of the mountain shall remove toward the north, and half of it toward the south.'"

"I have one, papa," said Lucy: "'And then shall appear the sign of the Son of Man in heaven: and then shall all the tribes of the earth mourn, and they shall see the Son of Man coming in the clouds of heaven with power and great glory.'"

"Listen to mine, dear children: 'And to you who are troubled, rest with us; when the Lord Jesus shall be revealed from heaven with his mighty angels, when he shall come to be glorified in his saints, and to be admired in all them that believe, (because our testimony among you was believed) in that day.'"

"This is a solemn subject, my children; for we are clearly taught that the Lord Jesus will come again in great pomp and glory to judge the world, and to take His people home with Him to the Church of the New Jerusalem, where they will be with the Lord in a state of unspeakable blessedness, during the outpouring of the last judgments. Once assured that we are His, we need not fear that day of wrath, for it cannot reach the redeemed in their glorious home. Now, Margaret, we will sing our Advent hymn."

Taking her seat at the organ, the voices joined in the majestic hymn:

"Once more, O Lord, Thy sign shall be
    Upon the heavens displayed,
And earth and its inhabitants
    Be terribly afraid:
For not in weakness clad, Thou com'st,
    Our woes, our sins to bear,
But girt with all Thy Father's might,
    His judgment to declare.

"Then grant us, Saviour, so to pass
    Our time in trembling here,
That when upon the clouds of heaven
    Thy glory shall appear,
Uplifting high our joyful heads,
    In triumph we may rise,
And enter, with Thine angel train,
    Thy palace in the skies."

It was a communion-day at St. Barnabas', and Dr. Hastings moved among his people with unusual solemnity, so weak that he was obliged to sit between the serving of each company as they surrounded the chancel rails. There was a stranger among them on that occasion, deeply moved by the solemn service, and as she passed down the aisle with the retiring congregation, she laid her hand on Mrs. Sherwood's arm, and said: "This is your dear pastor's last communion at St. Barnabas'; you will never see him here again."

It was a strange address from one unknown, but it made a deep impression upon the listener.

It has been some time since he has been at St. John's, over the hill, and in a day or two he proposed visiting the mission once more, Dr. Arnold accompanying them. Thursday seemed a tolerably mild day.

"I think that I may venture, wrapped up well," said the pastor. "I should like to have you with us, Emily; but your cold is too bad, and I think that you had better stay at home."

Accompanied by Dr. Arnold, Margaret, and Edward, they started for the mission, Dr. Hastings brighter and more cheerful than usual. The people were rejoiced to see the good pastor once more; for they had learned to value his ministrations, and to love him personally. Never had he preached Christ to them with more power and faithfulness than on that memorable evening. Many of the humble people gathered around him after service to inquire after his health, and to listen to a few words of Christian counsel. Edward brought up the carriage, fastening all the curtains tight, for it is snowing.

"Wrap your muffler close, papa," said Margaret; "you are a little heated, and I am so afraid that you may take cold."

Seated in the back of the carriage, Margaret kept a constant watch for fear of exposure to the air, for it was snowing hard now. He coughed several times more hardly than usual, and the affectionate daughter was troubled.

"Take one of these lozenges, papa. Do you feel badly?"

But there was no answer, as he coughed again in a manner that sounded unusual.

"Dear papa, tell me, are you worse?" said Margaret, in tones of distress.

"Do not ask," he whispered; "I must not speak."

Then came another clearing of the throat. Dr. Arnold looked round, but could see nothing in the darkness, only that silent figure that he felt was there. He whis·· pered to Edward: "Drive fast, something is the matter with your father."

The rest of the ride was in silence, Margaret holding her father's hand, her heart beating with vague apprehensions.

They are at home now; and Margaret, springing from the carriage, met Debby in the hall. In agitated tones, she said: "Rush quick for Dr. Lacey. Something is the matter with papa."

The tones of alarm had brought the wife out into the hall, to meet her husband with a face pale as marble, and a handkerchief saturated with blood. Suddenly she clasped her hands in agony; but he whispered: "Be quiet, my love; God reigns."

Quickly carried up stairs, he was soon placed in bed, and in another minute, Dr. Lacey was by his side. He had ruptured a large blood-vessel, and all night he lay pale as a sheeted corpse, forbidden to speak at all. The news soon spread in the morning; and for fear of agitation, the front-door bell was muffled, and Mrs. Lacey took her seat in the parlor, to answer the grieved and sorrowing people.

Father Morgan was summoned, and tears rained over the good man's face as he looked at the serene and patient sufferer on that couch of languishing.

"We must part with him, Debby," said the minister to the faithful servant. "Dr. Lacey says that he may rally again, and the lungs may heal, but his ministry is ended, and his days are few. He has been a blessed son to me, and his wife and children are mine as long as I live, and when I am gone, will inherit all that I have."

A lingering illness confined him to his room all winter, most faithfully nursed by his devoted wife and daughter, and favored by unbroken communion with his Lord and Saviour. March winds brought a renewal of all the alarming symptoms; and it was certain now that the beloved rector would never leave his room again. His people are untiring in their devotion, vying with each other in their ministrations to his comfort, especially Mrs. Sherwood, who, from the first, offered everything that was in her house for the venerated sufferer, and every day with her own hands prepared some little delicacy. Father Morgan, too, was the same devoted, untiring friend, coming every week to see the adopted son of his affections.

"Very gracious are the dealings of my Father," said the invalid. "Surrounded by the ministrations of beloved friends, fading so gradually, and sustained by unfaltering trust in the merits of my Redeemer, I wait peacefully till my change comes. My precious family I trust to the care of our common Father, believing that I shall meet them all in the many mansions."

"They are mine, Edward, just as much as though the ties of blood united us."

"I have had a blessed life, father — such a long and happy ministry among a devoted, united flock, many of whom I hope to present before our Saviour's throne as my own spiritual children. I leave dear St. Barnabas' in a prosperous state, and trust that none but a truly evangelical minister will ever occupy that pulpit."

Dr. Arnold is frequently by that bedside, and very sweet and holy is the communion between the two. At the close of one of these interviews, the pastor said:

"Call Margaret. I have something to say to her."

In a minute or two, Dr. Arnold re-entered, leading her by the hand. The father smiled.

"That is right — just what I desire. To none would I so cheerfully confide that hand as to you, my valued, long-tried friend. She is yours, Dr. Arnold, I hope in bonds as happy as mine have been. Kneel, my children, and receive a father's blessing." Laying his hands upon their heads, he continued, in solemn tones :

"God the Father, God the Son, God the Holy Ghost bless, preserve, and keep you ; the Lord mercifully, with His favor, look upon you, and fill you with all spiritual benediction and grace, that ye may so live together in this life that in the world to come ye may have life everlasting. Amen."

Margaret arose, and stooping over her father, kissed the placid brow, as he whispered :

"My blessed Margaret — my pearl. We shall meet there, where there is no more parting. Now, while I am able, I must see Warren. Send for him to come down on Saturday."

It was a solemn interview between father and son — a reviewing of the past years of his young life — a looking forward to the life that is yet to come.

"I wish that you could realize as I do, Warren, the fleeting nature of all earthly things ; for what is our life ? It is even a vapor that soon passeth away ; and then comes that unending life — our real life, Warren ! Could I only know that you were preparing for that endless state, how blessed, how happy should I be ! Edward and Lucy, I trust, are taking trembling steps in the narrow way, and you must not be left out, my eldest son."

Warren was deeply affected, for the father's holy life gave power to his words.

27

"I am not so thoughtless as you suppose, papa," was the reply. "My former habits of mind are giving place to a better state; but there are difficulties in my way which hold me back."

"Let nothing hold you back from Jesus, Warren. He is the only refuge of the soul. *I know* what he is in hours of weakness and trial. Make him yours, my dear son, by a living faith. Kneel, Warren, while we pray together."

In solemn words, full of tender feeling, the father poured out his soul in humble prayer; and Warren arose, deeply moved, and passed out into the orchard, where, for an hour, with folded arms and head bowed down, he paced up and down in sight of St. Barnabas'.

Allan, too, is at the parsonage, and Dr. Hastings is making a request of Father Morgan.

"Just one more hour of sweet communion, while I have strength," said the good man. "It has been so long since I have enjoyed the blessed privilege."

Assembled in that dying chamber, the emblems of a Saviour's love were spread out upon a small table, covered with a pure linen cloth. The wife, the children. Dr. Arnold, the Sherwoods, Mrs. Lacey, and three members of the choir, were there; while Father Morgan was to administer the sacrament. It was the sunset hour: and Dr. Hastings said:

"Turn aside the curtain, Emily. Let the last com

munion be in sight of dear St. Barnabas'. Those departing rays are so beautiful upon the old tower."

It was a sweet and holy communion; and the solemn hymn, selected by himself, was sung in sweet, low tones by members of the choir :

"O sacred head, now wounded,
    With grief and shame weighed down;
O sacred brow, surrounded
    With thorns, thy only crown!
O sacred head, what glory,
    What bliss, till now, was thine!
Yet, though despised and gory,
    I joy to call thee mine.

"Be near when I am dying;
    Oh, show Thy cross to me
And to my succor flying,
    Come, Lord, and set me free.
These eyes, new faith receiving,
    From Thine eyes shall not move;
For he who dies believing
    Dies safely through Thy love."

Warren stood apart, with head bowed down, deeply impressed by the solemn scene. It was a melting season —a time when the Lord Jesus stood in their midst, ready to bless the silent company. Very quietly, one by one passed around that bed, and, pressing the hand of each beloved parishioner, the dying pastor gave each his parting blessing. Solemnly, Dr. Arnold, the Sherwoods, Mrs. Lacey, and the choir passed down the stair-case and out of the parsonage door, not uttering one word; for they felt that they had seen the last of their beloved pastor.

"Just one more duty, Father Morgan, and then I have done with earth. I must see George Vincent before I die."

The young man was summoned, and Father Morgan met him in the parlor:

"You have come to see him die, George. It is a blessed death-bed, with nothing to dim its brightness."

Dr. Hastings received him with a smile. "Come here, my young friend: sit close by me."

Taking his hand between his own, he continued: "I thought of you, George, the other day, when we enjoyed such a blessed season of communion with our Lord and Saviour."

"Do you refer to the Holy Communion, Dr. Hastings?"

"I do, my son. I wish that you had been here. It was such a real communion with our Lord and Master; for here He was in spirit in our midst. Are you satisfied in your new relations, my son?"

The young man turned his face away as he replied: "I know that I am walking in the paths of the Holy Catholic Church, Dr. Hastings, and ought to be satisfied with that knowledge."

"You are on dangerous ground, George, where many

have stranded upon the shoals of Romanism.   Beware !
lest you follow in the wake."

"I have no sympathy with Rome, Dr. Hastings; but
I do desire to see the revival of old Catholic ceremonies."

"Beware lest you depart from the simplicity that is
in Christ.   Study the Epistles, George, and not the
fathers; for in the former only is infallible truth."

The young man listened seriously to the solemn words
of the dying pastor, remembering the early days of his
Christian life with secret feelings of unacknowledged
sorrow.

The last duty has been performed; and, day by day,
the angelic messengers hovered around that privileged
chamber.   It is known throughout Westbrook that the
pastor of St. Barnabas' is dying.   Prayers are offered in
all the churches; for he is much beloved by Christians
of all names.   Surrounded by his sorrowing family,
peacefully he passed to his everlasting rest; his last
words: "A sinner saved by grace.   Give Jesus all the
glory."

The tolling of the muffled bells, which had been silent
so long, announced the departure to a better world of
the dear rector of St. Barnabas'.   One by one, a weeping
company passed out of the parsonage garden; for many
had gathered day by day in the parlor, to inquire about
the dying pastor.

There is grief not only at St. Barnabas' but through

27 *

out Westbrook; for the community have lost a bright example and a valued friend. Arrayed for the grave in his surplice, his remains were laid in the parlor of the parsonage, where, on the day appointed for the funeral, they were visited by hundreds. Strong men wept as they gazed upon the serene and holy countenance; for one remembered how he had labored for him in hours of first conviction, another how he had stood by the death-bed of his loved ones, and committed them to the silent grave. Tender women were there, kissing reverently the pale, transparent hand that had so often extended to them the emblems of a Saviour's dying love; many joined by that departed pastor in the sacred bonds of matrimony, shedding floods of tears over the dear hands that had sprinkled baptismal water on the brows of their sweet infants, and in all their joys and sorrows bearing a part. For more than a quarter of a century he had broken the bread of life among the same people; and a tie so sacred is not broken without deep and tender sorrow.

It is the day of the funeral. The bells throughout Westbrook were muffled; and very solemn were the peals answered from churches of all denominations during the funeral ceremonies. The pall-bearers are selected from among the most valued of his clerical friends Members of the vestry are the bearers, and clergymen of all denominations head the solemn procession on its way to the church. The Sunday-school teachers, all wearing a badge of mourning, follow the family. It was indeed a solemn scene — the church heavily draped in mourning, the low wailing of funereal music, the weeping crowds, who gathered to do honor to his memory.

Three Bishops — Miles, Melville, and Lysle — occupied the chancel, and took part in the impressive service of the Church. Mr. Thayer attempted a few remarks, but was obliged, from excess of feeling, to bring them to a close. From the side windows of the parsonage the females of the family heard the funeral hymn, one frequently used by the departed at funerals:

"Vital spark of heavenly flame!"

and, with hearts bowed down by sorrow, saw the procession winding its solemn way to the grave-yard of the old church, where, amid the tears of hundreds, the dear remains were committed to the silent grave.

Now the widow felt that she was alone; for, while the remains were in the house, she could sit by them for hours at a time, reviewing all the past. But now she feels that she shall see that dear pale face no more!

The solemn tolling of those muffled bells is in harmony with her emotions; and long after they have ceased to vibrate on other ears will they continue to sound in the sorrowing widow's heart!

CHAPTER XXIV.

THE PASCHAL MOON.

" Thy Maker is thy husband."

A FTER a short period, the sad work of gathering together, all the sermons and letters of the departed occupied the widow for several days. Locking them up, she felt as if the last duty to the sainted dead had been performed.

Father Morgan has taken charge of the family, and advises Mrs. Hastings to remain at the parsonage until another rector comes. The vestry have generously voted her husband's salary for a year; and the assistant minister is in charge of St. Barnabas'.

Warren is in New York again, Allan at the seminary, Margaret a great comfort to her mother, and Mrs. Sherwood a most devoted friend. But the sorrows of widowhood are hers — sorrows with which a stranger intermeddleth not. She takes his place in the worship of the family, and misses the sweet words of holy counsel. She goes out into the kitchen to give her daily orders to Debby; but there is nothing for him who engrossed so much of their thoughts. She passes by the study-door

320

and often finds herself listening for the slight, hacking cough. She glances at the hat-stand in the hall, but neither hat, nor cane, nor umbrella are there; they are laid away among the treasures. She is in her little sitting-room after the labors of the day are over; but there is no quiet step now across the threshold — no tender husband takes his seat by her side when she is all alone, and laying his hand upon the forehead, or kissing the quivering lips, whispers, " You are tired, my love; I wish that I could lighten your many cares." These memories are often followed by a gush of tears, which will not stay.

The church is no less desolate. A stranger's voice falls heavily upon her heart, and a stranger's form fills her husband's pulpit. These are a widow's sorrows; but she has her comforts, too — a band of devoted friends, who cling to the rector's family, cherishing them for his sake; but, above all, the precious promises all fulfilled.

At the end of six months, a new rector is called — a worthy successor to the lamented Dr. Hastings. He is to be married at the end of a year; and, by Father Morgan's advice, is to board with the former rector's widow until his marriage.

It is a sore trial to the sorrowing widow to receive another into her family as the rector of St. Barnabas'— to see another in her husband's study; but Robert Murray is a man of lovely Christian character, and knows exactly how to respect the feelings of the min-

V

ister's widow. Delicate, modest, sympathizing, she soon learns to regard the young clergyman with a mother's tenderness; for there is an appearance of frailty about the new minister, which at once enlists her kindest offices.

He is in perfect sympathy with all the former rector's plans — thoroughly evangelical, spiritual, devoted. With peculiar wisdom, he carries out all the plans so successfully arranged by Dr. Hastings, so that no rude changes are made; and the people extend to him their fullest confidence and co-operation.

But Father Morgan is preparing for the change in the widow's lot, and has taken a new home in a pleasant part of Westbrook, where he proposes that Mrs. Hastings shall take into her family six young ladies to educate. The good man will come too, with his faithful housekeeper; for he is really in charge of the family now, although the thought of entire dependence is lessened by the charge that he so wisely suggests.

But the months roll on, and the day of departure comes at length. All the arrangements are made. On the following Monday, the family bid adieu to the dear parsonage, and the minister and his young bride arrive on the following Monday week.

It is Easter even. The widow sits alone in the summer-house, where, twenty-six years ago, she sat as a young and happy bride, in company with her beloved husband. The same placid moon is sailing in the heavens, smiling as calmly on the widow, as it did upon the fair young bride.

More than a quarter of a century has passed away, leaving deep in the sorrowing heart the memory of those blessed, happy years. She distinctly recalls the holy conversation of that sweet hour; how they talked about the paschal moon, and wondered if it shone that night upon the new tomb in the garden of Joseph of Arimathea. The hope of resurrection was blessed then. It is more than blessed now; for the pale moon shines upon the grave of her beloved to-night, and seems to say, "Thy husband shall rise again."

The church-door is open. She enters all alone, and sits down in the pew before the chancel — by the light of the moon, almost able to read the inscription on the marble slab back of the pulpit: certainly she reads the one cherished, honored name.

Margaret has missed her mother. Suspecting where she is, she enters the church. Jacob has seen the two, and follows:

"This is our last Easter evening at the dear parsonage, Jacob. Can't you blow the bellows for me? I want so much to play some of dear papa's hymns before we go out of our old home."

Jacob has done this work before, and is ready to oblige his young lady. She is seated now at the organ, has lit the gas, and, one by one, plays and sings the sweet hymns that her father loved so much. A light footstep

is near her. She knows that it is her mother, who in
silence sits there, listening to the sweet, solemn strains.
The music has called out the family—even Alice, who
has been drawn into the church too. The solemn moon
is shining down upon the pale and languid invalid; for
Alice has been steadily fading ever since her beloved
father's departure.

"Sing 'I would not live alway,'" said Father Morgan; and Jacob stood by, shedding silent tears, as the
holy strains filled the church.

> "I would not live alway: I ask not to stay
> Where storm after storm rises dark o'er the way;
> The few lurid mornings that dawn on us here,
> Are enough for life's woes, full enough for its cheer."

It was a precious hour in the blessed sanctuary, for
all in that company were partakers of the hopes of a
glorious resurrection; for Edward and Lucy were to
receive their first communion on the following Easter
Sunday, having both been among the candidates on the
rector's first confirmation.

"I wonder if the spirits of the just do visit this lower
earth, Father Morgan?" said the widow.

"We know not, Emily. The veil is very thin that
separates us from the world of spirits; and it did seem
to-night as if he might be here joining in our worship."

"We know that he is blessed, father; and though he

may not return to us, we shall go to him, and be forever with the Lord."

It is Easter morning, and the sweet chimes are ringing out the resurrection joy — a "joy unspeakable and full of glory" to weary pilgrims, foot-sore on their journey to the heavenly city — every member of the family at the parsonage surrounding the table of the Lord, save Warren; for Allan, at the seminary, is partaking of the Easter joy.

But Monday morning is here; and the removal is taking place. Some of the furniture belongs to the parsonage; but Father Morgan has supplied every deficiency at the new home, bringing all his own household goods. The last load has gone; and the widow takes one more farewell glance at the pastor's study, plucks a branch of apple-blossoms from the low, green trees, a few flowers from the garden paths, and goes out of her once blessed home to assume new relations and responsibilities.

Father Morgan has been very careful to select a home well shaded, for he knows how Alice would miss the green trees; and so they find themselves in the midst of a grove of lindens. She has a small room down stairs, where all her familiar objects are carefully placed — a neat green carpet and new curtains having been furnished by Mrs. Sherwood. We find the dear girl so comfortably fixed in her new room, entertaining Agnes

28

and her mother. Taking the lady's hand, Alice kissed it, and said:

"How can I ever thank you, dear friend, for all your goodness to me? Truly, goodness and mercy have followed me all the days of my life. Everybody is kind to Alice. There is nothing that I lack on earth, and so much in heaven! I ought to be a most grateful, happy Christian. I don't even miss the flowers from the parsonage; for every day, since the young bride came, they are sent to fill my little vase."

The family are settled. The six young ladies have arrived, and Mrs. Hastings finds her hands full of cares and responsibilities. Margaret is a great help to her mother; for she has a fine education, and a heart full of filial love.

The young pastor is highly gifted, admired, and followed by the crowd: but true friends are faithful to the departed rector's family, and Mrs. Hastings finds herself surrounded still by a choice circle of congenial, loving spirits. The good old minister is a father indeed; and Mrs. Hastings has long since proved the blessedness of the promise to the widow: "Thy Maker is thy husband."

Warren comes frequently on Saturday night to stay until Monday. Many are the sweet hours of affectionate intercourse between himself and Alice; and he never goes away now without leaving some blessed hopes in the heart of the dear invalid.

"Warren is so different," said the dear girl, after one

of these visits. "There are no more cavils now. I am sure, mamma, that he is an earnest inquirer after the truth — not in his own strength or wisdom now, but depending only on the Holy Spirit. All I want to make me perfectly happy is just to see dear Warren a Christian. He is so whole-hearted that I know he will make a bright and useful follower of our Lord."

The young minister's wife is a frequent visitor at Linden Grove, finding the friendly counsel of the widow invaluable to her inexperience, and she, in her turn, bestowing her confidence and love upon the inmates of the Grove. It is vacation now at the seminary, and Allan is about to pay his first visit at the new home. More than one looks forward to his return with joy; for it is certain now that Agnes Sherwood is to be the life-companion of the young man. The mother is pleased that it should be so, for she is a whole-hearted disciple, and knows no higher joy than to give her all to the service of her Lord and Master.

Alice has her couch drawn up to the window, that she might see the first glimpse of her precious brother.

"There he is!" said the invalid. "Dear, dear Allan!" and in the next minute she was folded in her brother's arms; for he had seen her from the window, and hastened to Alice first.

"How well you look, Allan!" said his sister.

The brother sighed; for he could not respond to the remark in the case of the pale shadow on the couch.

"I am not so well, Allan," said the sister, for she had interpreted the shade upon his face; "but, although the outer man is decaying, Allan, the immortal — that which is really Alice, is ripening day by day, and, through abounding grace, I hope, growing up into the perfect image of the Lord."

Allan saw that it was so. The knowledge that gave joy to the invalid awoke a pang in the brother's heart, for very dear was this precious one to the household. It is indeed a happy reunion; for, after one more term, Allan is to be ordained.

We will follow him to Englesby Terrace, where Agnes is waiting eagerly for his arrival; and yet, with the sweet shyness of girlhood, at the first glimpse of his approach, flies to her own room, instead of to the hall-door.

In a few minutes, we find her timidly entering the parlor, where we will leave the two to enjoy their first hour of reunion alone, where emotions, more than words, express their happiness.

"I came through New York," said Allan, addressing Father Morgan, "where I heard that George Vincent is very ill. I had not time to stop, or I would have gone to see him. He has been sick a long time."

"Poor fellow!" said the good man. "I am afraid that he is very uncomfortable; for he occupies a room, going out for his meals. I must go without delay."

Accordingly, by the next train, the old clergyman is on his errand of mercy. On entering the sick man's room, it was just as he had feared. Once a day the woman in charge of the apartments entered his room, placing his medicines near him, and then not coming again through the whole day. He had hired a little boy to bring him food from a restaurant near, but frequently of such a character as he could not eat; and he consequently suffered in every way.

When the door opened to admit Father Morgan, a flash of joy lit up the pallid face. Extending his hand in silence, he burst into tears; and, after a minute or two, said, kissing the wrinkled hand:

"You are very good, Father Morgan. How did you hear that I was sick?"

"Allan was passing through New York, and heard it. I came immediately, George, for I feared that you were suffering. Who is your nurse, my son?"

"I have none. Indeed, my physician, the woman that takes care of my room, and the little boy that does my errands, are all that I see, excepting Father Niles, who comes once or twice a week."

Father Morgan saw that the case was one in need of careful nursing; for the young man was laboring under a slow, wasting fever. Practical at all times, he immediately engaged a good nurse, went out himself and brought in the comforts that he needed, and, as the nurse could not come for two days, took charge of the invalid until she should arrive. Very tenderly he washed and changed the sick man, made up his bed

28 *

comfortably, put everything in perfect order, and then, taking his seat by his side, gave him slowly some very nice ice-cream. Very frequently the tears welled over the young man's eyes; it had been so long since he had experienced such tender nursing.

"This is so grateful, Father. I do believe that if I had such nursing, I should be on my feet again in a few weeks."

"Has your new faith been a rock to rely upon, George, in your hour of sickness and trial?"

The pale lips quivered, as he replied: "I have been learning the lessons of my childhood over again, dear friend; and all the time the sweet words of the quaint old hymn are with me:

"None but Jesus — none but Jesus
Can do helpless sinners good."

"God be praised, my son, for these hours of perfect retirement, that have brought back the old truths of the simple Gospel!"

"Yes, father, the old, old story of Judæa, the babe of Bethlehem, the child of Nazareth, the preacher on the Mount, the worker of miracles, the sympathizing brother, the great High-Priest, the Man of Calvary, the first-fruits of the resurrection, the God-man of Olivet, have all returned again — all embodied in Him whom we call Saviour."

"I have been looking for this, George. I knew that

tinsel and showy ritualism would not long satisfy a soul
that had ever had the experience of a heaven-born
faith."

"That is all true, Father Morgan; but I have found
that the symbols of the new theology teach lessons which
I cannot believe. I did not think so at first, and regarded the opposers as uncharitable and Puritanical. I
admired the music and the show; but, day by day, in
the quiet and self-communion of this solitude, these gew-
gaws have lost their charms, and, in the language of our
own sweet hymn, I can say:

> "As by the light of opening day,
> The stars are all concealed,
> So earthly pleasures fade away
> When Jesus is revealed."

"Let us praise God, George," said Father Morgan,
and, with an overflowing heart of gratitude, he bowed
before the mercy-seat, to return thanks for this deliver-
ance, and to pray for the guidance of that blessed Spirit
who only can sanctify and save.

"You cannot stay here, George," said the good man.
"As soon as you are sufficiently recovered, I will come
for you. We can make room for you at Westbrook, and
there you must stay until completely restored."

The nurse is fairly installed, with minute directions
and abundant means supplied, that the invalid may lack
no comforts; and then the good man is ready to return

"God bless you, Father Morgan," said the young man. "You were sent by Heaven I am sure, for you have brought life and light and happiness. I feel as if I had taken real steps now on the path to recovery."

"Farewell, my son! May God bless and keep you in all your ways, and spare your life to labor in his blessed service yet."

A few weeks of careful nursing did wonders, and Mrs. Hastings is ready to receive another into her family for the sake of Father Morgan; for he has his old propensity yet of gathering around him the children of a common faith, when the hand of suffering is laid upon them.

"Now you see, Emily, why I told you that I must have two rooms," said the good man; "for I have so long had a corner for the needy in my own home, that I could not be happy if unable to do so still. They shall never be any expense to you, and Hannah will take all the labor. I always loved George Vincent, and he has neither mother nor sister to care for him. I know a little about nursing, and he will be company for me when you are busy."

"I am only too happy, dear father, to aid you in your holy work: none that you bring can ever be an intruder here."

The good man was fully occupied with his charge; for his health had been seriously affected, and it would be months ere he would be fully restored.

Allan has returned to the seminary, where he is to

remain but one term more, and then he is to be ordained at St. Barnabas'.

Mrs. Sherwood is a happy, useful Christian: she has no time now for trifling over priests' millinery, for she is on a higher mount, and cannot come down. We find her very busily engaged now in founding a home for twenty-five orphan girls, who are to be clothed, and fed, and educated at her expense solely, and fitted for just such positions in life as their various talents indicate. And so the days roll on until the time for Allan's ordination has arrived. Bishop Miles, his father's uncle, is the ordainer, and the church where Allan had been baptized, confirmed, and where he had received his first communion, is now to witness his solemn ordination vows. It was indeed a blessed day. Here the mother saw the crowning of the father's holy work — here Father Morgan saw his own namesake set apart for the very highest of earthly callings — here Alice in her weakness was able to come during the ordination service only, that in God's dear house she might join her prayers with the church militant for the dear brother buckling on the armor of a youthful soldier of the cross. And here Agnes Sherwood lifted up her woman's heart of deep affection for him, with whom she hoped to share life's joys, and cares, and trials, and eternity's unspeakable and endless bliss.

Oh, these blessed communion-days! when we gather as one family around the table of our Lord and Master, to feed upon the heavenly manna of his blessed passion. How we miss the dear ones from our side, as year by year one and another have passed away to the church triumphant. It was so on this occasion; for here was the dear family of the parsonage, but the sainted rector was absent. Here was dear old Father Morgan; but who could say how soon the aged head, crowned with its halo of silver locks, might too be called hence. And sweet, fading Alice — in their heart of hearts, each one felt as they looked at the ethereal shadow, lovely still in its look of saintliness, that this was indeed her last communion in the church militant. The solemn service is ended, and as Alice passes out of the church-door, she said, in trembling tones: "Stop one moment: let me look once more on the dear old church."

Turning the carriage that she might be gratified, she looked sweetly, sadly all around, from ceiling to carpeted aisles, from organ to chancel, pulpit, reading-desk, and communion table — from pew to pew; and waving her shadowy hand, she said: "Farewell! dear, dear St. Barnabas'. God bless my father's church. God bless its pastor and its dear people, and bring us all home to the church triumphant."

Just then, Allan, accompanied by Father Morgan, came down the aisle.

"This is a happy day, dear brother. I wonder if papa" — she could say no more, for feeling choked her utterance.

Father Morgan spoke: "He is among the spirits of the just made perfect, Alice; and if they do indeed visit this lower earth, he is here to-day."

"We are a blessed family, dear father," said the invalid. "All partakers of the hopes of the Gospel, except dear Warren, and I feel that he will join us in our march heavenward."

"And so do I, Alice," was the good man's reply.

While the soft, low strains of the organ still fell upon the ear, the little carriage passed slowly out, followed by a deeply moved company, who felt that this was the sweet sufferer's farewell visit to St. Barnabas'.

CHAPTER XXV.

SUNRISE.

"Precious in the sight of the Lord is the death of his saints."

ALICE is fading rapidly now, is not able to ride out at all, and subject to terrible attacks of spasms, when drops of perspiration as large as peas are forced out upon her skin by these paroxysms of suffering. But not one word of murmuring ever escaped her lips. With hands clasped and eyes turned heavenward, she would lay for many minutes, the large tears falling over her pallid face; and the sweet, low voice comforting her mother and sisters, who witnessed these agonizing spasms. Sometimes she would press mamma's dear hand to her lips, and kissing it, would say:

"Don't weep so, mamma. Jesus comforts me. He gives me grace to be patient; and I have so many, many blessings! It can't be long, mamma, and then comes the 'joy unspeakable and full of glory.'"

Mrs. Sherwood and Agnes are untiring in their devotion, coming daily with their delicacies, never without flowers.

"You don't know how these sweet blossoms comfort

me," she would say. "They speak such a language of love to weary sufferers; for if God bestows such care upon these perishing flowers, Agnes, how much more will He take care of me, His weak and suffering child."

Mrs. Murray, the young rector's wife, is very good too, coming daily, or sending the flowers that Alice loves. When she has intervals of ease, the humble people, whom she has so often benefited, seek her couch.

Dan Galway, the man that she met in the lane and reproved so sweetly for blasphemy, is one of her most frequent visitors. Perhaps no scene around that couch of suffering is more affecting than the sight of this rough, strong man, sitting with his face buried in his hands, his breast heaving with sobs, listening to the kind and faithful words that fall from those pale and trembling lips.

"You have kept your pledge, Dan, I hope," said Alice. "You know that you signed it here, my friend, in the sight of Heaven."

"I have not touched a drop since that day, miss; and we have some comfort now. I bought my old woman a gown last week, and it would have done your heart good to see how glad she was."

"Remember, Dan, that you cannot keep your promises in your own strength. You must seek God's help, and become His servant."

"I am trying, miss."

"I can't talk any more now, Dan. Good-by."

29   W

"Good-by, miss. God bless you foriver and iver!"

Aunty Miller and Robert Jordan, too, come for their words of counsel. Nor is the sweet ministry of Alice Hastings confined to the children of the poor; for even Bishop Miles says that he has learned many a lesson of holy patience from that gentle sufferer; and Mr. Murray says that he always feels as if he had been inside of the gate of heaven when he comes from the couch of Alice Hastings; for many a holy text has he learned there. She has been a sufferer for eleven years; but her holy ministry is nearly ended, and Alice feels that it is so.

Allan is engaged to go out West as assistant minister in an important parish, and is to be married in the autumn, ere he leaves. He has just told Alice, who lay quiet for a minute, and then spoke:

"I did want to see you married, Allan," said his sister; "but I shall not be here in the autumn. I have just one request to make. Ere I become very weak, can't you and Margaret be married by my couch? Then I could be at the wedding."

"I will see, dear sister. I have no objections to offer."

Anxious to grant every request, all parties gave con- sent, Agnes willing to depart from etiquette to oblige the patient sufferer.

Father Morgan bestowed a handsome marriage-dowry on his namesake; and a very quiet wedding was solem- nized in the family parlor. The Laceys, the Arnolds, and the Warren family from New York, are the only guests.

Clad in a soft, white muslin wrapper, with a few white flowers in her hair, which lay in light ringlets around her face, a small bouquet in her almost transparent hand, Alice looked almost like an inhabitant of another world, so pure, so holy, so seraphic was her whole appearance. Propped up in her couch, she gazed around her with an expression of deep, unutterable love on the faces of the dear members of her household, about to take the solemn vows of marriage. Clad in their white marriage-robes, they entered the parlor, Margaret in her ripe womanhood on the arm of Dr. Arnold, followed by Allan and sweet Agnes Sherwood, never more lovely in appearance than on her wedding-day.

Bishop Miles performed the marriage ceremony, and Father Morgan gave the brides away. It was indeed a solemn service, and at its conclusion, Alice motioned to Margaret and Dr. Arnold to draw near.

"God forever bless my brother and my sister Margaret, and bring them safely to His everlasting kingdom." Drawing them down, she kissed them both, and laid a gold medallion in Margaret's hand, adding: "This is my little gift, dear; it will remind you of Alice when she is with the angels.

"Now come, Allan," she continued. "May God forever bless you with his richest love, and give you many stars in the crown of your rejoicing; and you, dear

Agnes, may he give you grace to be a faithful help-meet in the Lord to my precious brother." Kissing both, she added, laying a medallion in Agnes' hand : " There is my little gift, dear sister : cherish it for the sake of Alice."

No gift could have been more valuable, for the likeness had been taken ere the sufferer had become so much emaciated, and on the back of each was a lock of her own beautiful hair.

" Almost angelic ! " said Agnes, as she was looking at the sweet face when alone with Allan.

"She has seemed like one of those blessed ones for months," said Allan, in reply. " Truly we shall all miss that holy presence, although we should not desire her to remain in such a broken, suffering frame."

Allan is going to Englesby Terrace to stay until the time of entering upon his field of labor, and Margaret to Little Rugby.

" You will be very near," said Alice, as she kissed the two, "and I can see you every day: you must be sure to come."

Lucy is seventeen now, old enough to be very useful to her mother; but Margaret had been so much of a companion, that her absence was painfully felt in the home circle.

George Vincent has fully recovered, and is ready to take a new charge as soon as confidence is once more established.

Dr. Lacey warns the mother of a speedy removal of her beloved child. Margaret is therefore much at home, and Warren very frequently in the anxious circle. Very sweet and holy are these solemn hours; for no common tie unites Warren and his sister Alice. We will take a seat near them at one of these tender interviews. -The invalid is propped up, Warren's arm encircling the frail form, her head reclining on her brother's breast.

"We have passed a very happy life together," said Alice, "you have been such a tender, affectionate brother. I could not bear to think that we may not dwell together in the world to come. Do you ever think of it, Warren?"

"I must be truthful now, Alice, and own that the painful thought does sometimes cross my mind; but I am not what I used to be. Since our father died, the thoughts of eternity and its solemn realities are never absent from my mind, and the daily texts are themselves an ever-present gospel. For many years, Alice, I was encircled by a bristling fort of bayonets: you can never know, dear, how powerful the little shadowy hand has been in brushing them all away."

The tears were streaming over the sweet, pale face now, as she said: "Warren, I am happy now; this is all that I lacked in my cup of thankfulness."

"My former skepticism always had its seat in the heart, dear, for I was too proud to be saved in the same

29 *

way as the common herd of guilty criminals; but **now I** can sing:

> 'Jesus sought me when a stranger,
>   Wandering from the fold of God;
> He, to save my soul from danger,
>   Did redeem me with his blood.' "

Alice lay still a moment, and then said, slowly and solemnly: "A family in heaven, Warren; what blessed, holy hopes are ours!"

Very rapidly now the silver cord was loosened. The mother and Margaret, Mrs. Sherwood and Agnes, took turns in watching by the departing saint. It has been a day of great suffering; but the evening brought relief, and through the silent night the little feet were buffeting with the waters of Jordan. Toward the dawn of day, she revived once more, and whispered: " Put aside the curtains, mamma, that I may see the glorious sunrise once more; it is my last on earth — another morning, and I shall wake in the presence of my blessed Saviour, and be with my dear, my precious father. Do not weep, my dearest mamma: think how blessed I shall be. No more pain; no more tears; no more sin and sorrow — and then we all hope to meet there in that happy land, to part no more — no more — "

Leaning upon her mother's bosom, her dying gaze fixed upon the glorious sunrise, which now flooded the garden with his morning beams, Alice Hastings passed away to the land whose sun never more goes down behind the everlasting hills of the heavenly city.

It is the day of the funeral; and, arrayed for the grave, Alice Hastings seemed too lovely for the silent tomb. Beloved by so many, the sweet remains were strewn with pure white flowers, and lay in the parlor all day, visited by her father's parishioners. Warren is there with his mother.

"You remember my dreams of fame, mamma," said her son. "They all vanished by the bedside of that sweet saint, never to return again. I have only one ambitiou now, and that is to serve my Lord and Master in any station that He may appoint. This has been no sudden change, dear mamma. Ever since papa's departure, the world and its allurements have lost their charms. Fame is an empty cheat; and there is nothing real, nothing true but heaven."

Very touching and impressive were the whispered words around those pale relics, each one having something to tell of little notes, or kind benefactions, or gentle admonitions. One poor woman stood there sobbing with real grief: it was the wife of Dan Galway.

"An' shure she was the good angel that took my husband by the hand, and made him sign the pledge. He's niver touched a drap since that day. God bless the dear saint!"

Others told how she had taught their girls on Saturday afternoon, until she got too weak to labor any more.

Ah! here are two little girls, each with a bunch of sweet flowers to lay upon the coffin. Taking the cold hands between their own, they rained floods of tears upon them, remembering how many kind acts those pale hands had done for them in days gone by. Thus closed the gentle ministry of this saintly sufferer, perhaps more useful in her weakness than many a professing Christian in full health.

The bells of St. Barnabas' are muffled once more as the solemn procession enters the church.

"I know that my Redeemer liveth, and though after my skin worms destroy this body, yet in my flesh shall I see God."

For how many centuries have these blessed words poured their flood of light into the graves of beloved kindred, illumining their darkness, and filling the hearts of mourners with hopes full of immortality! So it was now, as the slow footsteps followed the dear remains of Alice Hastings up the aisles of St. Barnabas'.

Very sweet and touching was the funeral hymn:

> "Hear what the voice from heaven declares
>   To those in Christ who die;
> Released from all their earthly cares,
>   They dwell with Him on high."

By the side of her beloved father they laid the precious dust, in the glorious hope of a blessed resurrection. Perhaps none are so much missed from a household as those who require so much care and tenderness; for when the couch where Alice had lain so many years was really put out of sight, then it was that the great void left behind was truly felt in the household. After a few days, her papers were all locked up; but the pictures, books, and pretty ornaments all remained — her own sweet picture, that Mrs. Sherwood had secured before she became so very much emaciated, hanging on the wall.

There is to be the first confirmation under the new rector very shortly; and Warren remains, that he may join the company. Many an eye was wet with tears of joy, and many a heart went up in earnest prayer, as the manly form of Warren Hastings advanced to the chancel; for the people knew how the father's heart had yearned over this precious son. Father Morgan grasped his hand after the services, and, with a quivering voice, said:

"God bless you, Warren Hastings, and make you a burning and a shining layman in the Church of our Redeemer!"

Warren is at Little Rugby ere he returns to the city; and pacing the students' walk are two figures — the young man and his beloved preceptor, as in the days of boyhood, with arms encircling each other's waist. It is an interview full of interest; for Warren is telling the way that the Lord has led him, and Dr. Arnold is listening with a full heart.

"Do you remember the tryst appointed on the Adirondacks?" said the young man. "One can scarcely realize that nearly ten years have rolled away since that day. As it is so near, I will wait until we summon all the company."

"You are twenty-five now, Warren," said his friend. "What do you propose in the future?"

"To serve God in my vocation as a Christian lawyer; and in a place like New York I can find a large field, where I can labor in the Church of our Lord."

In a few days, the mountain travellers have all arrived at Little Rugby. Their meeting was in the students' walk, where they were warmly greeted by Dr. Arnold.

"Our tryst was appointed among the trees of the Adirondacks," said the professor, "and it seems appropriate that it should be kept amid the shades of Little Rugby. How well do I remember that summer day, the happy company stretched out upon the grass, each sanguine boy so full of joyous anticipations. Ten years have passed since that period; and the youth who made that appointment are all men now, ready to relate something of the inner life of those passing years. Now, Harry, let us hear your experience."

The elder Seymour was now twenty-five, and yet he looked like thirty — his face bearing the marks of dissipation; his hair thin and scattered; his whole aspect that of one who had drained the cup of sensuality.

There was no look of triumph as the young man spoke :

"I have attained what I then desired — live in the first style in a suit of rooms at the Metropolitan ; drive fast horses and fine carriages; have my box at the opera, another at the theatre ; am a member of the leading club of the metropolis ; am invited to all the gay balls of Upper Tendom, and have everything that the world can give ; but a broken, shattered constitution forbids enjoyment ; and to speak truly, sometimes I envy even the waiters at the hotel in their freedom from care, their robust health, and easy life."

"I see, Harry Seymour, that you have learned the truth of the proverb of the wise man, when he declared : 'Vanity of vanities, all is vanity!'"

Then George arose : "I too have reached the summit of my ambition; but I am not ready yet to agree with the wise man, for I find in the excitement of the gold-room enough to satisfy my desires : when I own two millions, I shall then lay out my plans for the enjoyment of my gains."

"And you call this, George Seymour, the life of an immortal?" said the professor, with a sad look upon his fine countenance.

Then spoke Allan Hastings : "I remember my wish," said the young minister. "To be just as useful and good as my father. It would be a most immodest declaration to say, that I have reached what I then desired ; but I am striving to follow in his blessed footsteps, have chosen his high and holy calling, and find God's service my delight. Thus far I have been greatly blessed in the companion which my Father has given me; and am looking forward to a life spent together in loving and serving our Divine Master."

"A wise and blessed choice, dear Allan," said Dr. Arnold; "full of peace here, and unspeakable joy hereafter."

And now spoke Archie Murray: "It was an humble lot that I desired," said the young man; "likely to be fulfilled; for as soon as I am ordained, I shall take charge of St. John's over the hill, and sister Annie shall be my housekeeper. I desire nothing more — just such a field as I should wish to cultivate: it is an humble, but a happy lot, for I shall be serving my Lord and Master."

All eyes now turned upon Warren Hastings:

"You all remember the proud boy that longed for fame, desiring to make his mark in the world. Those dreams have vanished like the mist of the morning; and brighter, holier aspirations fill the vision of my wiser hours. With the departing spirit of my sainted sister Alice, the last dream fled away; and now I am ready to buckle on my armor in the service of my Lord and Master. Henceforward, I am His, and His only."

Dr. Arnold had sat with his eyes fixed upon the

earnest speaker, every now and then wiping away the moisture that would come. Warren sat down, and the good man followed: "God speed you, my beloved pupils, in your heavenward march; you have chosen a wise and holy life; it will bring peace and usefulness here, and glory and immortality hereafter."

Ere the Seymours returned to New York, the good man sought to impress upon their minds the wretched, unsatisfying nature of their pursuits. They listened attentively, for they respected their former preceptor; but they were "joined to their idols." Fearful destiny! if God should let them alone.

It is communion-day at St. Barnabas', and, side by side, Warren and his beloved preceptor knelt at the chancel to receive together the emblems of a Saviour's dying love. It was indeed a blessed day, and arm in arm Father Morgan and the young man walked home together, talking of the things of the kingdom, and the blessedness of his new-born hopes. Once more in the office with Uncle Richard, he is daily wondering what great change has come over Warren, for "old things have passed away, and all things have become new." A faithful attendant upon the ministry of St. Matthias', he is at once engaged in active service for his Lord and Master: not in the high places of the church, but among the most abandoned, the most neglected, Warren has chosen his field, and by his energy soon gathers around him a band of faithful workers. Always decided,

30

bold, and manly, the same traits appear in his aggressive Christianity, and to all Uncle Richard's attempts to lead him in the old paths of worldliness and unbelief, he has the simple answer, *nay*, so that his uncle is obliged to give him up, with the sneer, that "Saul is among the prophets." Staying at his Grandma Warren's, the change is equally striking; for although his love of Protestant truth is stronger, his charity is broader, and the courtesy with which he treats his aunts' peculiar notions is so marked, that they are found, when alone, saying to each other:

"I do believe that there are hopes of Warren, sister all his sharp remarks are laid aside."

Neither was aware of the strong ramparts which encompassed Warren Hastings; for, "justified by faith, he had peace with God." And, from this eminence, he had neither time nor inclination to join in the childish play of processions and showy vestments and puerile ceremonies.

To return once more to Westbrook: — We find Allan preparing for his new field of labor. Englesby Terrace is closed, and the family are staying a day or two with Mrs. Hastings ere their departure. The dear circle is diminishing around the widow, and she realizes now that the pilgrim's lot is hers indeed. One by one the links drop off. Three in heaven, three in scattered folds on earth; but the hope of final reunion is ever bright — when the broken links shall all be joined again, and the family chain be once more complete, in the everlasting kingdom of the saints' inheritance.

The last religious service attended by Allan was the ordination of Archie Murray, who at once took possession of the mission on the hill. To him also was confided the care of Mrs. Sherwood's asylum during her absence from Westbrook. Thus the dear friends are parted, Margaret only within reach of the family circle.

CHAPTER XXVI.

REUNION.

" Hitherto hath the Lord helped us."

TEN years have passed away. Silver hairs crown Mrs. Hastings, who is still an interesting woman in her widow's cap.

Mr. Murray has closed his earthly ministry at St. Barnabas', and has been succeeded by Frederic Gray, a young and gifted minister, of like sentiments with his predecessors.

Allan Hastings has filled several important pulpits in the diocese of Bishop Melville. He has ministered with great acceptance, his trumpet never having given an uncertain sound in the serious controversy which has so long agitated our beloved Church, and has lately been elected Assistant Bishop to that good and holy man. By his own earnest request, the consecration is to take place at St. Barnabas', at which time there is to be a reunion of the friends of Dr. Hastings who are yet members of the church militant. The Bishop elect, his wife, and mother, are once more domesticated in the dear family circle; and Warren and his wife are there, too. Father

Morgan is living still, but very feeble and aged. He is cherished with the love of children by every member of that household.

The day of consecration has arrived, and a deeply solemnized company are assembled at old St. Barnabas' Bishop Melville, the defender of Protestant truth in the Great West, is there; and Bishop Lysle, the bold champion of the faith; but Bishop Miles has entered into rest. Dr. Nelson, with Luther's spirit; Thayer, the loving John; Vincent, fully restored; and Nichols, with his silver trumpet; but Musgrave and Winter and Harrington have joined the church triumphant. Brown is in a foreign land, missionary to the heathen; and the saintly Woodbridge is dying. About twenty of the former members of the convocation are present. More than twenty had entered the sacred ministry from the Church of St. Barnabas during the life of Dr. Hastings; but they are not all here. Five have entered their everlasting rest; some are too distant or too poor to undertake the journey; but letters come from all the absent, and only three have departed from the teachings of St. Barnabas'. All the rest are bearing a faithful testimony in their several fields of labor to simple Bible truths. Many, too, of the old communicants have passed away, and great changes are visible in the dear old church; but there are those present who remember Allan's boyhood, and their hearts are deeply stirred at the sight of the man of thirty-four, somewhat bald now, with his meek and holy aspect.

about to take such solemn vows in such momentous days. Not often do such scenes as these occur — not often that so many, endeared by such sacred ties, meet together in their march to heaven; and many hearts felt the sentiment of the sweet hymn, as the eye took in each familiar face:

> "Angels, and living saints and dead,
> But one communion make:
> All join in Christ, their vital Head,
> And of His love partake."

The music, the services, the sermon were deeply impressive, and the charge of Bishop Melville to the newly-consecrated Bishop full of power. Enlarging upon the dangers threatening our beloved Church, he called upon him who stood before him in his meek solemnity to see that his trumpet gave no uncertain sound, but to contend manfully, lovingly, and with the spirit of an Apostle, for the "faith once delivered to the saints," adding:

"These are no common days, beloved. Great and alarming errors threaten our *Protestant* Episcopal Church. We are called upon to withstand them with the spirit that animated Cranmer and Ridley and Latimer. Let us pray much, watch earnestly, wait patiently for the Moses that God may send. Let us not move before he gives the order; but when he does, without question, without delay, go forward; and God will be

with His own cause — not, perhaps, with the great mul
titude, but certainly with the little flock."

Many deeply affected listeners are in that densely
crowded church; but none more deeply solemnized than
two ladies in deep mourning, who occupy a pew near the
chancel. One is elderly, the other is no longer young;
but there is such an expression of sanctified affliction
upon the face of the latter as touches the heart at once.
It is Agnes Hastings, the wife of the newly-consecrated
Bishop, clad in the weeds of mourning for two dear
children, whom they have recently consigned to the
silent tomb, leaving her now childless; but she is a very
useful Christian, laboring wherever her husband's lot
has been cast in the service of her Lord and Master.

After church, Father Morgan, taking Allan's arm,
walked slowly down the aisle, and out to the graves of
the beloved, followed by all the clergy who were the
friends of Dr. Hastings. In silence they stood around
the enclosure; and Father Morgan said, solemnly:
"Blessed are the dead who die in the Lord, brethren:
let us follow the departed as he followed Christ."

On the following Monday, the party separated once
more — Allan, with Bishop Melville, to his new field of
labor, and other brethren to their respective posts.
Warren is a noble Christian layman in New York city,
using his bright talents for his Lord and Master,
rejoicing in "the liberty wherewith Christ has made
Him free."

In another year, we find Lucy at the parsonage once more as the wife of the new minister; and Mrs. Hastings in hearing of the chimes of St. Barnabas', in sight of her lamented husband's study. By especial request, Lucy was married on Easter-eve; for the mother has learned to connect important events with that glorious season. She watches year by year the same paschal moon, and remembers the eve of her wedding-day beneath its placid light, the eve when her husband's remains lay in the sorrowing parsonage, and the eve before her departure to another home.

Father Morgan is still an inmate with the family; for he is one of them in every sense but relationship. Every fine day he may be seen, leaning on the arm of Mrs. Hastings, walking in the orchard for exercise; and, in the sweet spring-time, a group of little children are sporting in the orchard again, plucking the fragrant apple-blossoms, while their elders watch their plays.

And so the grand-children of the former rector gambol beneath the same green trees as did their parents — Emily and Alice Arnold on every fine day visiting the parsonage; for they love to sit on Father Morgan's lap, listening with earnest faces to his stories about Grandpa Hastings and Aunt Alice, whose holy lives are a blessed legacy to the little ones.

Warren is indeed a noble layman, using his fine talents in the service of his Master, and Edward side by side in the same good and holy cause. St. Barnabas' is yet a noble witness for the truth — its talented young minister sounding a clear trumpet from its sacred pulpit.

Mr. Moncrief is still following after the fossils of a defunct theology, dispensing chaff instead of the children's bread; and yet the Judgment is speeding on. What will be the record when the Saviour comes to try men's faith?

Gertrude and Helen Warren are in the sere and yellow leaf, still devoted to the fopperies of ritualism; the Seymours worn out in the service of a cheating world — sensual, soured, disappointed; Dr. Arnold and Margaret at Little Rugby, filling up the hours of useful, happy lives; and Archie Murray at St. John's over the hill, laboring among the poor and neglected, gathering around him an humble, devoted flock of Christians.

The figures moving over these pages are not all imaginary; for they are representative men and women of a class living around us. We are bidding them farewell; but they do not vanish with our waking dreams. They are breathing, moving, acting moral agents in a world that is to pass away — their works to remain forever. It is sorrowful to see so much energy, talent, and worth bestowed upon such trifling, while above, around us, everywhere is such a treasury of boundless grace and mercy.

It is as though a shower of heavenly manna were falling daily at the very door of our tents, and we should crush it under our feet, or pass it by, to search in

the desert of Sahara for living water and the bread of
heaven. Full and free justification from all the accusa-
tions of sin is offered to us through Jesus our substitute.
This is the *heavenly manna;* and ritualism offers a series of
fasting, and penance, and painful, weary watching. This
is an *apple from the Dead Sea.* Adoption into the family
of God by faith in Christ Jesus is the gift of free grace.
This too is *heavenly manna;* and ritualism offers the
baptismal waters which fail to give the sweet assurance
which the soul needs. This too is an *apple from the Dead
Sea.* Gracious access to a throne of grace through the
one Great High-Priest is the great privilege of the Gospel — precious, *heavenly manna!* and ritualism dresses
up a man in priestly vestments, who leads the soul to an
imaginary altar, and a bloodless sacrifice thereon, who
tells the weary pilgrim that it is only through a human
priesthood that the soul gains access to the mercy-seat.
This truly is an *apple of the Dead Sea!* The immortal,
deathless soul wants something more than this. It wants
a conscious interest in the blood of the Lamb, "which
hope we have as an anchor of the soul, both sure and
steadfast, and which entereth into that within the veil."

To all these modern teachers of a buried theology
it cries out, perhaps unconsciously: "Sirs, we would see
Jesus!" — *Jesus* in all His offices, *Jesus* in His blessed
life, *Jesus* in His atoning death, *Jesus* on His mediato-
rial throne, *Jesus* and nothing else!

What shall we say then to that ambassador of Christ,

who holds up a screen between the beseeching soul and its Redeemer; and when he asks for Jesus, gives him incense, pleasant hymns, solemn dramas, imposing processions, and a human, fallible priest? To such, in the name of every redeemed soul for whom the Saviour died, we conclude with that language of entreaty: "Sir we would see Jesus!"—it is our heritage, our right.

THE END

Lightning Source UK Ltd.
Milton Keynes UK
UKHW022149021218
333278UK00005B/268/P